Pearls of Fire,
Dreams of Steel

Pearls of Fire, Dreams of Steel

short fantasy fiction

Deborah J. Ross

Published by Book View Café Publishing Cooperative
P.O. Box 1624
Cedar Crest, NM 87008-1624
www.bookviewcafe.com

ISBN: 978-1-61138-736-0

Cover illustration © 2015 Dreamstime
Cover Design: Amy Sterling Casil
Proofreader: Brenda Clough
Interior design: Marissa Doyle

First Book View Café edition published 2015

"Bread and Arrows" © 2003 Deborah Wheeler. First published in *Sword & Sorceress XX*, ed. M.Z. Bradley, DAW

"A Hunter of the Celadon Plains" © 2012 Deborah J. Ross. First pub-lished in *Sword & Sorceress 27*, ed. L. Waters, MZB Literary Works Trust

Table of Contents

Introduction

As I put together this collection of short fantasy fiction, I realized it comprises a retrospective of my writing career. Although it does not include my very first professional sale ("Imperatrix" in *Sword & Sorceress*), it spans the decades from novice to seasoned writer. To my delight, I found many of those early stories still spoke to me—delighted me—as much now as when I labored to create them. Often the output of a young writer will be justifiably relegated to the Trunk of Doom (hence the term "trunk stories"). When we're learning new skills, we need to practice, and not all of those early experiments succeed. More than that, in order to grow as artists, we need to take risks, to "push the envelope," even if it means falling flat on our faces, so to speak. But it does not follow that every early effort is best forgotten. Stories ignite within us, waiting to take shape on paper. Once we have acquired a certain basic level of craft, it no longer matters if this is our first sale or our fortieth. And one of the gifts of new publishing technologies is the ability to revive those stories, even from decades ago, so that new generations of readers can enjoy them.

"Storm God," "Fireweb," and "Dragon-Amber" all come from those early years, when I was trying out lots of new ideas. Astute readers will recognize a touch of a well-known American folk tale in "Storm God." "Fireweb" was an early exploration of the "wounded healer" theme, and also taught me that whatever

I thought a story was "about" when I started writing it, I was sure to be wrong; I developed the wisdom to let the "underneath" story tell itself. When I wrote "Dragon-Amber," it seemed as if everyone and their cousin was writing stories based on Anne McCaffrey's "Pern" series. True to my contrary nature, I insisted on something different. No oversized fire-breathing flying reptiles here, but a creature of magic nonetheless.

"Bread and Arrows" and "Nor Iron Bars" were written within a couple of years of one another. Both stories arose from a turning point in my life. When I wrote it, I had just moved from a large city to a redwood forest. I'd started a full-time day job to support myself and my younger daughter. It's about new beginnings, and also making choices that close off other avenues. "Bread and Arrows" echoes "Summoning the River" (*Transfusion and Other Tales of Hope*) in its journey into a dark place, grappling with loss and mortality. I also wanted a different role for the charismatic, sexually attractive stranger; Celine looks beneath the handsome exterior to the suffering man, and draws compassion from her own struggle. And the bakery salamander was irresistible!

Sometimes readers ask where I get story ideas, and often I honestly have no idea. I suspect the Idea Fairy leaves packets of them under my pillow at night. For "A Hunter of the Celadon Plains," however, I had been thinking about the place of women warriors in peoples of the steppe or plains. In *Azkhantian Tales* (later developed into *The Seven-Petaled Shield* trilogy), women used horsemanship and archery to compensate for lesser physical strength. In thinking of how the North American Plains peoples were able to hunt buffalo on foot, I kept the arrows but substituted long-distance running and superb tracking skills for the advantages of horses. Where the rat-thing that gnaws the bonds between worlds came from, I am not at all sure. Probably a nightmare.

Likewise, "Poisoned Dreams" came from a specific idea and then took off in its own direction. The Greek general Xenophon wrote (*Anabasis*) about a honey that intoxicated his soldiers: "A small dose produced a condition not unlike violent drunkenness, a large one an attack very like a fit of madness, and some dropped down, apparently at death's door." How could an author resist? But one idea, not matter how bewitching in itself, does not a story make. Hence, the fairy who is crippled in body but not in capacity for malice. I leave it to the reader to decide whether she has just cause.

"Under the Skin" also explores the effects of festering hatred. I wrote it not too long after my mother had been raped and murdered, and I wrestled daily—sometimes hourly—with raging fury. I remembered Agatha Christie's Hercule Poirot saying that if you invite evil into your heart, it will make a home there. The story first appeared in *Marion Zimmer Bradley's Fantasy Magazine* and when Marion selected it for *The Best of Marion Zimmer Bradley's Fantasy Magazine*, I sent her background notes for the introduction. "Are you sure you want to make such a personal issue public?" she asked, for the murder was not referenced in the original publication. I did and I do. The seductive nature of hatred thrives when kept in the dark. By putting words to page, the pain and anger lose their power over me, and others who suffer similar tragedies are invited along the healing journey.

"Silverblade," like several other stories in this collection, began as a dream. The scene with the land-crabs approaching and a child running to open the gates woke me in a cold sweat. Following the advice of Octavia Butler, I took what really frightened me and spun it out into a story. After its publication, a fan composed a "filk" song based on the story and sang it for me at a convention. Until then, I'd had no idea how deeply the story touched my readers.

"The Sorceress's Apprentice" is just plain fun.

"Our Lady of the Toads" had its origins at a late-night gathering at a science fiction convention. I was hanging out with Mike Resnick (who also wrote a blurb for my first published novel, *Jaydium*) and he'd just signed to edit an anthology of the *"Fantastic"* series for DAW. An invitation for *Witch Fantastic* ensued, and this is that story.

Ah, "Pearl of Fire," for which this collection is named: another dream, this one of looking into a mirror and seeing the reflection of a brass dragon instead of my own face. What to do with this image? By this time, I had 40 or 50 short story sales, and I realized that the story wasn't about an *outside* dragon, an independent creature, but an *inside* dragon. I also needed something that affirmed joy and life itself as a foil for the becoming-a-dragon theme: the love story. A few years after publication, the Pearl still had me in its clutches. The untold part of the story demanded with increasing urgency to be told. The heartbreak that conquered the dragon wanted its own space, and so "Pearl of Tears" came about.

When I wrote "The Casket of Brass," I was heartily tired of pseudo-medieval Western European fantasy. I had loved (a children's version) of *The Arabian Nights* (the original version being judged much too violent, not to mention erotic, for young minds). While flavored by those stories, this one takes off in its own direction, and certainly features stronger, more active women than Scheherazade described.

The last tale in this collection, the capstone, is one of my personal favorites. I have loved horses since I knew what they were. When editor Gabrielle Harbowy asked me to submit a story to *When The Hero Comes Home 2*, I knew at once that my hero must be a horse. I won't say more about it lest I spoil the deliciousness of the unfolding. Consider it a gift, to be savored as it is unwrapped.

So I offer you a potpourri—or bouquet, if you like—of tales of dragons and toads, horses and thieves, mothers and daughters, lovers and villains. Enjoy the journey!

Deborah J. Ross

Bread and Arrows

Celine knelt in front of the brick-lined bread oven, her head and shoulders halfway inside the fire pit. Her probing fingertips scraped against a cracked, unevenly heating floor tile. She took out her stone-wand, hoping she wouldn't have to dismantle the entire oven to make repairs. Nestled in a bucket of warm ashes, her salamander kept up an incessant grumble.

"Fire-go-out! World end!"

The string of bells on the front door of the bakery shop chimed gently, accompanied by the creaking hinge. Celine crawled backwards out of the oven and clambered to her feet. Basalt stood just inside the opened half-door, feet spread apart as if braced against a storm, an expression of disapproval twisting his thin lips.

As if I didn't have enough troubles! First, my moon cycles, then this accursed oven, and now him!

Celine tucked a stray curl back under her widow's coif and tried to pretend Basalt was really here to buy bread. There were a few long-loaves left, arranged on their wooden racks like giant's matchsticks, plus the raspberry tarte her friend Annelys had asked her to make for Herve's name-day and then not picked up. If Basalt would take the tarte and leave, he could have it.

"Cold-cold-cold!" Fireling insisted. "Waiting here for-*ever*!"

"Salamander in a snit again?" He leaned on the counter with what he clearly imagined an engaging leer.

"Did you want something?"

The leer deepened. "You know I do."

The curl of hair had unaccountably come loose again and Fireling's grumbling escalated to an outright whine.

"A long-loaf?" she asked. "Or this fine raspberry tarte?"

"Just say yes. You're already the envy of half the maidens on Merchant Street."

"FIRE-GO-*OUT!*" Fireling yelped.

"Either buy something," Celine snapped, "or get out!"

With a sigh he handed over the sols for a long-loaf. She wasn't quick enough to snatch her hand back and so he caught it and kissed it. When she retreated at last to the back room, her temper was as foul as the salamander's.

Long past dark, with Fireling once again settled in a bed of gently glowing coals, Celine carried the raspberry tarte down the narrow lanes to the inn owned by Annelys and her brother Herve. Throonish laughter filled the public room, with its low beamed ceiling. The dwarfish caravaneers were, Celine saw at a glance, already half drunk. The inn's ale-imps squealed in protest from their barrels as they churned barley-malt mash into more of the tangy brew. Herve's halfwit son moved through the room placidly refilling tankards. Annelys, a tray of bread and cheese aloft in each hand, cast Celine a despairing look and shouted above the din. Celine shook her head, *I can't hear you,* and made her way to the private living quarters. Two stools and a narrow table, set with cheese and a few apples, sat against the outer wall. Celine put the tarte down and sank onto the nearest stool.

Herve followed her with a tankard, which he placed before her, grinning. "All the luck!" He angled his chin back toward the public room as he sliced off a hefty portion of the tarte.

"Yes, you'll make a year's profits from just tonight," Celine said, grinning back. "Are you charging them double or triple? By the by, blessings on your name-day."

6

He planted a moist kiss on her cheek and hurried back to his customers. If Basalt had half his good nature, she might consider marrying him just to not have to work so hard.

What was she thinking? She'd already had one solid, decent husband. Oh, Jehan had meant to be kind, beating her less than another might and then only when he was drunk. The best thing and the worst thing he'd ever done for her was to leave her the bakery. So far, she'd managed to keep it going alone…

Annelys bustled in a short time later, flushed. "They'll be at it all night!"

"Yes," Celine said. Ale-warmth seeped through her. "Herve and I already discussed how much profit you'll make."

Annelys took a slice of the tarte. "Bless you! I haven't had a moment to eat. I was sure you'd sell it to someone else, I was so late."

"I almost did."

"Basalt?"

"I'd rather have splattered it across his face," Celine admitted.

"At least it's the shop he wants and not you."

Celine sighed and picked at a stray berry.

"What is it, my dear?" Annelys said.

"I don't know; I have been feeling tired with all the work. But Lys—my moon cycles, I've missed them twice now."

"Basalt?"

"Mother-of-God!" Celine sputtered.

Unspoken words hung between them. Instead of an unwanted pregnancy, did she face the wasting curse that had carried off Jehan's mother?

"Then you can do no better than to ask Old Magdalie. If anyone knows the truth of such matters, it's her," Annelys said, adding, "I'll go with you."

Close to midnight, Celine made her way through the hills

above the town. Occasionally, she stumbled and sent a rain of pebbles down the rugged slope. Annelys hummed and strode along, surefooted as the goats who'd made the path. Once Celine too had walked these hills as if night-nixie magic guided her steps. Now her body had turned clumsy as her own dough.

Along the path, night dew coaxed wild sweet smells from the sleeping flowers. Here and there, a herders hut or troll gate gave off flickering light. Goats shifted in their pastures.

Celine inhaled, feeling memories stir. She remembered as a child lifting her arms on such a summer breeze, taking aim with the bow she'd carved and strung herself. She'd painted eagles and dragons on her bow, pretending to give it enchanted powers. A willow branch, stripped to its pale core, became a milk-white steed to carry her on her adventures.

Where had those dreams gone? In the three years she'd been struggling to keep the bakery going, they had faded, as colorless as the petals of last summer's wind rose. All too often, these days, she longed only to sleep.

"There!" Annelys pointed.

Celine, seeing the spark of yellow light, felt something lift within her. She would have the truth from Old Magdalie and know what she faced.

The hut fitted snug against the rocky hillside, running into the body of the earth. A cat came running to them, collar bells tinkling. Annelys bent to pick it up and stood aside.

Backlit, the wise woman came forward. "Is that little Celine? And Annelys of the merry laugh? Oh my dears, it has been too long since these eyes beheld you." With a firm grip, she pulled both young women inside.

Celine smiled despite herself to see how little Magdalie had changed over the years. The old woman still had the same shriveled sweetness, like a sun-dried elf, the same bright eyes, the same wisps of hair which, so like her own, would never obey the dictates of modest city dress. Magdalie's fingers, smooth and hard as carved wood, cupped her face and Celine felt the sting of tears.

"Tell me, child."

Celine sat beside the fire, burning with a strange golden light so unlike the smoldering embers of the herders and villagers. Words spilled out of her mouth, out of her heart. The long days of sameness, the beatings, the slow grinding days, the endless work.

At Magdalie's urging, Celine stretched out on the thin pallet. Those hard fingers touched her with wisdom and knowledge, gentle even when the insistent probing brought pain.

Celine closed her eyes and began to drift, as if she were a mote on a river woven from the sound of Magdalie's voice and her own breathing. Eddies and swirls caught her up, carried her along. She felt none of the heaviness that had sapped her strength these past months. How she longed to rest, to lie safe and cradled in her grand-dam's arms…

She awoke to the sound of her own name. Magdalie bent over her, one hand clasped in hers. Beyond, Annelys held the black cat in her arms, her brow furrowed.

"Have I—I must have fallen asleep." Celine struggled to sit up. "I didn't know I was so tired."

"'Tis more than tired," Magdalie said. A strangeness in her voice stung Celine alert.

The world reeled in Celine's vision, but only for a moment. "My husband's mother died of the wasting curse, though she was a virtuous wife. I nursed her through her last days. I know what to expect. I will grow more tired with every passing moon and my body will wither away. There will be great pain."

"That can be eased."

"Can it?" Celine searched the wise woman's bright eyes for any hint of deception and found only kindness. Yes, she need have no fear of pain. And there would be no more struggle, no more unending days gnawing away at her spirit. No more Basalts.

"Is there nothing that can be done?" Annelys cried, as if the pain were her own.

"Nothing more *I* can do," Magdalie said, her eyes still fixed on Celine's. "There is something *you* can do, if you have the courage. Your death springs from your flesh, this much is true. But as a curse, its power is more than earthly, for the womb is the seat of birth as well as death. The old tales speak of a journey to the heart of the curse, a way to enter into its womb even as it has entered yours, to face whatever lies there. But this path is not for the irresolute. You will be tested in ways you cannot imagine."

"Tell us!" Annelys said.

"Do you wish this path?" Again, that piercing look.

Celine hesitated.

"What's the problem?" Annelys demanded. "It's a chance!"

"Leave it alone," Celine said, getting to her feet. "Life and death are not all that different. Why choose one over the other?"

"Why? *Why?* Are you moon-mad?" Annelys followed on Celine's heels.

It seemed the easier thing to let Annelys rant, to spew her own fears into the sweet night air. *They will lay me in the earth, and I will rest,* Celine thought. Whatever sustained her during the climb now left her utterly. She was tired, so tired.

Hot white light poured into her eyes. Celine struggled upright, slowly recognizing her room in the attic above the bakery. Someone—Annelys—had opened the shutters wide. Laughing voices echoed from the street below. Breezes bore the promise of the day's heat.

"I should have been up hours ago," Celine protested.

Annelys proceeded to haul Celine out of bed and into her overskirt and sabots. "It's Tourney Faire. Come on!"

Celine had intended to bake extra sweet twists to sell at the Faire. How could she have forgotten? There was no point in trying to start the day's baking now, so with a sigh, Celine allowed herself to be led into the brightness. Annelys tucked

Celine's arm in hers and they went along as sisters through the gathering throng that wended their way past the town gates, over the bridge with its mill and raft of shallow-bottomed barges, over the range of gentle hills and out to the great field. A miniature town had sprung up overnight, with pavilions, shade screens, pole corrals for the horses, flimsy booths and carts. Tinkers and traders called out their wares.

Celine knew many of the people gathered there, either from the bakery or the inn. Strangers smiled and waved to everyone on holiday. Annelys bought strips of striped ribbon, yellow for herself and blue for Celine. Tying hers in the loose curl that had escaped as usual from her widow's coif, Celine gazed at the mountains that lay on the other side of the town. How far away they seemed now.

Ryneld, the other public baker, had set up trays of meat rolls and fruit bread, charging extra. He smiled at Celine, once he realized she was not here to sell, and offered her an apple bun. She was about to ask where he'd found cinnabark so smooth on the tongue when she noticed his gaze. Basalt stood a little ways apart, talking with a man in Duke's livery.

Celine eyed the other baker speculatively. He had a son still young, but growing. Would he buy the bakery from her and run it with an extra apprentice as a second heritage? Shaking her head, she set aside the idea. He was not a man to try something new. And what did it matter what happened to the bakery?

Let Basalt have it, and every morning may he taste Fireling's wrath!

The thought of the temperamental salamander lightened her step. She and Annelys squeezed between the onlookers to watch the contests. Men and a few women, some in their masters' livery, sparred with staff or wooden sword or shot at targets set into bales of straw. Most used curved bows set with charms in carved shell or wound with colored threads for luck. In Tourney Faires past, archery had been Celine's special pleasure. She'd even entered a round or two, although her plain bow could not stand against the spells carved into a truly fine weapon.

Annelys clapped as the miller's son landed an arrow in the

red zone. Celine, who had never much liked the miller's son, let her eyes wander toward the waiting archers. One man stepped away from the next group, drawing her attention. He alone wore neither livery nor ordinary clothing, but a long vest of studded black leather over crimson shirt and leggings. Even from half the length of the field, she felt his eyes lock onto hers. She became aware of the milky skin at the unbuckled neck of his vest, the midnight hair tumbling over the broad shoulders, the slow curve of the lips as if in recognition. She swayed on her feet.

"What is it, my dear?" Annelys asked.

"Nothing." Doubt swept away the moment. *He must have thought I was someone else. It could not have been me such a man would want.*

And yet, her heart beat unaccountably fast when he stepped up to the line and dipped his bow in her direction in salute. Sun flashed on spiraling runes in silver wire as he took aim. His arrows went straight and true. The crowd cheered wildly.

Celine stood motionless as the victorious archer walked toward her. He bowed as if she were a great lady and not a widow with a shop. With sweet words he begged her pardon for his forwardness, asking only her name and the privilege of carrying her favor into the next round. While Annelys watched, open-mouthed, Celine gave him the ribbon from her hair, which he tied to a metal ring. His name, she found out, was Ian Archer, and that explained the odd lilting accent.

What was it Fireling chirped when she was warm and happy? *Fire-burn-bright! World-ever-flame!*

The salamander's joy filled her as she watched Ian Archer advance to the next round and the next. As if by magic, he always knew where she was standing, when she was looking at him. He would turn his head slightly, as if to say he were shooting just for her. All her life, it seemed, she had been waiting for something to happen to her, to carry her beyond the mountains, beyond the village, beyond the unceasing drudgery of the bakery, and here, on the eve of her taking leave of this life, he had come.

He went up to the dais where the Duke and his lady presented him with a purse and a garland of lilies twisted into a golden circlet. Then the crowd closed around him, as if he had been no more than a dream. Afternoon shadows lengthened across the tourney fields as the last rounds began. Faire-goers streamed back to the town to continue their celebrations.

"Ay me, I'm late!" Annelys said with a happy sigh. "We'll be all night working. Did you ever see such archery? Did you see how he looked at you? Oh, you *did!*" She giggled and threw one arm around Celine's shoulders.

"I feel—so strange. Lys, do you think he bespelled me?" Celine's feet lagged, as if something invisible tugged at her, pulling her back toward the mountains.

"If he did, it's one of the best, the kind to keep your dreams warm all winter! Your cheeks are brighter than cherries! You don't think—the pain, is it still there?"

Celine dipped her head. *But not for long.* Now she had a reason to try Magdalie's path.

Magdalie had left the door wide open to the patterned starlight. In the hearth, embers dimmed and hushed, falling silently. Only whispers broke the stillness as Magdalie recited words so old that no one now living had ever heard them spoken as language.

Once more, Celine lay on the pallet, her stomach still churning from Magdalie's concoction of herbs and ground resins. She clutched a talisman of intertwined hairs, one from the head of a crone who had died peacefully in her sleep, the other plucked living from her own head. This would serve as her guide for the inward journey. Returning to her body would be more difficult, Magdalie had warned her, for if she could not separate the hairs, or if she chose the one from the dead woman, she would wander lost between the worlds forever.

Dizziness crept over Celine, at first only the slightest

sensation of whirling movement. She'd felt this way before, just as she was falling asleep. Only this time, instead of fading into unconsciousness, the vertigo intensified.

Celine tried to open her eyes, but could not move. She could not swallow, could not see, could not breathe. She could no longer hear her heartbeat or the rush of blood through her ears.

Suddenly, she found herself sitting up. Her body, naked, had become pale and translucent as glass. Below her lay a fleshly form, eyes closed in a tranquil face, breasts rising and falling gently. Her ghostly fingers held the talisman, now no longer two entwined hairs, but a glowing rod of braided metal. It tugged at her grasp, as if eager to be off.

Moving cautiously, she got to her feet, letting the rod draw her toward the opened door. It pulled her down the path and straight for the steepest edge of the hill. But she did not go tumbling to her death on the rocky slopes below. She soared, spreading invisible wings across the sky.

The starlight intensified and with it came a sense of freedom, of leaving sorrow behind. Here she felt only peace, only stillness, and finally, as she grew quiet enough to hear it, the eternal, joyous song of the stars. A wordless song of delight filled her spirit even as the light filled her body.

By slow degrees, the light grew less brilliant and Celine became aware of a velvet darkness beneath her. By the time she touched the ground, she was once again solid flesh.

She landed with a jolt on a barren mud flat, clutching a tangle of greasy string in one hand. Wind howled through her ears. With an effort, she forced herself to her feet, looped the string around her neck for safekeeping, and began walking.

Celine had not gone more than a few paces when a flurry of ice pellets pelted her body. She gasped, doubling over and clutching her arms. Her skin burned with the sudden, biting cold.

Snow joined the hail. She hunkered down, hugging her knees to her chest. Her shivers grew more violent and then began to abate. Moments later, she lost all feeling in her fingers or toes.

She knew from her childhood winters in the mountains what that meant. The end was not far off, but at least there would be no pain. Soon she would feel calm and warm as her body surrendered to the storm.

As Celine drew her arms hard against her body, her fingertips brushed the string around her neck—the talisman, the guide that was to lead her back to life. Instead it had brought her here to die.

I was ready to let go of living. Now, for the first time, I wanted something for myself, something more than work and more work, men who want me only for what I can bring them—

It was so unfair, to have such a slim hope snatched from her. *I want a chance!*

The string glowed between her fingers, by degrees warm and warmer. Her trembling slowed and then stopped. The storm passed as quickly as it had come, the snow rapidly melting. She knelt on a shallow, pebble-strewn cup before the entrance to a huge cavern.

She stood up, still holding the talisman. As she moved toward the cavern, it gave off a sweet yellow light. When she turned away from the cave, the light dimmed. A guide she had been promised; a guide she had been given. Her heart lifted.

She stepped over the threshold. The arching doorway of the cave was the same grayish stone as the mountainside but inside, the rock turned blood red. Another step, and she was caught, jerked forward as if the cave had sucked her into its belly.

Celine stood about halfway down a slope leading to a cavern so vast she could not see its borders. Stalactites hung above her, so distant they resembled dangling threads. On the rocky floor below lay a huge lump of stone.

Like a skull it was, distorted and leering, far less human than the Throonish dwarfs. It stood about twice the height of a man, and its gaping maw was large enough for her to pass within. Two blunted, downturned horns adorned the top of the skull, and the deep-set orbits were tilted downward, the better to watch her approach. Poison-yellow light flickered within the eye

15

sockets. Glowing saliva dripped from the stone fangs.

Her feet froze to the path. The skull sat in front of her, unmoving and pitiless. Any moment now, her courage would surely break, and she would turn and run. There was nothing this lump of rock could do to stop her. But if she did that, she realized, or even if she stood here forever, she would never return to the human world, never stroke Fireling's smooth hide or smell the spice-buns she had made with her own hands, never travel beyond the mountains. Never laugh, never dream. Never see Ian Archer's slow smile.

All because she was afraid.

She had thought she had nothing to lose by undertaking this journey. Now, she saw as clearly as if engraved in letters of flame, how much she risked.

As she passed beneath the teeth, a drop of saliva spattered her shoulder. She screamed and clawed at it, but went on. The interior of the skull was still and black. Not the wondrous, living dark of the stars, but an utter absence of light and form. The stone skull, the red light of the cavern, even the glow of the talisman, all vanished as if they had never been.

Slowly her fears seeped away. She felt warmer, as if the darkness itself cradled her in loving arms. Her knotted muscles relaxed. Her eyes focused on a filmy wisp that suggested the lines of a kindly old face. Closer and closer the image came, until Celine felt the silken whisper of lips on brow, as she had often been kissed as a child.

A well-remembered voice murmured music to her heart, "Celine my baby, Celine my love..."

It was not mere longing that put those words into Celine's ears. She actually heard a voice—distorted and breathy, a melding of every loving phrase she had ever heard. She was a child curled in her grand-dam's lap, pressed against the softness of her body, fingers stroking her hair.

No drudgery, *no worry, only peace...*

She reached out, but her fingers grasped only air. She stretched further and took a step, then another, all the while finding only emptiness. There was nothing to touch, nothing to hold on to.

"Celine..." The voice seemed less human now, more like a twist of wind.

"No!" Celine screamed from the bottom of her lungs. "Don't leave me!"

Then Celine was alone in the darkness. Loss, sharper than the ice storm, swept through her. Wildly, she sobbed that she could not bear it, that she would give anything to be back in her grand-dam's arms...

Celine stood again in front of the skull rock, only now there was no light in the eye sockets and dull gray chalk filled the mouth. She could not travel that path again.

She still held the talisman, but the hairs were no longer tightly entwined. As she looked down at them, they separated entirely. They looked identical, two strands of colorless filament.

It would be so easy to throw one down without thinking, hoping it would send her back to her grand-dam and this time she would stay with her forever. She could convince herself that she had tried, but luck had been against her. It wouldn't be her fault she'd guessed wrong.

There would be no guessing. She must *choose* with all her heart and soul. The uncertain tides of life...or the empty promises of the dark.

Celine crouched on the threshold to Magdalie's hut, sipping goats milk from a horn cup. How thick and warm it was, with a tanginess that lingered on her tongue. One moment she felt weak as a baby, the next she wanted to dance. The heaviness, the unrelenting bone-deep tiredness of these last months, had lifted with the morning mist.

Here came Magdalie up the trail, mounted on Pierrot's

donkey and using a willow switch freely to keep the beast moving. She helped Celine on the back of the sturdy beast, which sighed in resignation. The thick wool riding-pad looked as if it had been freshly brushed.

"Pierrot will come to collect him tonight," Magdalie said. She tied two cloth bags, one on either side of the donkey's rump. "Now, you will prepare these herbs as I told you, and take them faithfully and—"

"Yes, yes!" Celine laughed.

She let the donkey set its own pace, watching the tapering ears bob with each stride. The sun was well up, and she wondered how she had never noticed the intense blue of the sky, the bright green of grass and vine, the almost-black green of massed evergreen forest. Night-nixies had left strands of glowing dewdrops wherever shade lingered. A tangle of wildflowers, grasses, fragrant herbs, mosses, and rotting wood lined the narrow path. Birds sang as they swooped and darted across the sky. She sang with them.

As she neared the town, though, she grew quieter. She felt remarkably well, but this changed nothing. Bread still must be baked, a temperamental salamander to be appeased, Basalt to be reckoned with...

With the thought of Basalt came that of Ian Archer. She smiled.

The town sparkled in the noonday sun, pavilions and booths still standing for a last half-day of merriment and trade. A pair of half-grown boys darted toward her, calling.

"Mistress! We'll keep your donkey safe, only five sols!"

"You give me the five sols and I'll let you ride him," she called back.

"Oh, it's the baker lady." One of the boys broke off the chase, his face falling. "She's a hard one."

A hard one. Is that what people thought of her? Ah yes, she must have been, to have endured first Jehan and then widowhood.

I did not come back from the skull cave to do more of the same.

Celine left the donkey at the inn, happily munching oat hay in one of the stalls reserved for travelers' mounts. Annelys was at the farmer's market, restocking after the Throons and fairegoers had eaten out their pantries. Herve nodded at Celine, beaming. A good soul, a simple soul. She wanted to kiss the bald spot on his head, but it would embarrass him too much.

The bakery welcomed her like an old friend, sagging against its neighbors as if it were too tired to go on alone. And yet, they leaned on one another, each knowing its own place—bakery, butcherie, epicerie, wine shop—each filling the street with its own constellation of fragrances. From the back, she heard Fireling's plaintive whine.

"Fire-go-out! World end!"

No, the world wouldn't end, but she hurried to the back of the shop to ease the little animal's distress. Behind her, the string of bells chimed gently. She paused with one hand on the bellows, knowing that this time it was not Basalt.

"My lady." Eyes of green flecked with gold like a far-off sea regarded her with a twinkle. A pulse leapt in the hollow of his bared throat.

But now she saw the shadows beneath those eyes, the tiny lines, the tightness, the tracery of silver in the midnight hair. The black leather vest was worn raw in places, and the ring where he'd tied her token bore a tangle of faded threads.

"I have no bread to sell today, sir."

"I have not come to buy bread." It was just the sort of phrase Basalt might have used, had he been a bit more polished. In a rush, as if looking into a mirror, she knew what Ian Archer had seen in her.

Not her, Celine. Any lonely, overworked widow, starved for a bit of romance, would do. But he would leave in a day or three, taking his tourney prizes with him. On to another faire, another widow, and then another.

For a moment, she considered, for Ian Archer was not Basalt. He would pay in earnest coin with those eyes, that hair, that musical voice. Those arms were yet strong, those hands skilled, knuckles not yet swollen with joint-ill. And if he found a night's solace in her bed and offered illusion in recompense, what harm could there be in that?

On the freezing plain, in the cavern, within the skull rock, everything had been so clean-edged, almost featureless. Even her emotions had been uncomplicated—hope, fear, love, loss. The outer world wasn't like that. Weeds grew in the cracks of weathered granite, dust fouled even the most carefully oiled gears. People said one thing and did another, meant well and yet brought sorrow.

While she was thinking, Ian Archer leaned on the counter, face tilted away from her. He took in a deep breath, released it in a sigh. The lines of his face and body softened. She brought out a short loaf from the last day's baking, one too stumpy for ready sale, and offered it to him. The crust crackled as he tore a piece off.

"'Tis good bread." He paused in his chewing, eyes thoughtful. "The flour is harder than we use in the Isles."

"We call it frost-wheat," she said, accepting a morsel in return. "It's a winter wheat, slow to ripen but with good bones, or so the miller says when he asks an extra sol for the grinding." Inside the shell of crust, the bread was still tender and faintly fragrant, reminding her of fields of waving stalks lightly dusted with snow. "But how does an archer come to know of such things?"

"In the village where I grew up—oh, a handful of cotts, not a grand place like this—my mother's family made the bread, everything from running the watermill to the real baking. I had no sisters, just a handful of rowdy brothers. We worked in the bakery from the time we could stand. The smells here remind me...I can almost feel the dough all silky in my hands...but that was long ago."

"And the archery? You could not have come to that late."

Dark brows tightened. "When the Boat-riders came sweeping down from the north, we all of us stood to the palisades. One day, I carried my father's bow."

And the luck-tokens carved into it had been real, so that even a young boy shot straight and true. But the father did not.

Celine saw what happened in his face, *They burned the mill, the cotts. I alone, I was left to make my way in the world.* Sadness shot through her like one of Ian Archer's arrows. How had he managed to live with such a burden? She felt a strange kinship with this man who had no place, she who had one that held her in a merciless grip. Once she would have turned away with a few meaningless phrases, to remember him only on the loneliest of nights. Now, on this day of all days, the rich chaotic pattern of her life came clear.

"Ian Archer, Ian…Baker." Gently she laid one hand on his, as if he were her brother. "I have a proposition for you."

Tiny brass bells jingled from the gray mare's harness as Celine rode briskly down the road that would take her away from the village. The long black vest fit surprisingly well when laced to her shape, and the bow case settled across her back as if it had always been there.

She'd left Ian Baker crouched over the fire pit of the main oven, getting acquainted with the salamander. Fireling, after yowling her distress, had favored him with a flick of her slender tongue, just quick enough not to sear his skin. He'd laughed, a merrier sound by far than all his flattering words. When Basalt came by the shop, expecting an even more worn-down Celine… Ah, but she left that moment to Ian to relish.

Overhead, the sky grew warmer and brighter, quivering with light. Within its case, the bow hummed sweetly to her in its own language; she remembered how it had warmed under her touch, inviting her to string it, test it, draw out its power with her own.

"No more tourney-faires for you, my beauty," she'd sung in her turn. "And no more endurance for me!"

Fire and moon! Dance through the air!

They were two of a kind, this enchanted thing and her. They

needed only an adventure worthy of their mettle. And if one did not come to them…well, then they would go out and make it!

A Hunter of the Celadon Plains

Spring Moon Rising climbed the hill behind her village to greet the sunrise. Below her, in every direction, stretched the Celadon Plains. Pale green grasses, heavy with beryl-hued grain, rippled across the land. In the distance, a herd of jade bison lifted their horned heads. The wind tugged at her long braids. The air smelled metallic, lightning edged with frost. In the Blue Beyond, a rapture was gathering, a turbulence of gray and silver. The storm was almost upon them, and it was a storm like none other.

Moon thrust the thought from her, lest it prove an evil omen. Her own restless spirit put such dangerous thoughts into her mind.

"Moon! There you are!" Cheeks flushed, Moon's eldest sister, Dew On Flowers, trotted up the incline. "Why do you stand here daydreaming, while the others are already gathered? Have you lost your taste for meat?"

Moon turned away to hide her moment of shame. It was irresponsible to keep the other hunters waiting once the sun was up. She did herself and her family no honor by behaving in such a selfish manner.

The two sisters hurried down the hill, settling their bows and arrow-cases across their backs as they went. At the outskirts of the village, they joined the other hunters. All together, the party numbered a dozen, somewhat more men than women, under the leadership of Uncle Lion Gaze. Although no longer as fleet he once was, he was such a crafty hunter that no one questioned his right to lead. Moon was the youngest, yet she had already killed two bison.

Under the direction of Lion Gaze, the hunting party set out toward the herd that Moon had seen earlier. They ran easily, at a pace they could sustain for many hours. They carried only what was necessary, their bows and arrow-cases, knives for butchering, and hand axes for cutting carrying-frames.

Moon skimmed the grass-laced earth, sweating lightly, her breath soft in her throat. Her spirits rose and the looming darkness overhead receded from her thoughts.

Several of the young men tried to speak to her. Moon knew they thought well of themselves, for she had seen the way the other young women of her clan looked at them, the sideways glances, the flushed cheeks. To Moon, however, they were as dull as sand. Why should she lay down her bow for someone she could outrun and out-hunt? She tossed her head, her braids flying, and refused to answer them.

"You are too picky," Dew said when they paused near the top of a hill. Below, the bison herd grazed, unaware of their presence. "Endless River or Snake Strikes could have any girl he wanted."

"Then let them!" Moon kept her eyes on the largest bison, marking him for her own. He was a massive-headed, shaggy bull, and his hide was so pale a green that he shimmered like moonlight. He would be strong and fast, so she must be stronger and faster.

Dew would not be diverted. "Think what you are doing! Do you want to end your days alone?"

"Stop worrying about me, sister. There will be time enough for marriage and children." Moon laid one hand on her sister's arm. "I know you are trying to look out for me, but I do not need a mother's scolding."

"It seems that you do, if you think a good husband will wait around for you while the long grass grows."

Moon sighed and made no answer. There was no point in arguing with Dew on the subject of husbands.

Quietly, they divided into groups and strung their bows. Moon struggled with hers, for it was new and the stiff wood resisted her. Hawk Wing made a disapproving sound.

"That's a man's bow," he commented, as if she did not already know. "It's too much for you."

Moon drew in her breath, deep into the pit of her belly, and the string slipped into place. She straightened and met his eyes. "A bow does not care who draws it, man or woman, mortal or god. It answers only to strength."

"Then it is a good thing we draw our bows with our arms and not our tongues, or you would outstrip us all." Lion Gaze came up to them. "Have you finished taunting your fellow hunters, my niece, and sowing rivalry instead of comradeship?"

Moon dipped her head. "I am ready, uncle." To Hawk Wing she said, "I am sorry for my sharp words."

"They were true ones." He turned, following the hunt leader.

They crept through the grass, keeping downwind of the herd. Not a sound betrayed their passage. One of the men startled a nest of plains sparrows that rose, crying out in the their shrill voices. An emerald-hued bison cow lifted its head, snorted, and then returned to grazing.

Dew crawled on her belly to Moon's side. "What did you say to Hawk?"

"Nothing of any importance. Look!" Moon pointed to the herd. The hunting party was close enough now to smell the warm animal musk and the scent of sweet crushed grass on the fitful breeze. The bull she had chosen stood a little apart from the others. His horns, wide and tapering, gleamed like polished bone, and the morning sun glinted on his golden eyes. Lush, curling hair covered his shoulders. He tipped his muzzle to the wind, black-rimmed nostrils flaring wide. Shaking his head, he rumbled deep in his throat.

He senses us, Moon thought. *He cannot smell us, but he knows we are here.*

Lion Gaze gave the signal. Everyone began moving, crouched down low. If they were lucky and the wind held, they might get even closer before the herd broke. This was the most difficult part of the hunt, when the possibility of discovery attended every step. No matter how well they read the temper of the beasts, no one could be sure if the herd would flee or turn and charge.

None of the hunters excelled Moon at stealth. Dew and Hawk and the two other men in her party dropped back, letting her take the lead. She slipped between the stalks of grass like a whisper from the earth itself. The smell of the bison filled her nostrils. She tasted their sweat, the dust on their hooves. The sound of their breathing vibrated along her bones.

She caught the subtle shift in that tremor, and froze. Even as she lifted her bow into position, her legs beneath her, the bull whirled and charged.

Moon surged upright. Adrenaline stung her blood. Her vision went sharp. The bull was closing fast, his head lowered, the tips of his sweeping horns aimed at the hunters. She drew the bow to its maximum tautness and held it, waiting for a target. From behind her, the others loosed a volley of arrows. One landed short and the others bounced off harmlessly. No arrow could pierce that thick hide or that massive skull.

Closer... Moon calmed herself as her arm muscles trembled under the strain. *If he turns but a little...*

"Aiee! Run!" Hawk yelled.

Moon heard their scattered flight, the cries of her sister, "Moon! Come *on!*"

The ground beneath her feet quivered like a drum. His hooves tore into the sod, throwing up clods and dust. Still she waited. At the last moment, when the bull was but a breath away from her, he swung his head to one side. One golden eye caught her in its gaze.

She loosed her arrow.

The arrow plunged deep into the bison's eye socket. He let out a fearsome cry. The reek of his blood shrilled in the air.

Moon scrambled out of the bison's path. Propelled by the momentum of his charge, he hurtled into the very place she had been standing and fell to his knees. Swiftly she drew another arrow and notched it to the bowstring.

Before she could take aim, the bull heaved himself to his feet. The shaft of her first arrow had broken off, leaving a bloody wound. He slung his head around, fixing her with his one good eye. In its molten-gold depths, she read terrible pain but also an unmistakable challenge. She lowered the tip of her arrow, fractionally releasing the tension on her bow. In that moment, the bull whirled away. She did not think an animal that size could move so nimbly.

Trailing drops of crimson, the bull galloped away.

Moon watched him go. Her heart clenched. To kill one of the bison was an act of courage, of daring, and also of necessity, an act that allowed her people to survive the frozen darkness of the Ice Raven. But to wound such a noble creature, to let it suffer…

In shame, she hung her head.

"Moon!" Rushing up, Dew threw her arms around her sister. "I thought you'd be killed!"

Someone else said, "What a shot! We will sing of it to our grandsons!"

"We will do no such thing." Moon unstrung her bow and slung it across her back. Blinking back tears, she averted her face so that none of the others could see. Theirs was the glory of the hunt, the herd now galloping away. "Go!" she cried. "The hunt calls you!"

Whooping, Hawk and the other young men darted off to join the others. Only Dew stayed behind.

"I must finish what I have begun," Moon said.

"I know."

"You have no duty to come with me. Your place is with the others."

Moon thought, *This will be my last hunt. It would be a mercy for the bull to kill me, so that I do not return to my clan in dishonor.*

In answer, Dew touched Moon's arm. She seemed to be saying, *My place is here, with you.*

Moon nodded. "Stay behind me. Do not risk yourself."

The plains wind sang in the braids of the two women. So soft was their tread upon the earth, the grasses parted for them. From time to time, they caught sight of the bull. Once Moon saw him stumble and fall. Her heart quickened and she pushed for greater speed, but when they reached the spot, they found only a circle of flattened, blood-stained grass.

The bull led them ever farther from the hills and plains of their home territory. At first, Moon paid little heed to the changing landscape. She scarcely noticed when the countryside no longer looked familiar.

Finally, Dew called for them to stop. "We can't go on like this." Wheezing, struggling for breath, Dew bent over. With one hand she kneaded the muscles of her side. "I don't recognize this place, do you? If we continue this chase, we'll become lost."

Moon shook her head. Her braids swung heavily, damp with sweat. "The bull cannot run forever. He must stop, and then I will end his pain."

"And what then, sister? How will we find our way home?"

"You have been strong and loyal, but this is not your search. I release you from it. Go back to our people in honor."

Dew's dark brows tensed. "I will not return without you."

Moon knew better than to argue with her sister. In such a mood, Dew could be as unrelenting as rain. So they went on, more slowly now.

The light of the Blue Beyond shifted. Day's heat seeped

from the earth, and chill gathered in the shadows. Above, the storm still had not broken. Clouds churned, heavy and oppressive. Dew, who had been trotting along silently, began to grumble. How would they track the bison in the dark? What if they met a pack of wolves or a viridine lion? What must the men think of them, to be gone so long and so far?

For a time, Moon would not listen. Twilight, pale and shimmering, washed the western horizon. The earth smelled cool and moist. She felt as if she could track the bull by the scent of his tread, the brush of his body through the grasses, and the lingering taint of animal musk.

At last, however, she relented and took heed of her sister's pleas. The ground turned rocky, rising sharply and making footing difficult. They entered a country of dense thorny brush reaching above their heads.

They found an open space and set about with their axes cutting dead branches for firewood, and living branches, thin and springy, for a shelter. They stripped off the bark to tie the branches together, and gathered moss and soft leaves for a bed. They had only a little water left, but Dew, ever resourceful, found a patch of juicy wild onions to roast.

After they had performed their evening prayers and banked the fire, the sisters retired to their shelter. Within minutes, Dew's soft breathing indicated that she was asleep. Moon lay on her back, gazing up through the opening between the roof branches. The tips seemed to be reaching past the roiling clouds, toward the stars perhaps, or the faint goddess-veil. She wondered if the bull were looking up with his single remaining golden eye. If he suffered. If he hated.

Forgive me, she thought, but she did not believe he could.

All the next morning, they climbed. The brush here grew sparse and twisted, so dark it looked black. They scaled a pass, traversed a valley surrounded by snow-topped peaks, and climbed again. Dew said no more about turning back. They needed all their breath for climbing. Wind blew constantly, at times threatening to peel them off the rock face. Moon's leg muscles burned. Her moccasins were meant for the softer terrain of the plains, and the stones bruised her feet.

Moon wondered how the bull could have come this far, what had driven him into such barren country, and how a beast his size, with such a wound, could navigate the narrow trails. Yet every doubt was answered by fresh evidence of his passing, the print of a massive cloven hoof, or a sprinkling of blood.

The mountains rose and rose, row after distant row, ghostly white. They rested more frequently now, and drank from rushing streams. The water tasted of rock and wildness, so cold that their lips turned blue. Days passed, and in between, they slept huddled in whatever shelter they could find in the shallow, wind-sculpted caves. The storm clouds covering the Blue Beyond darkened, so that noon took on the aspect of night.

Now that they had come so far, leaving behind everything they knew, Moon still refused to give up, for fear that all their suffering would have been for nothing.

Moon awoke to iridescent light. She crept out from beneath the overhanging rock where she and Dew had slept, blinking in the color-drenched brightness that swept across the horizon. Her belly cramped with hunger and every joint in her body throbbed, yet she stood, for a moment oblivious to all pain, caught up in the glory above her. Red and gold, blue and green and orange rippled like curtains waving in a celestial breeze. They beckoned her onward.

The trail led her upwards a short distance, then widened. For a moment, Moon thought she had reached the crest, for the lights now glimmered all around her. She breathed them in. A strange energy flowed through her.

A sound, a clink of one pebble on another, alerted her. She

whirled, reaching for the knife that was not there, and realized too late that she had left her weapons behind in the shelter.

Ahead she could make out only shades of gray and shifting silver. Something moved in the brilliance. She forced herself to stand still. Whatever it was, bow or axe could not harm it. Nor, she realized, would she wish to destroy a thing of such beauty.

Do not be afraid. The words shimmered in her mind.

The next instant, the brightness faded. A man stood there, tall and well-formed. Despite the cold, his chest was bare, and as he held out one hand to her, muscles moved easily beneath his smooth skin. By his features and fringed leggings, the cut of his moccasins and the slant of his eyes, he must be one of her own people, yet she did not know him. His braids were tied with feathers of deepest blue.

Moon had never seen such a color, except in the Blue Beyond on a cloudless day. Surely, this must be a god. Trembling, she dropped to her knees and covered her face with her hands.

His touch was warm and strong as he lifted her, but she would not look directly at him. She stammered, "How shall I address you, O god of the mountains?"

"I am no god," he said. His voice was deep and as beautiful as himself. "You shall call me Bluejay. What is your name?"

Moon looked up in astonishment. Truly, a god would already know her name and her quest, and all her hidden sins. As strange and beautiful as this stranger appeared, he must be as mortal as she herself. Emboldened, she answered his questions. Who she was, her people, what she was doing so far from her home territory.

"And now I cannot go back," she concluded. "I failed to find the bull and put an end to his pain. I have shamed my people."

"The bull you sought does not suffer."

"You may not be a god, but even if you were, I would not believe you," Moon said with spirit. "I must make certain for myself."

At that, Bluejay laughed. "Since you refuse to go home, will

31

you come with me on an even greater adventure? I have come here seeking such a hunter as yourself, one with heart as well as courage. I promise that if we succeed, and you still wish to return home, you will do so with honor."

Moon thought for a long moment. If Bluejay were not a god, perhaps he was a malicious spirit sent to entrap her. She had heard tales of such beings, songs sung around campfires in the Time of the Ice Raven. When she consulted her heart, however, she felt nothing but a surge of irrational joy.

"I will go with you, but first I must bid farewell to my sister."

Together, they went back down the trail to the overhang. Dew had made a fire, from what fuel Moon could not tell, and on that fire, a small bird roasted on a spit. Dew got to her feet and greeted the stranger, inviting him to share their meal. Politely he declined, for there was scarcely enough for one person, let alone three. He explained that he had come into this country to bring Moon back with him.

"You wish to marry her?" Dew said, eyes narrowing.

Moon began to protest, but Dew waved her to hush. If their mother had still been alive, she would have arranged the marriage contract. Dew was clearly determined to act in her stead.

Bluejay said that in his own country, the man presented the bride's family with a gift. Moon saw no possessions at hand, except possibly the feathers of startling blue tied in his hair. Yet the next moment, he was offering Dew a bison robe. It was expertly tanned, supple and sweet-smelling. As he handed it to Dew, his gaze met Moon's and she understood his words about the bull.

"This is a treasure!" Clearly, Dew was of the opinion that any man who owned such a thing must be wealthy indeed. She kissed Moon, bidding her to send word of her new life.

Moon took her bow and arrow case, her knife and hand axe. Following Bluejay, she continued back up the trail. For a long time, she was so beset with strangeness, she could not speak.

A storm came up suddenly, swirls of white and gray that

grew thicker with each passing heartbeat. Moon's skin went numb with cold. Ice congealed in the pit of her belly. Still Bluejay kept on. The blizzard did not seem to affect him. Moon struggled to keep up, although she could barely make out his figure.

Suddenly Bluejay came to a halt. Although the blowing snow obscured the terrain, Moon sensed that before them lay a sharp precipice. She could feel the shape of the mountains and the solidity of rock on three sides, but in front of them lay nothing but wailing emptiness. If she stepped off that cliff, she might fall forever.

"What is this place?" she asked through chattering teeth. "It seems to me the very edge of the world."

He held out his hand. "You are right."

Moon remembered thinking that whatever happened on the search, she would never return home. She had thought she would die on the mountain face of exposure or starvation. She had not the slightest idea then of journeying past the edge of the world. In spite of this, or perhaps because of it, she took Bluejay's hand.

The moment their fingers touched, a change swept through Moon. She no longer shook with cold and fright. Something immeasurably powerful, yet gentle as feathers, caught her, held her. The whiteness of the storm fell away and in its place, across illimitable spaces, she beheld colors such as she had never dreamed. Drawn by Bluejay's sure grasp, she soared like a frost falcon.

How long the journey lasted, Moon could not say. It seemed to go on forever, and yet when she stood once more on her own feet, only the span of a single breath had passed. Too amazed to speak, she gazed at an ancient forest.

She had seen plains trees, with their misshapen, wind-scoured branches and dusty leaves. Few of them grew taller than a man's height. Now she craned her neck, straining to see the tops of the giants that rose around her. Their trunks were straight and smooth-barked, thicker than a man's outstretched arms.

Moon and Bluejay stood in a little pool of sunlight

surrounded by dappled, blue-tinted shade. A jumble of lacy plants covered the forest floor. She inhaled, tasting scents that were pungent, unfamiliar, and deeply stirring.

Bluejay slipped his fingers from her grasp. "We're here."

"What is this place?"

"My home."

She stared at him for the first time. Far above, branches swayed in a wind, so that motes of light danced across his bare skin.

His eyes darkened. "You know there are many worlds, each with its own people, its own magic?"

"So our songs teach us." Her voice came in a whisper. "But I never guessed..." turning now, struggling to encompass the enormity and brightness of the forest, "...it would be like this."

"And in all these worlds," he went on, as if he had not heard, "what is the greatest danger? The most dire threat?"

"The Ice Raven, who brings dark and cold, the sleep of the soul," she answered as she had been taught. "It cannot be seen, or captured or—"

He cut her off with an impatient gesture. "The Ice Raven is a part of the natural cycle. The fallow times give the land its rest, and we take no harm from the long sleep. My people offer prayers at such times, blessing the Ice Raven."

For an instant, Moon was angry. Surely he was making fun of her, treating the beliefs of her own clan as ignorant super-stitions. Then she realized he was in earnest.

"What, then?" she asked. "If you do not fear the Ice Raven, what *do* you fear?"

"Something against which my people have no defense, no power." Bluejay paused, an unreadable expression passing over his features. "But you do."

Moon wanted to laugh. What could she do and what beast could she hunt, that this strong warrior could not? He could walk between worlds! Now he truly was teasing her.

Still, his expression remained grave, and she decided that no matter how far-fetched, he took his own words seriously. "What do you want from me?"

"Do you have the courage to face that which threatens all our worlds? Do you have the will to defeat it?"

Moon lifted her chin and took her bow in hand. "I am no magician. All I have are these, my arrows. They are yours to command."

"Then come with me."

Once more, Bluejay held out his hand. This time, as she slipped her fingers through his, Moon felt a faint quivering, but she did not know if it were her own or his.

No blizzard rose up to blind her, no wall of whiteness, no whirl of space and light. Instead, they rose gently, following the arrow-straight trees. The air grew fresher, warmer, yet wilder. Birds passed them, not the olive-drab sparrows of the plains, but creatures adorned with extravagant rainbow plumage. They swooped through the air, their songs rising and falling. Moon cried out in delight, and Bluejay grinned.

They left the birds behind and passed the tops of the trees. The branches were so far below that Moon imagined them as a soft carpet. Clouds wafted by until only the Blue Beyond lay above them. Such a blue it was, more intense than she had ever seen.

Moon kept expecting that the next moment would bring them up against a hard blue surface, as if the Blue Beyond were the inside of a bird's egg.

We are hatchlings struggling to be born, came his voice in her mind.

The end of their upward journey came suddenly. It was not at all what she expected. One instant, they soared gently through unchanging blue. The next, a strange uneasiness hovered at the edges of her senses, like a storm front poised to break.

Bluejay looked at her with a grave expression. "This is your last chance to turn back."

"I have said I will help you," Moon retorted with a touch of heat. Did he think her so lacking in honor that she would take back her word? Then she realized his words came not from any mistrust of her but from his own fears. He was tall and strong, clearly a warrior among his own people. Again she wondered what help she could give against an enemy that such a man as he dared not face.

As if reading her thoughts, he said, "Each of these wild worlds has its own form of magic. No matter how I appear to you, I have no prowess with physical fighting. My people's gift is the ability to travel between worlds. Yours—" and here he touched her chest over her fast-beating heart, "yours is courage. And you are the finest of them all. The only one who answered my call."

Before Moon could ask what he meant, he lifted his hand and under their feet stretched a wide path. One moment, it appeared to her as a beam of shimmering light, the next, a metallic cable, and still again, a twisted rope as thick as one of Bluejay's trees. Along this path, images rippled and flashed, the pale green plains of her own world, then an ocean of surging tides, beyond that, sweeping sun-kissed meadows, and in the other direction, row upon row of stone houses with glowing jewel-toned windows. The richness and beauty of the worlds captured her senses. She longed to visit them all, to walk those streets and glades and beaches.

"They are worth saving, are they not?" Bluejay asked.

Moon swallowed her answer, for no words could convey her emotion. Another breath, and she was able to say, "What threatens them?"

Bluejay pointed beyond his own world, where the visions disappeared into mist. "You will see for yourself. There."

Moon took her bow and strung it on the first attempt. Hawk had been wrong; it was not a man's bow or a woman's bow. It was a *warrior's* bow. Holding an arrow at ready, she moved toward the distant mist.

The haze began to flow and darken, like the storm on the

day of the hunt. It curled around her, dampening her skin, and shutting out all other sight and sound. Something moved within the shifting currents of air and light and power. She halted, holding herself still against the hammering of her heart.

A sound reached her, a gnawing, rending noise, as if the very fibers of the world were being wrenched apart. This was no bison, no wolf or eagle or emerald-striped viper, but something far more terrible. She moved closer, step by searching step.

A shape emerged as the mist grew thin and parted to reveal a beast. It was unlike any she had ever seen, fully as huge as a bison, but long-bodied and low to the ground. Dull black scales covered its body, except for the tapering snout and the whip-like tail. A stench hung about it, the smell of rotten things, of must and slime and places best forgotten. But worse of all were its eyes, lightless pupils ringed in blood.

Hooked claws and yellowed teeth sank deep into the shining rope. The beast twisted its head, snapping threads of light, then devouring them.

Awareness shifted the beast's eyes. It rose up, froth dripping from its jaws. Rumbling sounded in its throat. It extended its head, slit nostrils flaring wide, and bared its razor teeth.

For an instant, Moon's nerve almost failed her. How could she fight such a monster? Yet if she ran away now, as every instinct urged her, what then? The beast would destroy the paths that linked the worlds together. She knew, as certainly as if Bluejay had told her aloud, that all would then fall into darkness, a night without even the Ice Raven for comfort.

The beast was already moving toward her. Whip tail lashing, it gathered itself for a leap. Moon drew her bow. Her arrow sped true, but the beast turned at the last instant. Hissing and thrashing, the monster caught the shaft between its jaws and snapped it into a dozen fragments.

Moon slipped another arrow into place. Before she took aim, however, the monster leapt, quicksilver fast.

She ducked and rolled toward the beast. The claws of its hind paws raked her as it passed overhead. Something snapped—the arrow she had drawn, not her precious bow. The creature's body cast her into shadow and flooded her nostrils with its rank odor. Then it landed heavily on the path beyond her.

Moon scrambled to her feet to face the beast. As her fingers touched her arrow case, she realized that she had only one arrow left. Only one.

Fitting it to the string, she drew the bow.

Growling, the creature took a slow, menacing step toward her. She could not see a vital target, only rows of overlapping obsidian-dark scales. Its skull was thick and she did not think even her bow could drive an arrow through its ribs head-on.

She must choose her target. One more step and the beast would be upon her.

The monster halted, as if daring her to shoot. Its tail lashed the air. She faced it, unflinching.

One arrow, only one chance.

The beast tensed its muscles for another leap. Moon crouched down on one knee and shot upwards just as its forequarters lifted. The arrow buried itself in the thin skin just to one side of the breastbone.

The beast dropped, but Moon was already rolling free. The silvery rope shuddered under the impact, then began swaying and twisting. Clutching her bow, she flattened herself on its surface. Her vision whirled sickeningly. The entire universe seemed to have come loose from its moorings, bucking and heaving like a maddened bison. Below it, or perhaps above, for in Moon's disordered sight she could not tell, yawned an enormous whirlpool, an abyss of swirling darkness.

With a great cacophonous screech as if a thousand rusted bells rang out at once, the body of the beast slid sideways and disappeared into the void.

Gradually, the path of light grew still. Moon dared to sit up. Her cheeks were slick with tears, and the air stung her eyes. She bled from four or five shallow gashes on her arms, most likely from the beast's claws, although she could not remember being struck. Her bowstring had snapped, but the bow itself seemed to be sound.

She clambered unsteadily to her feet and retraced her steps. The path felt solid, resilient, but she was trembling so badly that the slightest tremor might topple her over the side. To her surprise, she saw no sign of the frayed strands from the beast's devastation. She hoped this meant the bond between the living worlds had taken no lasting harm.

The mist closed around her as she went on, but this time she welcomed it as a friend. It stroked her torn skin, drawing out the pain. She thanked it silently. After a time, so gradually she could barely discern the change, the mist lifted. Bluejay stood there, waiting for her.

Whether the battle with the beast itself had changed her, or whether it was something in the mist or the vision of worlds strung together by a rope of light, Moon now looked on the man before her with new eyes. When she had first met him, Bluejay had appeared as a warrior, a god. Certainly, the ability to walk the worlds was a magical gift. Yet he had sought her out to do what he could not.

"It's time for truth between us," she said. "Who are you?"

The air between them wavered like heat rising from the summer plains. Bluejay's form shifted and grew more slender. He was still tall, but his shoulders were narrow, his hands graceful and soft. He wore a shirt of azure wool, touched here and there with gold, and belted over narrow leggings. Thongs of dyed leather tied a cluster of blue feathers to one of several gray braids. His face was angular, with heavy eyebrows and a long, straight nose, very different from the features of her own people. A band of cloth covered one eye; the other, golden as a hawk's, met hers steadily.

"Do you know me now?" Only his voice had not changed.

Unable to speak, she touched the cloth over his ruined eye.

"A small enough loss," he said. "Only someone brave enough to face down a charging bull, and steadfast enough to follow an injured animal so far into the wilderness, could cross

39

the wild worlds without going mad. You see, I was right." With a small smile, he touched her cheek. "You were the one."

Moon dared not speak, dared not breathe. At first, his true appearance had seemed strange to her. Now she would not have him any other way.

Which of them, she wondered, had paid the greater price— he with his eye or she, having left behind her home, her sister, her clan?

"I will take you back to your plains." Bluejay held out his hand, "if you wish it."

Moon found her voice. "I wish to go with you, but not to return to the life I had before. I wish—I wish to see all those other worlds."

To walk those beaches and meadows, to explore those cities and forests...

She felt his heart rise in his breast, even as hers did. Warm fingers closed around her own. Together, they stepped out on the luminous road.

Storm God

Sevens. Damn! Dov stared at the dice and pushed Rion's shoulder aside, as if a closer look could change the result. The mage's teeth glinted in the shadow of his purple hood as he swept in the wager pile, and she saw her flame-opal disappear under his hand. The watching inn-rabble grew noisy in disapproval; mages were not popular in these parts.

"It isn't possible," Rion groaned. "He must have cheated."

"He didn't and you know it," snapped Dov, tossing a mop of lanky ginger hair back from her eyes. "Oh, how could I have let you talk me into this? You're always taking ridiculous chances and now you've lost my opal! Why did I ever listen to you?"

"It was your idea as much as mine. An easy mark, you said. I was ready to go home an hour ago, but you insisted we stay for one more throw. Just one more throw as long as our luck held." His dark eyes glittered in the inn's smoky light.

Dov jumped to her feet. He was right, of course, but that did not change anything.

Rion relented. "Love, I'm sorry. I know how much your mother's opal means to you, and I wouldn't have— There's nothing I can do about it now. It's done with, over."

"There're a few other things that are over and done with." She turned toward the inn door and the crowd drew back from her in sympathy.

"In the interest of domestic felicity," the mage said in his precise, dry voice. "Perhaps we could continue the game…" He moved his hand and the flame-opal sat alone on the rude wood table, shimmering crimson and gold.

Dov halted, keeping her eyes from Rion's stricken face. She had not anticipated arousing the mage's interest, but there might be some advantage for her in it. As long as she could keep him talking, she had a chance of maneuvering him into a bargain. He was not mortal, but that should make no difference. She sat down again.

"I suppose we could, if you made it interesting enough."

"Dov," Rion hissed, "we've nothing more—" She silenced him, still keeping her eyes on the mage.

"Games of chance do not interest you?" asked the sorcerer.

"Not nearly so much as contests of skill."

"Ah!"

"For instance," she leaned forward, resting on her elbows and studying the soot-grimed ceiling, "you've been boasting there are some things mortals just can't do. If you made it worth my while…"

"Are you proposing to turn lead into gold?" The dry voice reeked with amusement.

Dov shrugged. "Do I challenge you to shape honest iron, which you dare not touch lest you lose your arcane talent? No, I had in mind something I could do without the aid of magic."

"Then it's hardly worth the betting—"

"How about crossing the Turgian Marshes in a single day?" Dov raised her voice to make sure the inn-rabble could hear and witness her.

The mage's spine straightened perceptibly. "You can't do it. No mortal can."

"I will—for my opal and ten pieces of gold."

"Don't do it," Rion sputtered. "No stone is worth the risk. You'll never make it alive. Don't you know the horrors that lurk in the swamp?"

"Of course I do, the same as you. Whip-plants, were-foxes,

42

quicksand, vampire trees. Isn't that so?" she demanded of the mage.

"A crude approximation. The vampire are mythical and you omitted mention of the trap-spiders."

Dov blanched. She hated spiders and had blissfully forgotten them.

"You see how impossible it is," said the mage.

"These good folk heard my offer and they heard you say I couldn't do it," Dov replied. "Will they also hear you back down before a mere mortal?"

Slowly the mage shook his head. "If you survive and meet the time deadline, the opal is yours…and the gold."

Dawn filtered wan and yellow through the straggler trees bordering the Turgian Marshes as Dov adjusted the laces of her running boots and checked her knife in its hidden sheath. Rion shifted from one foot to the other, holding his tongue with visible effort.

"It isn't as if I'd never *been* in the Marshes before," she continued. "When I ran messages for Old Hammach over in Deever, I used to cut through them all the time. Most of the horribles aren't nearly so bad as their reps." She straightened up, shrugged her leather jerkin into a more comfortable position, and began a final inspection of her belt pouches.

"Listen, Dov—"

"Listen, yourself. I may have gotten out of condition since I took up with you and your crazy trading schemes, but I can still out run anything in the swamps. Why do you think they call them swamp *crawlers*? Not, I assure you, for their fleetness of foot. Besides, I know a trick or two."

"That's just the problem. You can't fool a swamp crawler the way you can a human mark. You think you're pulling one on that mage, cut he's the one who has you, not the other way around."

As if conjured by his words, the mage, robed as before in dusted purple, came striding over the grasses. The voice that issued from the darkened hood was brittle like aged parchment.

"Human, you are either foolhardy or extraordinary, possibly both. I will await you at sundown on the other side of the Marshes. Whether you arrive is another matter entirely." Then he vanished in the usual puff of smoke.

"Dov, it's only a game to him," Rion insisted. "He probably cheated us out of your opal just to force you into this ridiculous wager. It's not worth your life."

"This makes it all the better. Remember when you brought ice to Verbourg just because Rainold said it was impossible? The five bags of gold were nice, but you would have done it anyway."

"I didn't risk being eaten by a were-fox!"

Dov laughed. "Rion, I promise you that if anything out there eats me, it won't be a were-fox. One couldn't catch me if it tried." She leapt lightly across the borders of the swamp and called back, "They haven't any feet!"

Dov made good time through the morning, keeping to the threadwork of game trails that laced the Marshes. She had no difficulty avoiding the patches of quicksand with their coats of light earth and certain, sucking death. The sun rose higher, pale through thickening clouds. Desolate though the swamp might appear, it teemed with subtle, carnivorous life, no place for the unwary.

She glimpsed a were-fox curled near some brierbushes. Its whimpering, pitched to lure a predator to its end, aroused her pity at first. It looked exactly like a small wounded animal as it regarded her with bright, pleading eyes, its poison sucker-pads carefully hidden beneath furry sides. She laughed at its pretentious vulnerability and went on her way.

The whip-plants were another matter. She had just finished

eating her midday meal, sitting on a patch of salt-grass and congratulating herself on the excellent time she had made. Descending from the hummock, her ankle turned on the slippery grass, and she stumbled into a tangle of branches. It took her a moment to realize the grip on her arms and hair was not accidental. By then she was firmly held.

Dov lashed out at the bramble with a booted food.

"You idiot plant, let go of me!" The pliant vines curled around her, tough and resilient, well beyond her strength to break. She felt a slight, irresistible pull toward the central trunk.

"Of all the stupid—" she gasped. *Just when things were going so well, to be eaten by a plant!*

She twisted against the branches, feeling them yield and then tighten. They lifted her slightly and her boots slipped on the dry earth, her traction broken. Glancing toward the trunk, she saw a pulsating bulge appear in the dark brown bark. A slit of serrated pink appeared and dilated, puckering avidly.

Realizing that she had to act quickly, Dov raised her right knee to pull her knife from its sheath. The plant took advantage of her movement to draw her in closer, and she lunged at it, breaking its hold. It was designed to keep creatures from pulling away, not rushing toward it.

Screaming, Dov plunged her knife into the reddish heart of the whip-plant. Its branches lashed out with sudden, wringing violence, and tendrils fell from her as it rent the air with whistling wails. She scrambled to her feet, stunned at her luck. Resistance was what the plant was prepared for, and she had saved her life with outright attack.

Still gripping the hilt of her knife, Dov ran until her breath came in painful rasps and she could no longer hear the plant's torment. She hunched over, sides burning and heaving, staying on her feet despite the trembling in her thighs. Gradually her breathing quieted. She inspected her blade, finding no trace of the plant's sap on the metal, but she wiped it carefully on a patch of herbweed before putting it away.

From then on she went more carefully, her spirits somber. The cloud cover kept off the heat, and later it began to grow chilly. Dov again moved vigorously, jog-and-run as she had been taught, and the exercise kept her warm. She began to think that she might win the wager after all, if only to avoid spending the night in the Marshes. It would be a long time before she scoffed at their dangers again.

She did not see the earth-colored plasmoid lying in its rough trench until it was too late and she went slithering down the unnaturally slick slope. *Whomp!* The bottom ground me her with a tooth-jarring shock. The bars of the trap closed silently around her right thigh.

Dov pushed herself to her elbows, ears ringing with the impact of her fall. It was uncomfortably reminiscent of the time Rion had challenged her to cross the Whelan ice-lake (source of the ice they had shipped to Verbourg) and she had cracked two ribs falling on its uncompromising surface.

Her hip stung where she had landed on it, but the plasmoid trap held her so tightly she could not roll to ease the pain. She managed a sitting position, looking around her, and realized with horror where she was.

For the first time, Dov began to think Rion was right, that she had been risking her life foolishly. This was not her idea of a fitting end, dying alone in a trap-spider's den. She thought she was getting the better of the mage by counting on luck and her meager experience, amplified by boundless self-confidence. But she could not bargain her way out of *this* trap.

A roll of thunder sent her eyes heavenward. *All this, and a brewing storm, too!* she thought in disgust. The shallow pit in which she lay would give her scant protection against wind and rain.

Dov choked down a sob of anger, as much at herself as at the semi-living trap, and thrust her fingers at it. The plasmoid felt soft under her push, but its coarse suction-surfaces gripped her leather breeches still tighter. If she could slip something beneath it, she might be able to loosen its hold, but she had no lubricant to ease the process, nor could she reach the knife hidden in the boot top of her trapped leg.

Thunder again. "Oh, shut up!" Dov cried, her fingertips as well as her temper beginning to fray. "If you can't help, then keep your blasted nose out of it!"

"What's that you say?" rumbled a voice from above.

She squinted upward. "You didn't say that."

"Oh, but I did, small one. Haven't you heard of Kronk, the great and glorious Storm God?"

"Storm God, huh? I don't suppose you could get me out of this accursed thing before its owner comes to collect me?" Trap-spiders, according to those few who had lived to tell about them, were ten-legged, the size of a mastiff, and carnivorous.

"Ha!" clapped the thunder. "As if you were big enough for me to bother with."

Dov narrowed her lips to hide a smile. After Rion and the mage, how difficult could it be to manage a mere weather deity? "Of course," she agreed. "I'm only an undersized mortal, scarcely worth noticing. But then you aren't a *real* Storm God."

Thunder boomed across the sky, darkening as clouds massed to hide the sun. "Not a real Storm God? I'll show you who's real!"

Dov waited until the racket died down and her voice could be heard. "I'm only a powerless human, ignorant of the dealings of the mighty. But I've always understood that read gods do things like crack mountains and move oceans. You couldn't even move a small thing like me."

"Move you? A piddling little lump of flesh like you? I've swept whole armies away! Easiest thing in the world."

Wind hit her without prelude, bringing blood to her cheeks. The plasmoid, however, was securely anchored to the bottom of the pit, and even Kronk's single-minded blasting could not budge it. Finally the gale died down enough for her to shout, "O great Kronk, now I believe in your power. It is not for the likes of me to challenge the gods. Punish me for my impudence in any way you like—blast me, thunder upon me—"

The first few raindrops hit her like pellets. Then more fell, plummeting to sting her face and arms, but they were not enough to soak her leather breeches into slipperiness. Water began to drip from her nose.

Dov threw her head back. "O mighty Kronk, do anything to me you wish, but please not that! Anything but getting me wet!"

"Wet? I'll show you wet!"

Rain came down in sheets, quickly soaking her. Dov held her hands out, cupping them to splash her trapped thigh. The thin leather slid a little under the softening plasmoid.

The pit began to fill with water, and Dov's fingers slipped beneath the bars of the trap.

Only a few more seconds now...

Half-floating, she braced herself against the pit wall and looked up to see the trap-spider looming black and hairy, clacking its mandibles above her head.

Terror shook her. She'd played her gambit, relying on the pride and stupidity as well as the raw power of Kronk—and lost. Her death towered above her, insectile and odorous.

"Curse you, Kronk, you old rain-bucket!" she shrieked. "You're nothing but a weakling charlatan! You haven't moved me yet!"

The answering torrent lifted her on a swelling wave, and Dove gave a last thrust to slip the trap from her leg. She held her breath and curled beneath the water, reaching for her boot knife. The water carried her to the edge of the pit just as the spider leapt down and began to wade toward her.

As Dov struggled upright, the monster slipped on the slick mud, going down in a windmill of frantic legs. She hesitated for a moment before realizing that even if she could scramble out of the pit, the spider would soon be on its feet and after her. No escape lay in that route. She'd have to deal with it directly, just as she had the whip-plant.

Dov forced her way closer despite the stench of a thoroughly drenched creature of unclean living habits. Its wet, globular body gleamed like an obscene pearl incrusted with tortuous red veins. One hairy leg struck her below the diaphragm. She gasped, spitting bile, but she grabbed the foul limb with her free hand and kept her eyes on her target.

The trap-spider, as if guessing her intent, redoubled its thrashing. It lashed out at her with its poisoned fangs, straining to reach her. Dov twisted in even nearer and plunged her blade into its exposed abdomen. A quick jerk through the tender, unprotected vitals, and the giant arachnid lay twitching, the rain already washing its blood from her blade. She stood there trembling, scarcely able to believe how easily the creature had been killed.

Long moments later, Dov replaced her knife and wiped tears of relief mixed with rainwater from her face. She began to consider the benefits of a judiciously orchestrated weather deity cult. But first, a small test...

"O worthy Storm God! O great Kronk! Hear the words of this small mortal! You would be truly mighty upon the earth, but for one small failing. Your devoted worshipers will be terribly tired of being wet all the time. It's a pity you're powerless to stop what you start."

Rainbows hailed her as she ran laughing on her way to reclaim her fire-opal.

Nor Iron Bars a Cage

Tax collection day dawned clear and bright over the walled city of Ghillensa. Farmers arrived as the first light softened the ancient battlements; wooden gates swung open to admit a procession of oxcarts creaking under late summer's bounty, sacks of wheat and barley, tubs of pale gold butter, sheaves of clover grass to keep cattle fat over the winter, bushels of carrots and cabbages, kegs of country ale. A market had set up in the shadow of the gray-walled Affliction Tower where, it was said, kings had gone in and never seen the sun again until their ghosts wandered the endless corridors, so confused they did not know they had died. Others said there were no ghosts, only the endless, weary sighs of common criminals.

Tax collection day it was today, and Alaina bent over the slop pit behind her father's cloth shop, retching dryly. Nothing came up but acid. She knew better than to try even a mouthful of dry bread. Wiping her mouth on the back of one sleeve, she tucked the folds of her shawl into her wide belt, adjusted the money purse, and went back into the shop. The shop smelled of cedar incense, used to keep away moths. In the light from the mullioned front windows, bolts of blue and crimson cloth shone like jewels. As a child, she loved to bury her face in the fine wool, velvet, even brocade from far Eastern lands. How safe she had felt then, hidden.

A movement from the front of the shop startled her alert. A

familiar shape stepped away from the shadows and became distinct.

"Come on then, my dearling."

Her father's teeth glinted, although the light came from behind him. He held the book of records close to his belly and pulled the door open for her. Walking past him into the bright, dusty street, she drew in a quick breath. The heat of the morning struck her in the face.

"You are too warmly dressed," her father said, as if he had forced her to display his wares and thus increase their value.

The tax collector and his scrawny assistant had, as usual, set up at a table in the market square, so that everyone could see that the King's law knew no favorites and all their neighbors paid their due. This early, the line was short; many were still abed or about their morning marketing. The plain wood table was covered only by a runner bearing the tax collector's sigil: a double-headed axe. Here Alaina's father set his record book and a common clay token used by even those who could not read or write. The book with its tiny looped inscriptions was proof of his own stature, his learning.

The tax collector, a squat, grizzled man in his age-stained tunic, glanced past the book as if it were no more than a speck of dust. He picked up the token, studied it with lower lip outthrust and eyes squinted. "Miles the cloth trader. Fourteen princes of silver."

Exactly, Alaina thought, the same as it had been for the past ten years, since her mother died and she had been the one to accompany him to the market square on tax days. Behind her, a piglet squealed in its cage. Someone hawked turnips in a loud, hoarse voice.

The collector placed a ten-prince weight on the scales, then added four singles. The weights were soft lead, grimed from much handling but not so much that the stamp of the King's own treasurer, the likeness of a prince long dead, could not be clearly seen.

At her father's signal, Alaina took out the coin purse,

double-layered leather carefully stitched in compartment, holding their hard-earned silver. Like traders' coins everywhere, some were small, some large, some round, some oval, even a few Markoni squares. One or two were not coins at all, but silver buttons, and the collector let those pass. Silver was silver.

As she placed the silver pieces, one by one, on the balance pan, Alaina rested her gaze on the weights, lowering her lids so that the image blurred. She felt the familiar, sickening sensation of moving closer and closer until she was inside the metal, she *was* the metal. *Cold... Hard... Heavy...*

She moved among the tiny metal-demons, felt them crowding in on her, throngs so many she could not count them, dancing to their silent music, whirling fast and faster...

Dance with us! Dance with us!

Yes, she thought, and felt the cold metal bubble of their delight. *Dance... Lighter...* She nudged the demons with that special sense, the one she must never let anyone know she had. Dancing faster now, and lighter, as if she were Earth itself longing for Heaven...

Lighter...

The pan bearing the weights lifted, swung up and down. The collector signaled her father to stop, plucked a small coin from the tray and handed it back, holding it between forefinger and thumb as if it might bite him. With his free hand, he waved them on.

For an instant, Alaina could not move. The feeling of one-ness with the metal-demons ripped from her, leaving her senses raw and reeling. She swayed on her feet. Dimly, she felt her father's hand, hard as the lead and as cold, close around her arm. The tax collector might have glanced her way as they hurried past, although she could not be sure.

"What's wrong with you?" her father hissed, as soon as they were out of easy hearing. "Do you want to get caught? Do you know what they will do if they find out about you?"

Hanging, hair and nails pulled out by the roots, molten lead on her eyelids, skin flayed in strips and salt rubbed in... She could recite the

53

words in her sleep, her father had said them so often.

Alaina didn't bother with an answer. She knew better. She steadied, but the old familiar feeling had wrapped her stomach in its vice-like grip, as unrelenting as her father's grasp of her arm. *Don't be sick again*, she pleaded with herself.

He let her rest for a while in the back of the shop. She drank the thin, sour beer because she knew she must. Weakness would not spare her, would only make things worse. Finally, warmth spread from her belly and loosened her muscles. She could breathe again.

That afternoon, a lady and her retinue came in, not a real lady but a spice trader's wife, newly rich, but with ready money to spare and a taste for colorful gowns. The price of the fabrics would go far to replenish the coffers drained this morning. Yet Alaina knew it would not be enough to please her father.

For a while, Alaina lost herself in the choosing of the cloth for the lady's undergarments, chemises of smooth, tightly woven linen to lie against tender skin. She brought out bands of colorful embroidery, stiff with patterning of grapevine and peacock feathers, and tatted lace brought by barge and caravan from the far mountain kingdoms. Time stood still as the beautiful edging strips and fine cloth moved through her hands. At last the lady sighed with contentment, looked toward the bustling street, and turned to go.

Her father bolted the door behind her, signaling that the day's business was done.

"You fool! You simpering, fainting fool! You could have given yourself away! And then where would I be without you?" He rubbed his hands together, soft merchant's hands. Alaina could not take her eyes off his hands. She wished she could cry, but found no tears waiting.

"Yet," his voice softened, crooning. "You did well. I'll wager your curse saved us five solid princes. I might not have to beat you after all."

She kept her eyes lowered, so he would not see the hope that always flared up when he said those words. Flared and died, this time like every other. Her vision went white and she sank to her knees, knowing there was no escape.

Pounding woke her, not throbbing pain from her back and thighs but waves of sound. She started to swing her legs over the side of her narrow trestle bed. A cry tightened around her throat. She quashed it, forced herself to move slowly. It was past dawn so she must have slept, finally. She heard her father's snoring from the other side of the thin wall that marked off her tiny room.

"I'm on my way!" she called out.

She'd slept in her clothes last night, full skirt and long-sleeved blouse gathered high around the neck despite the day's heat. She knew from experience that was easier than having to put them on the next morning. Now she eased herself to sitting, shifted her weight forward, straightened up. The stairs were the hardest part. They always were.

"I'm coming!" she yelled as the pounding redoubled.

"We know you're in there! Open for the King's men!"

She flung open the shop door and let her face twist into a scowl, part genuine pain at the day's brightness. Two guards stood there, alike in blue and silver tunics, nondescript breeches, scuffed boots. One had a sword scar across one cheek.

"My father's still abed. What do you want?"

"You are Mistress Alaina, that stood with him at the tax collector yesterday."

"Yes, of course." Her impatience now gave way to dawning fear.

"Then it's you we want."

They took her, manacled her wrists together as if she were a common thief, would not let her stop to put on her boots so that she had only time to slip her feet into the wooden sandals she saved for muddy days. "Father!" she called, but before he could shuffle downstairs, cursing, the King's men had dragged her through the door and on to the street.

"What's going on? Where are you taking me?" She stumbled. Her neighbors stared. "I haven't done anything!"

Streets and facades blurred by, the faces of the curious, carts and strings of pennants above, smells of fresh-baked bread and overripe fruit, wet wool hanging to dry, boiled cabbage. The guards half-carried her the rest of the way to the King's Voice, court of the western part of the city. She had been to this building with its carved frontel once or twice before, always in her father's shadow.

Spectators jammed the courtroom, eager for amusement. The King's men pushed Alaina forward. She looked around wildly, recognizing no one. A clerk bent over his desk with a stack of curling foolscap to one side, his pen scratching furiously. The tax collector's assistant stood to the side, along with a priest barely old enough to grow a beard. The Voice herself was an old woman with beetle-bright eyes and a mouth like a dried prune. She got up from her darkwood chair, carved all around with bound demons and the saints who had bound them, and peered into Alaina's face.

Please, Alaina prayed, closing her eyes, *let me not go back*.

The Voice made a *h'rumping* sound as she lowered herself back into her chair. "Explain to me again how this child managed to cheat on her taxes."

My father's taxes. Her mouth would not move. Her throat closed up.

The tax collector's assistant said ponderously, as if that were the only speed he knew, "The cloth merchant was to have paid fourteen princes in silver. After he and his daughter left I re-weighed their portion and it came to only nine princes. *She* was the one who carried the purse and placed the silver on the scales."

The Voice peered at Alaina with those too-bright eyes for a moment. "Is this true? Come on, girl. Speak up! Do you have anything to say for yourself before I sentence you?"

Words rushed to Alaina's mind, excuses, pleas for mercy—

her father was poor, it had been a hard year, the prices of wool were so high, she hadn't meant to do wrong, she would never do it again—

Let me not go back…

They took her away with a word from the Voice and the pounding of the staff that sealed her fate to the King's word. To the Tower of Affliction they took her, in whose shadow she had lived her whole eighteen years.

In whose shadow, she thought as the doors clanged shut and the other prisoners, a wave of stinking, starving woman-flesh, drew nigh to drown her, she would die.

That night, Alaina lay curled on the mat of straw in the farthest corner from the door, wishing she did not have to wake up ever again. *Let her sleep, poor child,* said the crone with more gaps than teeth and a welter of festering sores across her chest and back, and gestured to herself. *Soon enough she will come to this.*

But it was not day, not yet. Around her, sleepers sniffed and whimpered, coughed and snored, shifted on their thin pallets. Alaina pushed herself to sitting. Her wrists smarted where the manacles had torn her skin, and it would be several nights before she could lie on her back.

She thought of praying that she might die here, this night and in this place. But her prayers, said by moonlight or not, had never been answered before. There was no reason to think they would be now.

Without thinking, she let her senses wander until she touched the metal-demons in the lock. It was iron, not lead, and she liked its subtle liveliness. With her mind, she followed the shape of the lock. How easy it would be to slide this piece here, to lift this other one.

And where would she go, even if she passed this locked door and the next and the next? Back to her father? To starve on the street?

She stared at the beam of moonshine coming through the single narrow window. No light-demon dancing here, but only a silent song, waves of movement and delight. Exhaustion weighed her eyelids, leaving them heavier than any tax collector's weights. The light grew, reached for her, luminous and piercing like an angel's song...

She awoke again to the clamor of her cellmates rising, complaining to themselves and each other about the hardness of the floor, the body lice, things she didn't understand. Thirst rasped along her throat but her legs and back were less sore than the day before. Somehow she found herself near the front of the throng as the guard passed a basket of bread and a bucket through the door and locked it fast. Alaina gathered up two chunks of bread, one in each hand, then backed off as the other women pressed forward, scrabbling for their share. She looked around, wondering how she was to drink.

"Here you are, dearie." The crone appeared at her elbow, holding out a battered tin cup. Alaina dropped one of the pieces of bread into the crone's hand and took the cup. "That's the way, that's the way."

Alaina realized as she scooped up the brackish water that without the exchange, the crone might have gotten only the hard crusts at the bottom of the basket. With friends, one might survive a long time here.

Alaina turned to find a place to sit and eat. She bumped into an older woman, a good head taller than she, with heavy shoulders and cropped pale-red hair jutting at all angles. The woman's face and most particularly her nose bore a ruddy tint.

"Give that here. I'm hungry."

Alaina handed over her chunk of bread without a blink; she had no appetite for the dry, musty stuff. But she hesitated to surrender the cup. She was so thirsty. The smell of the water rose filled her head like perfume. She licked her lips. Then, without thinking, she lifted the cup and drank deeply. She heard gasps around her as she gulped. Someone jostled her, breaking her balance. She lowered the cup. Red-hair glowered at her and Alaina realized how much bigger and more powerful the other woman was. Strangely, she didn't care. What could the woman do to her that had not already been done?

Water had dribbled around the sides of the cup as Alaina drank, wetting her chin. Now she wiped the back of her free hand across her face.

"What's wrong with you, girl?" came a voice behind her. "That's Maryam the Sword! She'll beat the stuffing out of you!"

Maryam's eyes narrowed. Alaina could well believe the older woman had been a pirate, a soldier, a berserker. But still there was no fear in her; it had all been used up.

"You want water? Here it is!" She downed the rest of the cup over Maryam's head. A gasp rippled through the cell.

"Fight!" someone shrieked.

"Call the guards! She'll kill the child!"

Maryam shook her head, scattering droplets. Her pale-red hair stood up in spikes, like a dozen devil's horns.

Do it, Alaina silently urged her. *End it.*

Somebody by the door was taking bets on how long the fight would last. A clatter down the corridor indicated the approach of the guards. Yet it seemed to Alaina that the cell, that all the world, held its breath.

Maryam leaned forward, scowling down at her. Alaina could feel the heat from the other woman's body on her own face. Suddenly, Maryam threw her head back and laughed.

"Ho ho, ho jo! A fearless one, this!" Still laughing, she turned away to her own pallet by the front wall. The others shrank back from her. She stretched out her legs and gestured at Alaina. "Come here, Little Dragon, and tell The Sword how you came to be in this vile place and who it is that beat you so."

Alaina, who had no idea what to do now that she was going to live, crouched beside Maryam. "How did you know…" she said timidly. *About the beating?*

59

One glance at Maryam's eyes told her. *She knows what it feels like inside her own body. She knows how it is to wake the next morning, to be afraid to move, even to breathe. She knows the footsteps that come in the night.*

The gates to a flood she did not know existed opened inside Alaina. If she could have thrown herself into Maryam's arms and sobbed like a baby, she would have, but she sat, back straight and eyes level, as if they were the only two in the world, and told her story from the beginning, all except for her witch-sense and how her father forced her to use it. Her father's warnings still echoed in her heart, what became of witches.

When she got to the morning and the tax-collector, Maryam stopped her.

"In and out of these places I have been, more times than I can count, Little Dragon, and only one rule have I ever kept. Whatever brought you here, or me, or any of us, that we leave behind."

"Oh." Alaina saw that it didn't matter to this squat ugly woman what she had done, what demons she danced with or why, only who she was right now.

In the nights that followed, as she lay in her pallet that was now next to Maryam's, Alaina sometimes heard the swordswoman cry out in her sleep. A soft cry, not enough to waken anyone else, yet it penetrated into the very marrow of Alaina's bones, where her deepest nightmares hid. At first, Alaina covered her ears with her hands and shivered until she sank back into her own uneasy dreams.

One night, she could not shut out the sound, and she could not bear to hear it. Demons not of metal or of light but of pain, of wordless, endless pain, called out to her. Their voices tore at her soul. Her vision went white and she sank down among the demons, opening herself to their claws and fangs, knowing there was no escape.

Numb endurance was the best she could hope for…or was it? Little demons they might be, little motes of memory, edged like the sharpest knife, but she had some power over demons. Did she dare use it on another person and take the awful risk of be-ing recognized and called out for a witch? Yet did she have a choice? Was it so wrong, so evil to want to ease such terrible pain?

She reached out for them with her unnamable sense, deep into the mind of her sleeping friend. They did not dance, like Earth, nor did they sing, like Light. They collided with each other, swirling, tumbling, shrieking in their own language.

Alaina seemed now to be floating in their midst, surrounded by the chaotic frenzy. They took no notice of her, and she realized that the moment she feared them, they would rise up to drown her. She nudged them as lightly as she dared.

Dance…?

The agitation intensified, whirling, twisting even more franticly now. She could almost see waves, ripples of something that was neither demon nor space between them. She saw it, in a moment's clear vision, like a river in which they struggled, lashed out as if shadow-boxing. Their passion whipped the waters into a foam, dark and poisonous. No, no dancing.

Alaina heard the whimpering again, somewhere beyond the raging, frothing seas of demons. She knew that sound, knew what it was like to long for sleep that never came, knew the pain that had no words. Gently, she reached out to the child beyond the demons, imagined pulling her into strong, safe arms.

"Rest now, my small one, my treasure." In her mind, she said the words she wished to hear a hundred times. She heard them in her mother's voice. *"Quietly, gently, rest…"*

As she spoke, the waves seethed less powerfully, as if calming slightly under her words.

"Quietly now… Gently now…"

She went on speaking in her mind, cradling the invisible child. Slowly, in groups and patches, the demons slowed their terrible whirling. The waters between them grew clear, waves becoming ripples, ripples becoming stillness. The voices of the demons faded, except where they blended into a rhythm that built and faded as smoothly as a song.

"Quietly now… Gently now… Rest now…"

She fell asleep, rocked in the comfort of her own words.

Movement woke her shortly before dawn. The slit of a window through which she had seen the moonlight on her first night in Affliction Tower now admitted the creamy glow of dawn. She sat up, rubbing tear-grimed eyes. Around her, sleepers lay in dreamless sleep. Maryam stood facing the window, one hand clenched tight in a fist, the other covering it. She turned, bowed slightly to Alaina, and lowered her hands.

Pale eyes bored into Alaina's so that she wanted to look away, hide, but something in that searching gaze held her fast. Then Maryam nodded, as if satisfied, and the moment faded.

The guards came tramping down the corridor, four in formation and not one or two as usually came. In their footsteps, Alaina heard their numbers and their fear. The other women felt it, too, for they froze in their games of knucklebones and chance. Tin cups and dice disappeared. A few scuttled to the corners. Maryam, who had been standing in the exact center of the cell on one foot while breathing noisily and waving her arms in a complicated pattern, came to attention and turned to face the bars.

"Oh—ho—ho—" the crone cackled. "There'll be a hangin' sure enough this day."

"Quiet, old woman," Alaina snapped, and received an injured glare in return.

The guards arranged themselves, two on either side of the barred door, the other two a pace behind them. They looked more frightened than grim to Alaina, and it came to her, watching with curiosity as one guard took out a scroll and proceeded to read it, that these were no different from the two who had dragged her here. It was she who had changed.

"Maryam the Sword, accused mayhem and berserker, leman to the dread pirate Caribe, late of the King's Fifth Company of Swords, graced with the Ribbon of Fortitude and since disgraced by crimes against God and His Majesty, stand forth!"

Maryam did not move. The guard looked up from his text and squinted in your direction. "That *is* you, isn't it?"

"All but the leman part," she answered equably. "*That* I never was."

"You are to come with us," he said, still reading. His comrade fumbled with the keys and finally got the door open.

Alaina stood and watched, open-mouthed, as Maryam strode through without a backward glance. Behind her, one of the women muttered a prayer for the dying and the lost. Alaina turned, eyes half-blind, to find the crone holding out her hands.

"Ah, dearie, don't weep for that one. It's a better world she's goin' to than she's ever known on this side."

She's to be hanged—

"The only way out of here," some other woman said. "Ten years and more I been, and never saw no one walk to the gallows like that one."

"Aye and a raw lump she was, too," another replied.

"You could see the death in her eyes, that one, when she looked at you."

"She was kind enough to the child—"

"After she near to eaten her for breakfast!"

The voices went on but the words brought Alaina no more comfort than the bony arms around her shoulders. The prison cell which had become a sanctuary in an instant turned desolate.

She cried herself to sleep that night, not caring who heard, her fellow prisoners or the guards or her father for all she cared, that night and the next and the next. The demons whirled and the waters frothed, but they could not touch her. Never again would they touch her.

I will die here, she thought numbly. *I will die alone.*

They came for her a fortnight later.

Down one corridor and then another, up a flight of stairs, a landing, then two, through more twists and turnings than a badly snarled loom, Alaina followed the pair of guards. They'd manacled her, the way she'd come here, and the chain jangled with her step. She wished she'd had the courage to witch the locks, that first night in Affliction Tower, though that might have brought her a quicker death.

She found herself wishing that Maryam had said goodbye, even a turning of the head, a word or two.

Alaina had only a vague notion of where she was in the tower. By now, she could not have retraced her steps for any amount of princely silver. She assumed they would take her to the battlements, where she had seen the bodies of traitors swaying in the wind. Yet after ascending a flight of stone steps and then another, their path wound on the same level. Her eyes stung with the brightness of the day, crossing a courtyard where a pair of well-dressed ladies, probably noble prisoners, sat beneath a long-dead tree, bent over their needlework. Something within her stirred as the guards paused to unlock a barred gate and then a heavy wooden door.

A public flogging before they hanged her? She shivered with outrage. For the first time, she believed in her own innocence, knew in the very marrow of her bones that she had done nothing to deserve such a punishment.

There was no flogging pole, no stocks, no barrel for dousing. No gallows. Alaina saw only a few ordinary people looking curiously, not at her but at the guards, and a knot of fighting men in swords and leather vests. Their loud, percussive voices rose above the noise of the street.

The guards removed Alaina's manacles. She wondered if she

ought to be afraid. She could not understand what was happening. Was this some new form of torture? Her native wit urged silence.

They retreated through the open door, leaving her alone. A heavy hand gripped one shoulder from behind. She closed her eyes, steeling herself for the worst.

"Little Dragon!" Strong arms enveloped her, almost lifting her from her feet. She smelled newly polished leather, soap, steel oil.

Maryam set Alaina down, grinning. Alaina had mistaken her for one of the men with her pale-red hair hidden beneath a helmet that flourished a wildly crimson plume.

"What are you doing here?" Alaina blurted out. "You're dead!"

That brought a fresh round of laughter. "It matters not what Mar has done—

"—merely opened up the bag of a windbag for the wind to come in!"

"—compared to what we might refuse to do the next time his Royal Backside gets himself in a mess," one of the men said.

"Blaw, now they're saying it was all a mistake!" the second of the three men said.

"And what are two less mouths to feed?" Maryam said, keeping one arm around Alaina's shoulders. "What think you of her, my mates?"

"Little dragon indeed, to naysay you hung over!" laughed the third.

"And you," Maryam turned to Alaina, "will you take the freedom of the streets or go with us to far Kurestan, where there is a king's son needs rescuing and many locks to be picked?"

Two thoughts warred for Alaina's attention, the first that Maryam had somehow contrived her release, that she was not to be executed after all and the second—

She knows! She knows and she does not care!

"Little Dragon," Maryam said in a lowered voice. "Think

you I would not know the touch of a healer's mind, I who have seen fields run red with blood, and darker things done when there is no moon? Think you I would not know the value of that gift, wedded to courage such as yours?"

For answer, Alaina slipped her thin small hand into Maryam's calloused one and followed her into the bright, unforeseen day.

Poisoned Dreams

Toward dawn, all conversation along the battlements trailed into silence. The priest had made his rounds an hour earlier, shriving those who asked and silently blessing those who did not. Fighting men, archers and swordsmen and those who worked the great cauldrons of pitch and boiling oil, looked out over the darkened fields below, counted the campfires they could see and wondered how many more remained hidden. They tightened their belts around hunger-flattened bellies and checked their weapons one more time. A few glanced nervously over their shoulders, not toward the high tower where King Reyesmond the Second met with his council of war, but toward the main hall and the kitchens beneath it.

Deep within the ancient bulk of the castle, a strange, misshapen figure crouched by the scullery hearth, tracing runes in the ashes. No one drew near to hear her whispered chants. The cook and all his assistants circled wide as they rushed to prepare hot drinks and a meager breakfast for the fighting men.

At the first stirring of the single uneaten cock, the fay lifted her head and turned eyes like milky opals toward the east. The delicately pointed ears that protruded through her matted amethyst hair quivered. Ember-light reflected dully from the loop of iron around her neck, no thicker than a wire and joined by only a twist of rawhide that even a child could have pulled loose. Purplish discoloration spread across the moony skin from under the wire, leaving cracked, oozing scars. As the fay bent over the ashes once more, the movement shifted her tattered cloak to reveal the wings that hung, crippled, down her back.

With one finger, she traced over the runes, coaxing them from luck to dread and from dread to cowardice and from cowardice to mortal terror. The King had commanded her to work a charm of victory for the morning's battle and so she would, but he had not said *whose* victory.

The fay did not look up at the sound of boots on the stone stairs. She did not need to, for she could hear in those footsteps the echo of another's tread, the grandsire dead but not forgotten. The door flung open, the cook bowed and drew back as a young woman in half-armor strode it. Her dark hair had been braided tightly against her head and she carried a short sword as if she knew how to use it. Her surcoat bore the King's arms, with a unicorn as her own insignia. As a child, she had loved unicorns; the fay had seen her watch for them by moon-light and creep out of bed to hear a traveling minstrel sing of them.

"King's-blood," the fay hissed, her purple lips drawing back to reveal needle fangs. "King's-kin, King's-daughter-who-would-be-a-son. What petty errand has he sent you on now?"

Valry King's-daughter lifted her face, pale and resolute. The fay could sense the sadness in her and had tried many times over the years to nurture it into something more, into resentment and bitterness, a canker of malice that would poison everything the princess touched. She had tried without success, as if a unicorn truly stood guardian over the young girl's heart.

"My father bids you come to him."

The fay's knobby hands moved in a rune of Night, the sort that sent never failed to send the menials scurrying away. The princess stood firm.

"My grandfather bested you and bound you to his service by cold iron. My father's pleasure," she hesitated for only an instant, "is to keep you. And you will obey him, Old Broken Wings, if I must drag you before him on your belly."

At the mention of the old King, the open sores on the fay's wings throbbed, oozing a thick, dark liquid. She scented the grandsire's blood in the young woman's veins. Shuddering, she heaved herself to her feet and hobbled from the kitchen as quickly as she could.

In the King's Council chambers, candles cast wavering shadows across the tapestried walls. Pages darted about to replace them and cut away the night's drippings. Maps and charts lay scattered over the central table.

As the fay entered, guarded by the King's daughter, captains and councilors alike froze as they were. Some looked up. A few of them blanched. Only the King appeared undisturbed but the fay could feel the terror gnawing deep within him. She grasped it and felt it tighten like a hangman's noose.

He resisted her, as he always did, for he was his father's son. But he had watched his father, in the fullness of his victory, ask the fay what his own future was to be. He had seen the joy bleed out of his father's life when she told him what his death was to be—a lingering nightmare of pestilence and senility. And in all the years he had been King, all the years since his father's death, all the years he had kept the fay prisoner, he had never asked her for his own future.

The King now gestured the fay to approach. She read in his eyes what she had sensed in the night, that reinforcements had arrived, strengthening the usurper Duke's position. She reached out to his heart again and tasted the twisting, dark temptation to kill her with his own hands, rather than allow her power to fall into his enemy's.

"O great king and son of my conqueror," she said in her sweetest voice. "What is your desire?"

The King hesitated for the slightest moment before replying. He must have spent hours considering the question, the exact right phrasing to obtain the answer he so desperately needed. "What must I do to win this battle?"

Oracular compulsion knotted her throat and her lips moved

without her will. "You must open your gates to them."

"What!" the senior captain leapt forward. "Surrender?"

"Treachery!" someone else shouted. "The witch-demon cannot be trusted! She is too dangerous to let live!"

The fay drew herself up to her slender height, gathering her cloak around her. "By the cold iron that binds me, I have answered truly. But I can only answer what I have been asked."

"This is true, Father." Valry King's-daughter stepped to his side, her brows drawn together in thought. "But the answer does not necessarily mean your surrender. Perhaps she has seen some moment in negotiation, a truce—"

Just then the doors burst open and a grizzled sergeant rushed into the room, his face as red as if he'd run all the way from the farthest battlement.

"Your Majesty—they're gone! Every last jack of the Duke's men, gone! The whole field, empty!"

"Empty?" the King repeated.

"Aye, all but a few piles of baggage not even big enough to hide a man in. As well as we can see in the dawn light—it's a miracle, it is!" Then, perhaps recalling his position and the august company to whom he was speaking, he broke off and bowed deeply.

"Perhaps a miracle," the King said wonderingly. His eyes flickered over the fay's impassive face. "Let us go down and make sure."

Remnants of campfires and abandoned equipment littered the field, furrowed by hastily filled latrine trenches. The marks of heavy wagons and shod hooves scored the earth. The King and his retinue strode back and forth, amazement melting into triumph as they examined what had been left. The fay, with the King's daughter watching her, followed behind them.

Scattered about, they found jugs of beautifully worked pottery, decorated with flowers and stylized bees and giving forth the enticing aroma of honey.

"Why leave them here?" one of the councilors wondered.

"As a gift," another answered, giddy with relief. "In homage to our superiority!"

Unsmiling, the King shook his head. "We might have prevailed, had it come to a fight. But it was no sure thing. They were as resolute as we, and better supplied. Why would they give up, and leave these here for us?"

He touched one finger to the smooth wax of the seal. His courtiers gathered around, waiting for him to order the jars opened. They had all been on painfully short rations and now the sweet heavy scent of the honey made their mouths water. Someone's stomach rumbled hopefully.

The King gestured the fay forward and showed her the jars. "Our enemy has left us this, but for what reason? Is the honey poisoned?"

A ripple of compulsion sent the fay's wings trembling. "It will not kill you."

"Yet there are other ways of bringing a man to harm," the King said thoughtfully. "Is the honey tainted with magic?"

Again the fay answered no. Relief spread across the King's face. The courtiers nudged each other, faces relaxing into smiles. One bent to pick up another jar.

"Father." The clear voice of Valry King's-daughter made them all pause. "Is not this honey *too* tempting? Would you risk the fate of the realm on the word of a sworn enemy...or the word of a fay?"

The King's brow furrowed. "She has said it is safe."

The princess shook her head. "No, she has said only that it was neither poisoned nor charmed. If it is indeed safe, let *her* taste it for you..."

She took the jar from her father's hands and with one swift movement stabbed her thumb through the wax seal. The smell of the honey enveloped them, cloying and beckoning. The distilled sweetness of a thousand flowers, a hundred summer days, filled their nostrils. Tension-weary muscles melted.

Unsmiling, the princess held the jar out to the fay. "...if she dares."

The fay narrowed her opal eyes. She had known, the moment her wings were broken, how much greater was the cruelty of humans than that of her own kind. She had known the trait would not die with the old King. Now her hands quivered as she accepted the honey jar, for although she did not know how it would come about, she was certain that her prophecy of the opened doors was true. She dipped one fingertip into the smooth thick honey and lifted it to her lips.

For a moment the world rippled around her like reflections seen on wind-kissed water. Something stirred deep within her, something long buried. Her vision swam with glittering lights, burning pale and pure like the stars above her birth. The pain in her wings eased as if they'd suddenly healed. The perfumes of asphodel and night-blooming jasmine filled the air; she drank them in, filling every pore of her being with their scent. A soothing chill shot through her; she had almost forgotten what it was like to feel pleasure.

Sound jarred her ears, grating and barely understandable, like the buzzing of insects. Reyesmond's voice: "Take the honey and the traitor inside."

Then from a far distance came the music of silvery bells and voices calling out in a familiar lilting cry. "Come! Come to us!"

I am here! she cried out from the very depths of her being. She lifted her wings, stretching wide the folds of patterned gossamer membranes. They caught the breeze; her body seemed weightless. On tiptoe, she raised her arms, poised for flight.

For a single moment, she heard the voices singing the name she had not heard since the old King had broken her wings. The name she thought she would never hear again.

"Come, oh come to us, O beautiful one, O Miranthea of the Silken Wings! Quickly, come to us!"

I am here! O my brothers and my sisters, I am here!

⋅⟨≈⟩⋅

She came to herself again, confused and sick at heart. Pain clenched her, the old pain in her wings as fresh now as the day the old King had shattered them. Her nostrils flared, filling with the stench of human bodies, grease and filth and dried sweat.

Stay, O my sisters, stay for me!

In an instant she realized where she was, the little room that had been given to her but which she rarely used, preferring the oracular ashes of the scullery. A grim-faced guard stood just inside the doorway. His voice still echoed against the bare stone walls and it had been his words that had woken her. For the first time in thirty years of captivity, she could not sense what was going on. All her defenses had been stripped from her, leaving her naked among her enemies.

Valry King's-daughter strode through the doorway. Her armor shone, as if catching invisible light. Or perhaps it was only the brightness of Miranthea's fading dream, she could not tell.

"Come with me, Old Broken Wings. My father is about to open the gates."

Briskly, Valry King's-daughter led the way to the battlements overlooking the central courtyard. Miranthea looked down and saw the bodies lying on the ground, their limbs contorted as if by hideous convulsions, but now motionless, yet with her fay's sight, she saw the life burning in them. The unbarred gates gaped in invitation. Everywhere she looked, she saw more men waiting, hidden behind half-opened doors and wagons, their weapons ready.

"A clever trap," she murmured. The guard had withdrawn, leaving the two of them alone on the parapet. "Worthy of the foulest treachery of men."

"If we are treacherous," said the princess, watching the fay with her cold gray eyes, "it is because we have learned it from you."

Miranthea faced the granddaughter of her conqueror. Once she would have silently cursed her, or tried to twist her words, using her hatred as both sword and shield, but now she could only stand there, defenseless against her own memories. Again she felt cold iron ripping through the delicate membranes of her wings. She heard the slender bones snap. The echoes of silvery voices faded from her ears.

The princess flinched as if she'd been physically struck. What did she see in Miranthea's eyes? Perhaps she was remembering the nights she danced in the moonlight on her balcony, singing for the unicorns. Or perhaps of all the times her father had turned away from her because she was not a son.

"My grandfather should have slain you. My father should have freed you."

"They were men and fools."

"But I am neither."

A shiver went through Miranthea's broken wings. Below, the Duke's men strode into the courtyard. Their voices rang out, as if they had no further need for stealth. Their laughter rose to the battlements. The captains lifted their pennons. One of them took out a small horn and blew a fanfare as their Duke rode past the gates on his high-bred white stallion.

Suddenly another horn blared out from the high tower. The portcullis, its rope cut, dropped with a thunderous noise. The men lying on the ground leapt to their feet. The King's archers appeared on every parapet and rained their arrows down on the men below. Laughter turned to screams, shouted orders, each contradicting the next. The Duke wheeled his mount, rallying his men. But half his army was still outside the gates and the rest in disarray, scrambling for cover.

At a second blast from the King's horn, armed men jumped out from behind half-closed door, from posts and wagons, and hurled themselves at those besiegers who had managed to find shelter against the arrows. Three that Miranthea recognized as the King's best swordsmen rushed at the attacking lord. One ran the white stallion through the belly and the animal went down, screaming. The others hauled the lord to his feet and held him, arms behind his back, sword edge across his neck.

Even as the attackers surrendered and were led away,

Miranthea could not take her eyes away from the dying stallion. It lay there, twitching, its moonshine coat befouled and bloodied, until one of the King's men slit its throat.

Miranthea followed the princess into the great hall, where Reyesmond sat on his father's throne. The captains drew back from her, making ward-off signs and crossing themselves. She stood in her allotted place while the King heard his adversary's formal surrender. The penalties were the usual—the Duke's firstborn son as hostage, a modest forfeiture of lands and an oath of loyalty. The son, who'd acted as lieutenant, was of an age that Miranthea guessed he'd be wed to Valry as a way of permanently solving the problem.

And then who will have won, King's-daughter, and who will have lost?

"And now, we come to other matters," the King said in his sternest voice. "Matter of justice, matters of vengeance for darkest betrayal. We speak now not of the ambitions of men, but of the treachery of immortals. Stand forth, and hear the charges against you." He pointed at Miranthea, who hobbled forward. "But for the quick thinking of our daughter, we would have eaten the poisoned honey. We would now be on our knees, listening to our fate, instead of sitting here in judgment. You have forsworn the oaths you gave to my father and committed the most heinous crime of treason. What have you to say for yourself?"

Miranthea lifted her chin. With the slightest movement, agony surged through her crippled wings. "I told only the truth."

"Only the truth! Enough to get us all killed! The honey was gathered from dream-poppies, as well you knew! One taste and a man is lost, his body living and his mind enslaved! Yet you kept this secret from us." The King's face reddened and contorted. His courtiers drew back, murmuring. "Is there any reason I should not have your head stricken from your shoulders as you stand?"

Hope shivered through Miranthea. She could survive as she was before she tasted the honey, half-dead and the rest numbed with hatred, but she could not endure this new awareness that pierced every part of her, the knowledge of what she had been. Perhaps if she goaded him hard enough, the King would indeed cut off her head.

"You'll never be rid of me, never!" she shrieked. "Dead or alive, I'll haunt your nightmares forever!"

The King drew his sword and stepped down from his throne. His eyes burned as if his soul were on fire.

Miranthea threw her head back and cackled with joy. "I've won! I've won! You cannot escape me now! The unholy curse will be on you and yours until the end of time!"

The hall fell silent, the courtiers holding their breath. Fear rose up from them like a charnel stench. Swiftly Valry moved to her father's side. She lay one hand on his sword arm. Miranthea could feel the tenderness of that touch. The King paused and looked down at his daughter, as if seeing her for the first time.

"Have I not served you well?" the princess asked. "And may I not ask a reward for my good counsel?"

After a long moment, he bent his head in agreement.

"Then give this wretched creature to me. Let *me* be the one to pass judgment on her."

A ripple of surprise passed around the room. The King threw his head back and laughed. "My daughter! Her courage is worth twice any man's!" He pointed to the fay with his sword. "She's yours."

As Valry approached, Miranthea spread her lips in a soundless snarl, baring her needle fangs. She spat out a challenge. "Let us see what you are made of, King's-spawn. Is your courage, too, so small that you dare not strike me down, though I am unarmed?"

"I will not bandy words with you, Old Broken Wings. Only sentence you as you deserve."

With a swift, savage movement, Valry King's-daughter

grasped the iron ring. The iron wire bit deep into Miranthea's flesh, causing her such agony she could hardly breathe. Somehow she managed to stumble along as the princess dragged her from the hall. The King and his courtiers followed on their heels.

They halted by the gates. The portcullis had been raised and one gate opened to permit the Duke's men to surrender. The princess released the fay and thrust her through the opening.

Miranthea staggered, momentarily overwhelmed by the bright hard light, the scent of the tramped fields and the lingering taint of blood from the courtyard. The princess slid her sword free and laid the tip against Miranthea's throat.

"Kill me now and be done with it," Miranthea hissed. "Show mercy in this, at least."

Slowly the princess smiled. With a flick of her wrist, she cut through the leather bindings and tossed away the iron wire. "You have the freedom of the road. May you live long to enjoy it."

Miranthea gasped at the sudden disappearance of the pain she had lived with for so many years. Even as she tried to straighten up, her muscles cramped, as if her spine had turned to stone. Her wings ached and she became acutely aware of her crooked limbs, the sloughing, pitted skin, the matted hair, the ash-filth calluses on her hands and feet.

Where could she go? Where in all the wide world was there a place for what she had become? Who among her own kind would welcome her now?

The princess reached into the pouch at her waist and took out a small crystal vial, sealed with wax and hanging from a loop of braided silk. She placed it around the fay's neck, saying, "A parting gift, something to remember me by."

Through crystal walls, the honey glowed like a pool of molten light. A smell, cloying and compelling, wafted upward and seeped all through the fay's senses. Visions of heart-tearing beauty clawed at her. She reached one hand up to the seal and felt the wax soft and yielding to her touch. How easy it would be to push through it, to dip a finger into the golden elixir, to hear beloved voices calling her name, to stay forever with them...

Miranthea's fingers closed around the vial. A hard snap would break the cord, but she knew she would never do it. Just as she would never surrender to the dreams within. But she would live with it every moment of her immortal span, the memory of all the beauty that had ever been hers, lost to her now and forever.

The voice of Valry King's-daughter pierced the waves of longing, pitched low so that only Miranthea could hear. "You are like this honey. True and false, sweet and treacherous. I would not harm you for myself, but as long as you are here, my father will be tempted to use your powers. He will fear you, and that fear will eat away at him until there is nothing left. I love my father. No matter what the cost, I will not permit you to destroy him."

Miranthea lifted her head and her wings stretched, aching. Everything had come clear now, in the light of memory. "Think on this, O princess. Think long and hard on this. If I am evil in the eyes of men, is it not because of what men have made of me—cruel, scheming, treacherous? Did I agree to have my wings broken, my life taken from me, to live as a slave, forever cut off from my kin? Did I choose what I have become? And which one of us now is truly innocent?"

Tears glowed in the eyes of Valry King's-daughter, but she made no move to wipe them away. She might have what she desired, her father's high regard and ridding him of the fay, but at what price? Unlike Miranthea, she had freely chosen cruelty. Out of love, perhaps, but chosen it nonetheless.

What unicorn now would come to lay his head in her lap...except in her own poisoned dreams?

The fay nodded. "And so you have your birthright, King's-daughter, King's-heir. May you live long to enjoy it."

Without a backward glance, Miranthea of the Silken Wings turned to make her crippled way through the dust.

Silverblade

Silhouetted against the twin-mooned amber sky, a woman in trail-stained leathers reached the last dusty ridge, moving quickly despite the sword strapped across her back. As she stood panting at the edge of the cliff, she shook lank, ginger-colored hair back from her face and shaded her eyes with one hand, scanning the valley from the strip of harbor to the abandoned farms to the inland hills behind her. Below, tantalizingly close, sat the Western Keep that she had been summoned to fortify. The ancient stone walls looked sound enough, invulnerable to assault. Any human assault, that is. The Dark Ones inching their way up the valley were another matter.

People called them *dragons* or *devil-spawn* or simply *monsters*, but no one knew what the Dark Ones truly were. Taller than a haystack, blacker than pitch, relentless, untiring, armored with impenetrable carapaces and capable of spitting fiery acid, they seemed more insect than reptile. Some said that Barzon, Duke of the Eastern Marches, had bargained with a necromancer for their aid, that they had swallowed him up and seized his lands for their own. Whatever the truth, the western kingdom of Creston-var now also lay waste and Wynne's Queen in exile.

Wynne cursed under her breath as she hurried back down the trail. These days it seemed she'd spent her whole life fighting the Dark Ones, although she'd never faced more than a single one before.

She found her team resting in a dry riverbed beside a clump of thorn trees, a dozen men and women armed with rough-forged bronze or iron swords. Their single remaining pack animal bent its scrawny neck to nibble the yellowed grass. Aldair, Wynne's second, heaved himself to his feet.

"How close?" he asked.

"An hour away, maybe less. There's no way we can reach the Keep before they do. Not with enough time to bar the gates after us. They'd be fools to let us in."

"They'll take the Keep at the last," he said. "You know that, Silverblade."

Silverblade, he called her, calling her not by her own name, but by her sword.

Wynne felt his aged eyes on her, measuring her as they had not done since she was a skinny, arrogant teenager, demanding sword lessons from her mother's old teacher. What did he see when he looked at her now—Wynne herself, or only his memories of her mother, who carried Silverblade before her? Did he see anything at all beyond the sword?

She ran her fingers through her hair and rubbed her neck. "There's precious little to live for these days, old friend. The Queen safe on the Islands. Sarai and the other youngsters at the Keep. A good death with as many demons as we can take with us…" But it was the sword speaking, not the woman.

Wynne frowned. She didn't like to break her team up, not even so close to their goal. The day before, they'd finished off a cluster of demons that had strayed from their convoy. But they'd lost two good fighters and one, the boy who'd joined them just a few months ago, down with a splintered lower leg. Nathi was swabbing his broken skin with a poultice of the last of their healing herbs. The pungent smell tinged the air.

"Jon, Nathi, Tia, you come with me," Wynne said. "Aldair, you and the others make for the Keep. Put the boy on the pony. We'll try to buy you enough time."

They settled into formation behind her, these three who'd been with her the longest. As they broke into a run across the valley floor, Wynne reached over her shoulder to draw Silver-blade. It felt light, almost alive in her hands. Her mother had said it held magic, although Wynne doubted it. The blade was no ordinary metal, certainly not iron, or even costly southern steel, but silvery-white, razor-edged, never rusting.

Tia-the-dancer ran silently in her usual place at Wynne's side. What she would have been if the Dark Ones hadn't come boiling out of the east ten years ago—a real dancer or just an ordinary farmwoman with a fat husband and four kids—Wynne couldn't guess.

The convoy crept along the unpaved road that led to the Keep gates, the three giants moving in a single file, rattling and hissing. Their bodies slithered over the naked red-dust path on huge segmented claws. The smaller demons spread out, killing every living thing they found; others nestled amid the Dark Ones' weirdly sculpted projections like deformed wings. Some looked like goblins, others horned scorpions. As Wynne's team approached, they scuttled to the ground and took up defensive positions.

Jon and Nathi veered towards a man-high demon, while Tia slashed at another with her short bronze sword. She danced away from its clumsy swipe, drawing it off to give Wynne a clear field.

Wynne scrambled up the nearest Dark One, leaping from one ornate chitinous shape to the next. The giant monster swerved and one eyeless, wedge-shaped head whipped around on its articulated neck, its jaws snapping and reeking of brimstone. She kept climbing. Where the weight-bearing claw joined the main body, she found a flexible collar as long as her forearm. The chitin resisted her thrust for a moment, then the blade slid in, as if slicing a fruit with a stiff rind but succulent interior.

Suddenly Nathi tripped, and the nearest demon lunged for her. As Jon yelled a warning, Tia-the-dancer darted in, stepping lightly off the angular claw. She somersaulted through the air and landed at a run just as the demon swiveled towards her, spitting acid.

Wynne heard Nathi's cry and knew she'd been wounded. She jerked the sword free in a spurt of yellow blood, jumped down and sprinted away. The Dark One came to a hissing, staggering halt, both heads thrashing, limping heavily on its crippled claw. Abruptly, the demons broke off their attack and came swarming back.

"Come on!" Wynne called.

Jon hauled Nathi to her feet and sprinted after her, Tia guarding the rear.

The convoy had still not moved by the time the four humans reached the Keep. Nathi, although still on her feet, was stumbling, and they were all breathing hard. The parapets looked empty, as if deserted. For a moment, Wynne wondered if the Keep folk were too frightened to let them in. Then the gates parted and Aldair beckoned to them.

Behind him stood the rest of Wynne's troop, a few oldsters, a scattering of grim-eyed fighters, many of them crippled, a handful of frightened children, strays or orphans probably. They were maybe thirty in all, counting the older children. The Keep was designed for a much large force; beside the enormous well, a handful of striped goats looked up, tails flicking.

"Momma!" Eight-year-old Sarai, her hair an unruly crop of sunshine, catapulted across the courtyard, scattering chickens. It had been a year since Wynne sent her daughter to the fragile safety of the Keep and Sarai had lost all traces of her baby softness. For a moment she looked utterly unfamiliar, a changeling. Wynne saw not a slender child with serious eyes, but the shadow of a man now dead. She was only seventeen during that brief loving, snatched between battles across the midland plains. Her mother was still alive then, and Wynne not yet Silverblade.

Wynne gave Sarai an awkward pat on the shoulder before she turned back to Aldair.

"Is this—there have to be more than this. What about the other northern companies—Lauren's, Sell's? They started out before us."

"They never came, Warlady. We held on as best we could."

One of the Keep folk stepped forward. She peered at Wynne through her one remaining good eye, the other hidden beneath a knotted scar. She carried a short dagger around her neck. "The Queen set off for the Islands with at midsummer. She took the best of what we had left." There was no hint of censure in the old woman's voice. "Everyone thought we'd be reinforced before now."

Wynne glanced at the walls, measuring how few could defend them, marking the position and steepness of the stairs. The granite stones had been fitted so closely that not even a sprig of wall-ivy could take root.

"Supplies we got," the old woman said, "but empty walls can't keep those devils out."

"We can hold them, if no one gets careless." Wynne let the sword speak again. "Aldair, I want sentries posted and hot food for our people. A healer for Nathi, if there is one. How's the boy with the leg?"

"He can't fight."

"Then put him where he can do some good. Get everyone else on the walls, the older kids as supply runners. You know what to do."

He nodded and headed off toward the main hall. The Keep folk dispersed, leaving Wynne standing there with Sarai.

Wynne looked down at her daughter. "I—ah—don't have time to play now."

"Oh, Momma, I'm too *old* to play. Can I see the sword?"

Wynne pulled Silverblade over her shoulder and held it flat as sunlight danced over its silver-white surfaces. "Some day it will be yours."

"Is it really magic?" Sarai reached for the hilt.

"Don't—" Wynne started to say, *Don't be in such a hurry to grow up.* But the words seemed as futile now as when her own mother had said them.

A short time later, Wynne sat in the central hall, eating stew with cracker-bread and hot spiced fruit. Above them, the minstrels' gallery sat forlorn, perhaps dreaming of the days when Queens listened to music as they dined. A few weavings remained on the walls, too worn to be worth hauling away; some bore the coats-of-arms of noble families that no longer existed. Nathi, her thigh bandaged, sat across the table. Wynne remembered that she'd lost children to the Dark Ones.

"—says it's all over now, but I know she's wrong because we never had *Silverblade* fighting with us before," Sarai chirped. "I'm going to kill giant monsters when I'm big. Just like Momma!"

"Leave the Dark Ones to grown-ups," Wynne snapped.

Sarai favored her with an indignant grimace. "You're going to kill them all and not leave any for me. That's not fair!"

Aldair nudged Wynne's other elbow and said in a low voice, "You were just like that at her age." He added, to Sarai, "There'll be plenty to go around, little love."

A voice ghosted from outside: "They're here!"

Wynne scrambled to her feet. Sarai pulled at her sleeve, as if wanting to begin killing immediately.

"No," Wynne said in as gentle a tone as she could manage. "I need you to be a good girl and go with the others. I can't fight and keep an eye on you at the same time."

The girl's gray eyes smoldered. "Don't *need* an eye kept on me!"

"A good soldier follows orders, no?" said Nathi, drawing Sarai towards the inner chambers. "Your mum's our captain, did you know that? We all do what she says."

Wynne glanced over her shoulder, startled by how easily Nathi managed Sarai's mood. But she had no time for wondering now. She hurried out into the courtyard and up the narrow stairs to the parapet. The Dark Ones had already reached the trampled ground below the gates. Demons swarmed up the walls, soundless except for the unnerving slither of chitin over stone. The rigid tips of their claws found holds in crevices too shallow for human fingers and toes.

"Here they come!" Aldair shouted.

Wynne's heart pounded and her muscles quivered in anticipation. She sliced through the probing claw of the topmost demon and sent it toppling to the ground. The fallen demons picked themselves up and began climbing again, making made hissing, creaking noises. Down below, one of the two unwounded giants spewed acid on the metal bands, while the other began battering at the gates.

Wynne chanted her battle-cry as she slashed and thrust at the demons. The sword sang in her hands, warm, supple, a thing of living light. Deep within her, something answered. Quicksilver scintillated along her veins. She could feel its fire streaming all through her, down her arms and legs.

The Dark One kept pounding at the gate, sending ominous echoes through the courtyard. Demons kept coming and Wynne kept fighting. She lost her sense of time. Then suddenly, for a moment, the parapets were empty. Wynne glanced around for her team and could not see Tia-the-dancer anywhere near her post. Jon and Nathi, stationed too far apart for decent teamwork, shouted encouragement to one another.

Breath rasping in her throat, Wynne lowered her sword. There were no demons within attack range, and the booming at the gates had stopped. From the courtyard came a high-pitched wail, a child's imitation of her own war-cry. A small, golden-headed figure darted towards the gates, staggering under an unwieldy bronze sword.

Wynne raced down the stairs, taking them two and three at a time, slipping and stumbling but somehow keeping her balance. She sprinted across the yard, reaching the child just as Aldair appeared on the other side of the courtyard.

Sarai turned a suddenly whitened face to her mother. "I was going out," she faltered, "to fight. Like you, Momma." Her lower lip quivered. She dropped the sword.

Outrage drove Wynne beyond speech. She could not think of what to say. She stood there, shaking Sarai with one hand while brandishing a naked blade in her face, and trembling with anger as much as her daughter was with fear.

"Silverblade!" Aldair halted at her side and pointed to the gates.

Wynne stifled a cry of alarm. The massive wooden gates sagged at their hinges, no longer capable of resisting a determined thrust. The metal, pitted and eroded, smoked. Outside, the giant thrust itself against them with renewed vigor.

The other defenders had come down from their posts into the empty yard, the livestock having disappeared at the first assault on the gates. The wounded and children stood in a knot just outside the hall. The old woman who spoke for the Keep stepped forward. Her face was ashen. "This is the end, isn't it, Warlady? Do you think it's any kinder to them," jutting her chin in the direction of the children, "to be hunted one by one? Wouldn't it be easier to go all at once?"

Wynne glanced down at Sarai, now standing in the curve of Aldair's arm, looking up at her with mixed tears and rebellion. A little dagger hung from her neck, a dagger like everyone in the Keep wore. Silently they waited for her signal.

She lifted the sword above her head, tilting it so the metal gleamed in the sun. This time, its beauty seemed a pale shadow, its promise of magic a hollow lie.

What's the use of fighting on? The very best I've been able to do is wound them. Not kill, only slow them down. Here is not one but three, and such darkness in my soul...

But something made her hesitate for a few crucial moments. The bronze hinges shrieked like an animal in agony. The gates splintered and gave way.

"Get behind me—all of you!" Wynne shouted. She heard rather than saw them obey.

Demons swarmed through, spreading out to half-encircle the stunned humans. Majestically, the Dark Ones swept in to take possession of the Keep. Their segmented necks swiveled from side to side, blind heads bobbing.

There was a quick movement near the top of the foremost giant as a demon that had nestled there broke free and clambered to the ground. It stood on two legs, had two arms and a discernible head. An eerie parody of speech, distorted by the chitinous coverings of its head, issued from it.

"Par-r-rley."

Wynne almost dropped her sword in astonishment. In all the years she'd fought the Dark Ones and their demons, she'd never heard them make anything like human speech, only that infernal hissing and booming.

"Stay where you are!" she cried.

Slowly the words came, strained but decipherable. "We wish—a trade. We offer—safe passage."

"Given half a chance, we can outrun them and reach the Islands," Aldair said.

"What do you want?" Wynne called out, not taking her eyes off the manlike demon.

The demon raised one claw arm and pointed at her.

Behind Wynne, Nathi cried out and someone else shouted, "Never!"

Wynne hesitated. Could she trust them? No, but she could bargain with them long enough to let the others escape. Then... Her blood turned cold. What could they possibly want with her? A war trophy, a slave?

I will do it, no matter what the cost. I will buy life for Sarai. Then I will find a way to die.

She thought she would tremble as she nodded, but she didn't. She turned her head and saw Jon standing beside Aldair, and Nathi beyond him with tears in her eyes. Tia would have chosen death rather than this moment.

Wynne kept herself and her sword between the Dark Ones and the refugees. They left behind everything but their weapons. The demons scuttled back and forth at a careful distance, but made no effort to interfere. Step by step, the ragged band crept across the courtyard and through the ravaged gates.

Once they were in the open, Wynne paused, looking over the narrow valley leading to the harbor. She didn't want the others to leave her alone, and yet they must. And quickly, too, before the full impact of what she'd done overtook her.

Sarai, her face covered with dust and tears, wriggled to the front. "Momma, why are they letting us go?"

"They're letting *you* go, little love. You must be brave and strong."

What am I doing to her, so young? Will she spend her life trying to live up to her martyred mother?

Even as I did?

She bent to kiss the child's forehead and then handed Silverblade to Aldair. "The Dark Ones may have me, but not the sword. You must keep it for Sarai."

Aldair met her gaze. All the color had bleached from his eyes and he looked like a man at the end of his strength. Perhaps he was. He'd trained two generations for Silverblade, only to see them die.

Sarai slipped her hand through his elbow. "Will you teach me to use it, the way you taught Momma?"

Aldair squared his shoulders and placed his hand over hers. His eyes looked grim and sad; he would find some way to go on. The next moment, Jon and Nathi hurried the rest of them toward the harbor.

Once back at the Keep, the Dark Ones gathered around her. Their bulk blotted out the sun. She shivered from an inner chill. Without the sword that had never left her since the day she took it from her mother's body, she felt naked. She'd borne Silverblade so long, she wasn't sure who she was without it.

The manlike demon raised both upper appendages to the knobs along its vestigial neck. With a crack and a twist, the entire head section popped off.

A human face emerged, milky and withered, crowned with wisps of hair. A scar ran across one temple and down the cheek. His eyes shone dully, and his mouth was compressed into a lipless line.

"Who are you? Are you," Wynne wet her lips, "a prisoner, too?"

"A prisoner? No…" Without the echoing effect of the helmet, his voice creaked. His expression seemed hollow, as if all emotion had been stripped from him.

"Where are we?" he asked, looking up at the empty parapets.

"The Western Keep. Creston-var." She blinked, realizing. "You mean you *don't know?*"

He shook his head, his pale eyes wandering. "I was like you. Once." His breathing took on a new, hoarser quality. "I had a name. Barzon. I had…sons."

Barzon! The Duke who made a pact with the black wizard? "What are you doing with the Dark Ones? What do they want? How do we fight them? How do we win?" Wynne wanted to grab the old man and shake the answers out of him. Her fingers curled into fists, but she kept them at her side.

"That was all a long time ago. They put things in my mind. Dreams. I woke up and I was old. I don't know where my boys are. I have to find them." His skin turned gray, his lips almost blue. A light sheen of sweat covered his face. "Come on, it's time."

Wynne drew back. "Not until you answer me—what do they want with us? With you, with me? How can I fight them?"

Barzon's words wheezed through his throat, one rusty syllable at a time. "If you see them. Tell them. I did it all for them."

It was no use. Whatever was left of the old man's mind was now lost in the past.

Before her stood an unwounded giant. It held a helmet, breastplate, gauntlets, other things that looked like armor. Wynne froze. It was one thing to see Barzon peel away his armor, and quite another that in a few moments she herself would be encased—no, *entombed*—in chitin.

The demons inched closer, forming a funnel towards the giant with the armor. Wynne recoiled, but found herself held fast. Barzon, behind her, grabbed her arms and pinioned them in a grip like a death rigor.

"They have—no purpose—of their own." Barzon's breath hissed in her ears.

The Dark One extended the helmet towards her, closer and closer until it was only inches from her face. Gasping, Wynne threw her head back. The chitin brushed her forehead.

Wynne suddenly found herself floating above her body. Strange sensations flooded her, so vivid they seemed like her own memories... Darkness, a fire-lit cavern. Slow waking, each moment an avalanche of pain. Compulsion: resistance. Sleep rising again in her—then a kernel of will—alien, irresistible, coruscating through her like lightning. Daylight, gold. The slow march from marsh to plain, scything through field and underbrush alike, stripping trees until only stubble remained. Pausing to sweep away the soft-bodied pests, to mend wounds from their prickles. Moving on and on, driven by the burning, tenacious ember.

Still Wynne struggled to hold on to her own human thoughts. It would be so easy to let go, to drift on the dreams...

The helmet dropped lower. Somewhere within her, a last spark of resistance flared. She looked on the bodies in the Dark One's vision, tossed aside like so much garbage. A patch of straw-colored hair caught the light. Like Sarai's hair. Like her mother's.

The first Silverblade had taken most of a convoy with her when she fell. When Wynne pulled her from the pile of tangled bodies, all she could think was, *Where's the sword that will make me Silverblade?*

I am still Silverblade!

Wynne twisted away from the helmet with all her strength. The light was so thick and bright she staggered under its weight. She ducked, then lashed out with a snapping side kick that send the helmet flying from the Dark One's claws.

She grabbed Barzon's shoulders and shoved. He cried out, a harsh, gurgling rattle, and crumpled to the ground. His weight jerked her to her knees. His face had gone from blue-tinged to waxy, and only a crescent of white showed between his half-closed eyelids. His mouth fell open, his lips pulled back slightly from his yellowed teeth. He lay utterly still, not a flutter of his eyeballs, not a quiver of breath.

The demons scuttled back. Wynne knelt and touched one finger to the side of his neck. His flesh felt like warm clay.

She was still close enough to the giant to smell its dry, slithery scent. Dimly she felt its obsession falter.

Drawing her legs under her, Wynne lunged for shattered gates. Sarai crouched behind a massive fallen beam, staring at her with such awe-struck worship that Wynne's heart leapt in her chest. Had she ever looked like that, watching her own mother fight?

Once she'd moved, the demons leapt into action. Two of them circled her, cutting her off, closing in, one to each side. Wynne retreated one step, then another.

Suddenly, a demon spotted Sarai and swerved toward her.

Wynne jumped in its direction, then skittered to a halt. What did she think she was doing? Attacking it with her bare hands? Behind her, the Dark Ones boomed and hissed.

"Run!" she cried.

Silverblade! Without thinking, she reached for the sword that was not there.

Sarai pulled the dagger from around her neck and scrambled to her feet, plain in the demon's path. The demon stretched out its serrated claws and scuttled closer. Sarai held her little blade in front of her. Her face had gone white, mouth set, her stance steady as she waited for the demon to close the distance.

Even as she screamed and hurled herself after it, Wynne watched the next few moments unfold in her mind, as she'd seen so many others in the past. The ebony claws ripping flesh, the spurting blood, the heart-sickening *thump!* as the body— Sarai's body—hit the ground. The pale-gold hair tangled in the dust.

The Dark Ones loomed above her like a wall of tidal blackness. She could feel their desperation like caustic over her skin. They would bury her under their hissing, thrashing mass, and buy her death with their own.

Silverblade! The world turned molten. Fire raced along her veins. Air sizzled past her ears as her feet pummeled the earth. She brought her hands together as if grasping a sword hilt—

Flames burst from her fingers, forming a blade of pure white light. Wildness, hot and sweet like fire and music together, surged through her, sweeping away every other feeling, searing her to the core. She gave herself over to it.

Chunks of chitin armor went flying and yellow blood sprayed the ground as Wynne sliced through the demon's head section. She whirled, faced the black wall of Dark Ones. The other demons, in retreat, huddled at their feet. They cast eerie shadows in the light of the blade.

Wynne's body shook with the power coursing through her. Madness or funeral pyre, she didn't care, just so long as the Dark Ones kept shuffling backwards.

"Momma?" A small voice cut through the roaring inferno.

The fire raged all through her now, consuming her from within as it leapt ever higher and brighter from her hands.

"Momma, come now!"

The flames faltered and the image of the sword dimmed. Wynne's vision cleared. She felt as if she were waking from a fever. She wavered on her feet. Her nostrils filled with the stench of burnt chitin.

Wynne sprinted to Sarai and pulled her towards the gates. Demons rumbled after them, claws churning the dust. Sarai scrambled to keep up, then slipped suddenly and fell. Her hand jerked from Wynne's grasp.

Grabbing Sarai's wrist and ankle, Wynne heaved the child's body across her own shoulders and raced for the harbor. The road sloped downward, uneven. She stumbled, regained her footing, somehow held on to Sarai. Pain shot through her thigh muscles, but she kept moving, one step after another. Each breath seared her lungs. She heard only the sound of her laboring heart.

They were near the bottom of the long sloping trail leading

to the harbor. A few oar-boats bobbed alongside the low wooden pier. In the other direction, the Dark Ones were just starting down the last incline.

As they reached the pier, Wynne made out the outlines of the nearest islands jutting above the glass-calm sea. The oar-boats all looked reasonably seaworthy. Sarai leapt nimbly into the nearest one.

Wynne guided the boat away from the pier and aimed it towards the nearest island. The oars slipped through the water with a weight and rhythm of their own. The air smelled fresh and salty-wild. Sarai sat in the back of the boat, hands laced around her knees, sea-breeze ruffling her yellow hair.

Wynne rowed with all the dregs of her strength as the Dark Ones clattered on to the pier and stopped there, hissing, eyeless heads thrashing. She felt in her bones how much they hated the water. She felt, too, the fervor seeping from them. Without Barzon's consuming ambition, without her own hatred to drive them, they were rapidly sinking once more into somnolence.

Wynne's spirits soared as she realized what she'd done. Now she could lead her people from the Islands to beat the Dark Ones back to the wastes that spawned them. Sarai's children would farm their own lands without fear.

"Momma." Sarai's eyes were as bright as stars. "I saved your life back there, didn't I?"

Wynne's mouth smiled of its own accord. *My warrior daughter.*

"So I'm the next Silverblade, aren't I?"

Wynne rocked back with the motion of the boat, for a moment unable to speak.

"So when do I get the sword?" Sarai asked.

Not while I'm still Silverblade!

She couldn't tell any more whose voice echoed through her mind—her own, her mother's, Sarai's. If she'd had the sword at that moment, she would have thrown it into the ocean.

Her arms kept rowing of their own accord. The waves rippled against the sides of the oar-boat. Sarai sat there, eyes glowering, arms folded tightly across her chest.

"It's—it's not—we don't need the sword anymore." Wynne stopped. It was no use. Her words sounded hollow even to her own ears.

Sarai's lips were drawn tight and her eyebrows pulled together until they looked almost straight.

I should have died like my mother. It's too late.

Numbly, Wynne pulled the oars in and let the little boat drift along the current. Her arms felt so heavy, her vision blurred. Wetness slipped down her cheeks. Sea spray, nothing more.

What if she had let the fire have her, would it have been any worse? Would she have felt so empty, so barren of heart, so like a burned-out shell?

Sarai slid forward in the boat, slipped her arms around Wynne's waist and laid her head on her breast. At first Wynne sat stiffly, as if she didn't know how to hug back. She felt her daughter's breath, coming in jagged little gulps. Then something broke open inside her and she too began to cry.

The Sorceress's Apprentice

With every tug and shove of the scrubbing brush across the mosaic floor, Tahanna cursed softly under her breath. She'd been all afternoon preparing Vashkiri's audience chamber for the petitions that the old sorceress received on the first day of every month. Her knees ached, her back ached, her hands were chapped and raw. She could have gotten the job done in half the time with a simple spell, but Vashkiri had forbidden it.

She was tired of cleaning—there was still the great carved chair to polish—tired of wearing apprentice's drab and, most of all, tired of studying magic every minute she wasn't cleaning this or carrying that—and then never being allowed to use a scrap of it.

Tahanna sat back on her heels and pushed a wisp of sweat-dampened hair back from her forehead. She longed to sit in the great chair and try out a spell, any spell, just to hear how it sounded in her own voice. There would be no harm done, and she'd revoke it right away. But no, she repeated to herself for the thousandth time that morning, *Vashkiri had forbidden it.*

Fire and Darkness! It was so unfair.

Savagely, Tahanna attacked the rich dark wood of the chair with citron oil. Then she paused, the polishing cloth hanging limp in her fingers. A seductive thought snaked through her mind. What was she studying all this magic for, if not to use it? How would she know she was good enough if she never got to try? Would there ever be a better time than now?

Clinging to her new determination, Tahanna strode off towards Vashkiri's private tower. She raced up the stairs, taking them two at a time. Her heart pounded as she reached the top. Her mouth went dry, but she kept on going.

Vashkiri the sorceress stood just outside her door, leaning on her ebony cane and looking for all the world as if she'd been waiting for Tahanna's arrival. Her robe of gold-stitched silk brushed the floor. Her black eyes snapped as they fixed on Tahanna's.

"Vashkiri—*magistera*—" Tahanna panted. A spasm of doubt curled around her tongue. She'd forgotten the faint smell of burning copper that always clung to the sorceress, forgotten how small and frail and terrifying she was.

Tahanna took a deep breath and silently recited a charm for fortitude. Her tongue unfroze. "The time has come for me to begin exercising the art you've taught me." Her voice rang out in the hallway, more powerful and resonant than she'd ever heard it. "I've worked hard for you for all these years. I've memorized every spell you've taught me. I know all the pre-cautions and counter-indications, all the possible cancellations, nullifications and synergies. But you—you never let me try out the tiniest bit of it! Well, that's got to change. You've prepared me to work the true magic—now let me do it!"

For a long moment, Vashkiri did not move. Her face, as usual, looked frozen into a permanent expression of disapproval.

Tahanna's stomach tightened in dread. She'd gone too far, she knew it. Vashkiri would surely kick her out now, if she didn't turn her into a gerbil first. But whatever happened, she'd been right to stand up for herself.

"You think you're ready to work the true magic, my girl?"

Tahanna raised her chin defiantly. "Yes. I *am* ready."

The pleated leather of Vashkiri's face folded into a smile. "Perhaps you are right. Perhaps it is time."

Tahanna stared in open-mouthed astonishment as the old sorceress went on, "You think you have earned the chance to prove yourself. Then you must take my place in the great chair tomorrow and I will take yours in the scullery." She turned her back on Tahanna and made her way down the passageway, her cane tapping. "Oh yes, it will be a welcome change to be scrubbing floors again."

Fire and Darkness! Tahanna murmured reverently. *A miracle!*

Tahanna awoke before dawn. Vashkiri's big bed, heaped with plushy sheepskins, was almost too comfortable to sleep in. With a twinge, she thought of the cot in her own garret, the thin blanket, the chipped bowl. The next moment, she noticed the curl of jasmine-scented steam arising from porcelain ewer on the marble wash stand.

It was true, it was all true! sang through her mind as she bathed and dressed. No more endless lessons without the ghost of a chance to use them. No more scrubbing that any farm brat could do better. No more rough canvas next to her skin, but finest silk. Vashkiri's wardrobe bulged with a dozen ceremonial robes, each more gorgeous than the last. She was still debating between the peacock-patterned gold and the rose-petals-on-snow when a soft tap sounded at her door.

"Who—who is it?"

"Breakfast, magistera." The door swung open and Vashkiri hobbled in. She wore a shapeless smock over peasant-style pantaloons and carried a breakfast tray in both hands. Tahanna's mouth watered at the sight of dewberries in clotted cream, buttery crescent rolls and cinnamon tea. She stammered her thanks as Vashkiri left, and only when she was sipping the last fragrant drops of tea did she realize that the old woman hadn't used her cane.

She had too much to do to wonder about that, dressing her hair and figuring out how to put on the traditional regalia—tiara and veils, pectoral, arm bands, wide-collared cape. She had arranged everything securely enough so it wouldn't fall off when Vashkiri returned to tell her that the petitioners had arrived and were waiting in the antechamber. Picking up the heavy, elaborately ornamented Wand of Office, she went to take her new place.

Tahanna settled herself in the great chair and surveyed the audience chamber with satisfaction. The mosaic floor she'd worked so hard over yesterday now shone as if she'd coated it with glass. Not even Vashkiri could have found fault with it. The petitioners had better be impressed. And they would be, Tahanna reflected. Vashkiri's audience chamber was the jewel of her entire castle—spacious and elegant with its carved ivory-and-sandalwood screens and, best of all, its superb acoustics. Any incantation spoken under its arching roof would sound awe-inspiring.

Tahanna drew a deep breath and motioned to Vashkiri to let the first petitioner approach. She studied him as he strode across the expanse of gleaming tiles. His turban was of cloth-of-gold, as were the sash around his ample belly and his curl-toed slippers. Rich men made generous gifts, Tahanna thought. She determined to do her very best for him. She would not take any shortcuts, she would carefully consider all the implications of whatever spell she used. She would show Vashkiri she could work the true magic as well as any seasoned sorceress.

The rich man sweated as he recited the ritual greeting. Tahanna made him wait a suitable time before she asked what he wished. His request sounded simple enough. He had a hoard of gold that he valued above anything else and he'd been terrified that someone might steal it. He'd hired extra guards and bought new and bigger locks, but still he couldn't sleep at night.

Tahanna kept her face stern as she considered the problem. She could cast an invisible wall around the treasure, one that would keep out even the most determined thief, but then the owner wouldn't be able to get in, either. An obvious pitfall. She deliberated and rejected several spells before selecting one. As she recited it, her words resounded through the chamber. Was that truly her voice, so rich and vibrant? She hoped Vashkiri was eavesdropping.

Feeling pleased with her solution, she received the next petitioner. They came in together, a group of elders from a farming district five hundred leagues away. Tahanna was gratified they'd come so far to seek her help. Their problem, they told her, was the flocks of dragonets that had taken to ravishing the entire asparagus crop. Tahanna personally could live without asparagus but, *Each to his own*. A simple repulsion spell ought to keep the fields free. She was careful to shape the spell to be specific to dragonets and not to farmers or honeybees or anything else that rightfully belonged there.

The tiara and pectoral had become unmistakably heavier as Tahanna watched the elders leave. Her arm ached from holding up the Wand of Office and she wished it had fewer focusing gems and glitter-byes. Unconsciously, her mouth curved down at the corners into an expression of disapproval. She recited the charm for calming the nerves, but couldn't tell if it worked or not. She was so tired, all she wanted to do was crawl away somewhere and sleep. Why hadn't Vashkiri told her she'd feel like this?

Struggling to regain her poise, Tahanna stiffened her spine and signaled for the final petitioner.

As the tall young man approached, her heart beat faster. His short, simple tunic and sandals revealed muscles shapely enough to make a sculptor swoon. True, his legs were a little hairy and he could use a shave, but his eyes were huge and dark-lashed and brooding. She wondered if there were some way she could keep him at the castle while she solved his problems, but Vashkiri would undoubtedly forbid that, too.

Slowly he raised one hand to her. On his palm, she saw a glowing pentagram.

"By my magic, I have already divined your problem," she said grandly. "You are a werewolf."

"Aye, such is my curse." Tahanna found his outland accent as charming as his figure.

"Each passage of the moon's fullness, like to a woman's ripe belly, then must I suffer the most dreadful transformation," he went on. "A wolf I become, aye! a furred beast—huge and slavering, belling my sins to the naked sky. And—" with a wink that turned Tahanna's knees to water, "—keeping the neighbors awake all night."

Although her head was spinning from the intoxicating presence of the young werewolf, Tahanna applied herself to solving his problem. She couldn't remember any references in the texts to an un-werewolfing spell—it was probably too specific—so she blended together several elements, for size, hairlessness, bloodthirstiness, everything else she could think of that might pertain to wolfhood. She checked it twice before pronouncing it.

When the werewolf had departed, with a breath-taking grin, Tahanna sat in the great chair for a long time before she could summon the strength to stand. Her skin exuded the faint odor of burning copper. Despite her weariness, her spirits soared. She'd done it—worked the true magic. Now, where was old Vashkiri to see it?

Vashkiri stood waiting, arms folded and face bland, in the servant's entrance. As she helped Tahanna up the stairs to the bedroom tower, she said nothing at all about her performance.

Over the next week, Tahanna did little but eat ravenously and sleep. She kept expecting Vashkiri to send her back to her own garret, but night after night she slept in the sumptuous bed, bathed in the scented water, ate the delectable food. After a few days, her hopes began to rise. Perhaps the old woman had meant the change to be permanent...

Tahanna realized she had passed the crucial test and was now a full-fledged sorceress. A true professional. She began taking exercise daily, as well as applying herself once more to her studies. There was so much more to learn, now that she'd proved herself worthy.

A month later, Tahanna sat alone in the great carved chair after the last petitioner had departed. Her bones ached with weariness, but her senses were still clear. The endurance exercises she'd been practicing since the last audience day had helped greatly. Her skin and hair reeked of the smell of burning copper.

But there was no denying what she had to do next and no graceful way out of it. What could she say to Vashkiri, "You were right and I was wrong and can I please have my garret back"? She'd been so sure she was ready, so pleased with her command of magic. And what a mess she'd made of it!

Slowly, as if all her joints hurt, Tahanna took off the ceremonial regalia and placed them on the chair. She had no right to wear them now. She searched the audience chamber. After a few moments, Vashkiri appeared at the servant's entrance and asked, "You wished to see me, magistera?"

As Tahanna approached the old sorceress, she found she couldn't look Vashkiri in the face. Her shame was too painful to bear.

"I'm not ready to do magic after all," she said. "Everything I thought I did so well has turned into disaster. They're all back, all the people I tried to help last month. I couldn't think what to do, so I told them all to come back tomorrow. And all the new petitions, the ones I granted today, *they'll* be back next month."

"If that's all it is, you don't need me—but supper does. It won't make itself, you know." Vashkiri started off down the rush-floored corridor toward the scullery. There was a new spring in her step, a new roundness to her cheeks. Without glancing back at Tahanna, she added, "You'd better get right to work. You'll have a bit of research to do, figuring out what to do before tomorrow morning."

"You don't understand!" Half in tears, Tahanna ran after her. "You don't know what I've done!" She blurted out how she'd protected the rich merchant's gold from thieves—thanks to her, it now smelled like a combination of wet dogs and rotten cauliflower. No one, not even the rich man, could stand to be in the same room with it for more than a few seconds at a time.

The old sorceress picked up an empty bucket in each hand and started toward the courtyard well at a surprisingly brisk pace. "I daresay he'll find a way to live with it," she said. "Either that, or live a little poorer."

"But he came to me for help!" Tahanna wailed. "And what about those poor asparagus farmers? How was I to know the dragonets also ate cabbage grubs? Without them, the grubs have multiplied like crazy—every cabbage-patch in the district is infested with them now! The farmers will be ruined because of me!"

"Did you revoke the dragonet repulsion spell?" Vashkiri asked as she put down the buckets in front of the water pump and began working the handle vigorously.

Tahanna shook her head. "I wasn't sure whether to do that or set a new one for the grubs. I thought you would—"

"*I* have enough on my hands, just keeping this place running, thank you," Vashkiri replied tartly.

Tahanna followed her back to the castle kitchen, where Vashkiri dipped out a panful of water and began scrubbing potatoes. Tahanna sat down at the table and absently began peeling one.

It took her three tries to summon enough courage to admit her last failure. The werewolf no longer assumed a lupine form with each full moon. No fur, no slavering, no huge monstrous beast. He now turned into a tiny hairless lapdog. And he still

102

kept the neighbors awake all night.

At this confession, Vashkiri put down the potato she was scrubbing and covered her face with both hands. Slowly her shoulders began to shake and a strange sound bubbled up from her throat. But her expression was perfectly serious when she lowered her hands.

"Surely you must agree," Tahanna said, "I'm not ready yet. Maybe I'll *never* be ready."

"My old teacher said exactly the same thing to me forty years ago when I wanted her to take the job back. As I remember, what I'd done was a spell to make hidden things visible. A wealthy merchant had died and his son couldn't find the will. The poor lad thought he was coming to me for help."

Tahanna blinked in surprise. "What happened?"

"The lawyers discovered papers proving him illegitimate." Vashkiri's black eyes twinkled. "Now listen to me, my dear. You'll be just fine. Trust me. Besides, I've been waiting for years to retire. I'm certainly not going to give it up now."

"But—but—it's criminal negligence to turn me loose on these people! I haven't the faintest idea what I'm doing."

Vashkiri shook her head. "My dear, neither does anyone else at your stage. You are no less competent than I was when I demanded my chance. There is nothing I can tell you that will teach you better than having to mend your own mistakes. You'll make more of them, never fear. Some worse, some better. Probably none less memorable. But remember this—the most terrible thing that can happen is that people will learn better than to seek magical remedies for problems they ought to be solving for themselves."

The old sorceress reached out and patted the young sorceress affectionately on the cheek. For a long moment neither said anything. Then both of them shrugged and got back to work.

Fireweb

The selith came down hard, three-pronged hooves battering the dusty road. He bounced stiff-legged, recovered, and then arched his neck for another wrenching buck. The modified scales along his crest struck Orlly across the face, and she lost her temper.

"Of all the stupid, hell-stinking conniptions to pull! Get your head up where it belongs, or I swear I'll make you wish you'd never seen the ground!" Screaming at the top of her lungs, Orlly hauled on the reins, using all her strength to jerk the selith's head around. Rebellious, the animal bared his teeth.

"Don't even think of it!" she shouted, booting the selith's tender nose. He squealed in pain, giving her the chance to pin his bony head to one shoulder.

Orlly's arms ached with strain as the selith halted, sides heaving. She loosened her grip on the near rein, allowing the animal to stretch his head skyward in a gesture of surrender. Then she directed her gaze to the cause of the crisis. A young woman her own age stood not two paces beyond the selith's bucking orbit, waiting quietly in her leather and knotted silk armor.

Orlly's anger surged again. "You blockhead! Don't you know better than to run right up to a selith? Now I'll have to settle him again, and he was just barely fit to rent as it was. That's two days' hire you've cost me, plus whatever business I've lost after that little show. If you can get your worthless legs to carry you, take yourself from my sight before I get really angry."

The young swordswoman's mouth twisted, but she kept her hands at rest, well away from the hilt of her sword. "Let me make it up to you. You seen competent enough, and I want to hire a guide and mounts. I'll pay you for the two days' rest as well as a trip across the Pass."

"Done!" cried Orlly. She kicked her feet free from the stirrups and jumped down. "Where exactly are you bound? I'll need to know how many are in your party, any beasts you may already have, and your level of conditioning—"

"I suggest we begin with names. I'm Valeria Langua dy Ostrander," the swordswoman said with a friendly smile.

Orlly ducked her head, resenting not for the first time her single, ordinary name. "Orlly" was honorable enough, being the name of her maternal grandmother, until her death the head-woman of the tiny farming village where Orlly had spent her childhood. She might have claimed the village as part of her name, had she left it by choice. Her face hardened reflexively, but she made an effort to keep her tongue civil. "Call me Orlly. Everyone does."

"That's sensible. Mine's such a mouthful, I shortened it to Val. Can you imagine someone trying to get in all those syllables in the middle of a sword fight?" She laughed lightly.

Orlly stared at her. *With a name like that, dripping with gentility and old family honor, she jokes about chopping it.* "Where we off to?"

"Kasimire, through Breakheart Pass."

"I *know* where it is," Orlly said.

Val's pale violent eyes flicked across Orlly's face, but her friendly tone did not change. "There's me and two guards, we'll have our own kits and clothing… And an elthim." Orlly drew a quick, astonished breath, but the swordswoman went on conversationally, taking her arm and steering her toward the nearest ale-house. "She's old, in her fourth cycle, so her speed may be our limiting factor. I don't know how fast laden selithi can travel, but it's vital we not overtire her."

Orlly gulped as Val urged her to sit down and called for ale.

106

She had never seen an elthim, but in her childhood village they had been legendary, the tattered fragments of a once powerful, magical race.

Val took two tankards, paid for them, and shoved one in front of Orlly. "How soon can we start?"

Orlly sipped her ale, a rare luxury for one who lived by nothing but her wits and her selithi. "Depends on how quickly 'we' can make peace with 'our' mounts."

Val laughed with uninhibited gusto. "And I thought you were only pretending to be angry at me to ask a higher price! You mean that display of riding wasn't an advertisement for my benefit?"

Orlly shrugged. With ordinary handling So would not be fit to hire, but she could use her special gentling techniques and then ride him herself. "He could carry me. I wouldn't trust him with a stranger. But I have only the three selithi for four riders. I'll have to buy another."

Val handed her a small, promisingly heavy purse. "Buy what you need. You can give me a reckoning tomorrow when we set out."

"What's to keep me from taking this and not showing up?"

Val downed the last of her drink and stood. "You'd miss the rest of where that comes from. I'll see you at dawn at the northern gates." She sauntered out of the inn, leaving Orlly to enjoy the rest of her ale.

Orlly pulled tight the last strap on the new selith's hackamore in the dawning light. Val's generous purse had bought a strong young female, plus extra blankets and good food; she had even managed to justify the purchase of a new double-lined riding cape for herself. The other selithi, Sa, So, and Sy, stood quietly, heads together. So, the fractious male Val had startled into rebellion, kept one ear swiveled hopefully in Orlly's direction. She had spent hours the night before, stroking him, finally smoothing his restive spirits into contentment.

Orlly sat the elthim first, tall and silvered in the strengthening light, arms and torso concealed beneath a flowing, intricately embroidered robe. Her four clawed paws moved with deliberate, almost delicate grace, and her beautiful but inhuman face reflected only serenity. Val trotted at her side, talking animatedly, while two male guards brought up the rear. Orlly stepped away from Sey, the new selith, and assumed a characteristic posture, hands on hips, with elbows thrust out.

"Elth'ua'lth, this is Orlly," said Val, "who will be our guide. Orlly, this is *H'ma* Elth'ua'lth, and Taggart, and Dev." Taggart blurred in Orlly's sight as young and dark; Dev was middle-aged and looked competent in a grim sort of way. She took in their faces from the corners of her vision as she stared at the elthim.

"You are welcome to my presence, my child," spoke a melodious, three-toned voice. "Am I to yours?"

"Y-yes," stammered Orlly, furious at her own awkwardness. The elthim, with her calm and kind words, reminded her too much of the healer Ama, who had sheltered and taught her.

Orlly said, "Each selith bears food for five days; that's twice as long as the trip usually takes. We can night-over in the travelers' shelters, so we can sleep out of the wind. Let's get going."

Orlly had managed to recover her emotional balance by the time she had the three humans mounted and had swung herself on So's back. She could feel the results of her work in the steadiness of his gait as he stepped out at the head of the line. Next came Taggart on the gentle Sa, then the elthim, moving with a curious gliding pace. After her came Val on grizzled Sy and the veteran Dev on Sey.

They rode easily through the wildflower-dotted foothills, the well-marked trail gradually thinning to a ribbon of itself. Orlly left the head of the train to let So stretch his legs and to check on the others. Taggart would have saddle sores before the end of the day, but he had the sense to leave Sa's head alone, and the selith bobbed along contentedly, happy to be out of the bustle of the town.

The elthim paced steadily along the steepening trails. She had shed her cloak and packed it in the bags strapped to her slanting back. Orlly had heard legends that once elthim lived side by side with humankind, scarce even then, but each one using her magical powers to secure the safety and peacefulness of her territory. *If only my village had had a resident elthim*, she thought in a burst of private grief, but their ways had faded long before her birth.

Orlly touched So into action beside Val's Sy. "We'll stop for midday meal soon. There's a flat place not too far ahead, although no water."

Val glanced around her, scanning the peaks. "Don't the selithi need to drink?"

"Not now. There's a spring farther up, and they'll drink a day's worth there. After that, we'll go more slowly, but we should reach the shelter by dark."

Orlly squinted up toward Breakheart Pass. From this angle, she could not see even the beginnings of the cleft through the tall Killian Mountains. She need no fear bandits with three armed fighters in her party, even if the elthim did not exude a mystical aura of protection. As yet, she was not in territory familiar enough to remind her...

The rest of the journey would be a constant battle to forget that on the far side of the crest of the pass lay a narrow, almost invisible thread of a trail, and at its very end, nestled in a valley of hidden green, her heart's unattainable desire. And she could never go back.

On the grassy flat, she jumped from So's back and began unpacking food. "Leave the reins tied around their necks so they can browse," she told the others. "They'll stay close, and the green feed will do them good."

The three warriors sat around the elthim, who seated herself gracefully with her clawed feet drawn up under her body. The men relaxed, chatting as they broke open their packets, but Val squashed together some waybread and cheese, and ate while she paced the green borders of the flat.

Orlly was too awed by the elthim to feel very comfortable in her presence and had no wish to socialize with the soldiers. The selithi welcomed her to their midst, rubbing their bony heads against her thighs.

So came alert first, ears cupped toward the upward trail. Sey, the new female, whickered as her head spun around. Orlly reached a hand to calm her, but as soon as she touched the animal, she knew something was wrong.

The next sound was Val's warning shout. Dark-sheathed riders galloped down the trail, mounted on heavy lowland solethi. The omnivorous cousins of the selithi bared their fangs and screamed as their riders spurred them on.

Val had drawn her sword, running to encounter the first rider before he could reach the rising elthim. In a lightning arc, she slashed through the reins. The over-weighted soleth stagger-ed, fighting for balance. Val glided to one side, avoiding the beast's massive shoulder, and dispatched its rider with a sharp upward stab. His whip dropped from his hands. The soleth scrambled over his body as he fell.

Taggart and Dev had each taken a defensive position around the elthim. The three remaining riders reined their mounts into a circle around them. Orlly shrunk against So's quivering flank, her childhood nightmares vivid before her eyes.

One of the dark riders wheeled his soleth toward the selithi, brandishing his whip. Orlly looked up to see the rider's masked face for a terrible instant before the whip lashed around Sa's off hind leg.

Sa cried out in pain as the rider jerked on the whip handle, wedging it against the high pommel of his saddle. A sickening snap, and Sa fell heavily to the ground, her cries escalating to pure agony. The pungent smell of the selith's blood stained the air.

Orlly heard Val's piercing shout, then a thud, and the rider toppled from his prancing soleth, whip slipping to the ground.

The hilt of a long throwing knife protruded from his back. The two remaining riders wheeled their mounts and fled, followed by the riderless solethi.

In the sudden silence, Sa's anguished cries shot through Orlly's heart like a charring blast. She knelt at Sa's side. The raiders had bought their own deaths; her animals, innocent of all malice, were another matter.

Sa lay on her side, the splintered bones of her leg protruding from the mangled flesh. Her cries had subsided to a croon, her eyes glazing over as if she were already dead.

Orlly took Sa's triangular head in both hands, and brought her around to stare directly into her eyes. "Peace, peace, my beauty, my love," she whispered. "It will all be over soon."

Sa's eyes darkened, clearing, and she grew quieter. Orlly felt her own throbbing grief calm under the certainty of what she must do. She slipped her knife from its sheath in her boot and pierced the selith's carotid artery. Sa quivered but did not struggle. Orlly held her as the blood flowed down slope to pool beneath a large rock. Finally Sa gave a relaxed sigh and closed her midnight-colored eyes.

Orlly laid Sa's head down as So's anxious whicker reached her. She went to him and led the three remaining selithi away from the pool of blood. Val looked up from where she knelt beside Taggart. The cloth of his sword arm shone red. Val slit the fabric and drew the strips back from the wound. Orlly's throat convulsed as she met Val's eyes. She could not speak.

Elth'ua'lth said, "They will not come again."

"No," Val agreed. "He'll send worse. We've no time to spare now." She finished tying the makeshift bandage around Taggart's arm. "We'll have to leave them as they lie." She nodded toward the two inert bodies.

"They were human, however misled. Should we leave their bodies, the temples of their spirits, to the scavengers?" asked the elthim, her face still reflecting unearthly calm.

"They were Bakkar's henchmen, sent to delay or destroy us!" Val cried. "If we stay to bury them decently, we give him time to

111

summon what we cannot face. We might as well turn around and go back now."

The elthim moved to her side, resting one hand on the swordswoman's shoulder. "If our pursuit of the greater good, we must not lose sight of the particular." She raised her head toward the peaks. "Yet I think your words carry wisdom, my child. Since secrecy will no longer serve us, speed must."

Val helped Taggart to his feet, looking toward Orlly. "We've got to move on fast. I'm sorry about your selith, but on the whole we came off lightly. It's too bad we couldn't have caught one of their beasts to use instead."

"You knew about the attack," Orlly said. "You knew there was that kind of danger, and you led me right into it without telling me. How dare you risk my selithi like that?"

Val's face clouded as she took Sy's reins and led him to Taggart, helping the injured man to mount. "No, I didn't know, not precisely. Besides, that's part of the 'dangers of the trail,' isn't it? Surely you realized that an armed guard must be armed *against* something." She strode over to Sa's body and, with a grim, set face, began dividing the food parcels and tying them on the three remaining selithi.

Orlly turned her face to the elthim. "With your magic you could have stopped the attack—you could have saved Sa." She added, with wrenching bitterness, "Aren't we good enough for you to care about?"

"All life is sacred, daughter of the mountain. The loss of your beast diminishes me as much as you. What would you have had me do?"

"Blast them into nothingness, shrivel them in their saddles before they could draw their whips, I don't know. You're supposed to be so powerful, so magical, so wise. You tell me what's to be done."

"Oh, my dear." The elthim laid one small hand on Orlly's shoulder, looking down with eyes soft and gray. "There have been such stories told of us, and you have unwisely put your trust in them. The powers I have are not the sort that could blast an assassin from his saddle, even if it were lawful to do so. I am not magical, at least not in the sense you mean."

"Then you could not have protected Sa…"

"I might have eased her passage, but you yourself had the love to do it better. Your parting gift to her was closer to magic than you know. It was of the heart, which is where true enchantment dwells."

Orlly moved away from the light touch. Despite all the tales of their legendary abilities, the elthim had been powerless to act. Just as the people of her village had been powerless against the army that had marched across it.

She thought for a moment of gathering her remaining selithi and heading back down the mountain to safety. The elthim, Val, and the others could fend for themselves. Their future was none of her concern. They could bring her nothing but sorrow. Yet honor stopped her, for she was pledged to their care from the moment she had touched Val's purse at the inn. Her best course would be to get them all through the Pass as soon as possible.

The elthim still fixed her with that deep gaze, moonlight dancing behind her silvery eyes. Orlly muttered, "What's the use of magic, then?" Before the elthim could reply, she turned back to Val. "I agreed to guide you, not fight assassins. If I am to risk my selithi, as well as my neck, I'm entitled to know what more to expect. And why."

"This attack means we've been found out," Val said, "and we have no time to spare. Come, I'll walk beside you. Fall in behind us, Taggart," she called, "and then Elth'ua'lth. Dev, guard our rear."

"Right." He reined Sey into line behind them.

"I should have warned you earlier," Val admitted, "but I had hoped my fears were groundless. It's my business, not yours, to plan Elth'au'lth's defense."

"Who would want to attack an elthim? Even if they aren't magical?"

"Long ago, my people used to listen to their wisdom. Elth'ua'lth's line-of-descent was pledged to the service of Kasimire long generations ago, when it was still a village. The elthim arbitrated, judged, and ensured peace with neighboring settlements. Then the world changed, the towns grew, and the elthim faded into their own retreats over the years. Men learned to fight."

"That's nothing new."

Val went on, her voice still even and measured, her breath in easy rhythm with her stride. "There's a dispute now over the rightful heir to the Kasimirsh crown. It's the usual tangle of collateral branches and power bids, such a mess I don't think it's possible to tell whose claim is more legitimate. But once Konray and Vistiane decide to fight it out, the whole country will fall into civil war. That must not happen," she said fiercely.

"You're not much of a peace-keeping force," Orlly observed.

"I bring Elth'ua'lth in response to the Regent's summons. If Konray and Vistiane agree to her arbitration, as I pray they will, countless lives will be saved. If one agrees, the other will be forced to, if only to appear devoted to the welfare of Kasimire. They both know that no matter who wins, the country will be devastated, easy prey for greedy neighbors."

"Who would sabotage such a noble mission?"

"Bakkar, Duc dy Lanola, and rumored to be a black magician. He tried to marry Vistiane a few years back, but she knew he was only after power in Kasimire, and she most undiplomatically laughed in his face. Now he can just wait until she and Konray thrash it out, and then destroy their exhausted armies. To do that, he's got to make sure Elth'ua'lth never reaches Kasimire."

Orlly felt a sudden fury spark within her. Her village had been only one of many tiny obstacles in the way of an army bent on such a cause, caring only for its own purposes. She thrust the memory from her. "Since you came from Kasimire, you crossed the Killians yourself to find your precious elthim. Why did you need a guide at all? You could have bought your own selithi, or walked on your bare hands for all I care, without dragging me into your troubles."

Val's face clouded and she moved her right hand toward the hilt of her sword, but she drew in her breath and answered evenly, "I never intended you to fight our battles. That's what Taggart, Dev, and I are for. You're being paid well for your work, and I did need a guide. I didn't come over the Killians. I went around through Norroway and the Salten Lakes. I had to follow the retreat path of Elth'ua'lth's line-of-descent in order to locate her."

Orlly lowered her eyes to the steepening path before her. It was hard to stay angry at one who admitted so casually to a legendary quest. She bit her lip at the unfairness of her feelings and forced herself to say, "I can see why assassins are of no importance to you after the Norroway cannibals and sea-dragons."

"The people are Norroway may be strange to us, but they're not man-eaters, and I saw only one sea-dragon from very far off. It was small and quite shy, more frightened of us than we of it. Have you never traveled, and found that the tales that frightened you as a child were but fantasies to beguile the credulous?"

"I was told stories, the same as any other youngster," Orlly retorted. "Who knows if there are true monsters in the world? I only know that some of them wear a human face."

"Yes, there are those for whom laws exist only to be broken. I think there will always be a need for a good sword in a steady hand to keep the peace."

"What could you possibly care for peace? You who march to war as to a pleasure faire! You who brandish your sword and throw knives into men's backs as if they were so much target practice! You—"

"But I'm *not* like Bakkar's raiders. I'm trying to *stop* a war! I serve the cause of peace."

"Do you think Sa gave a fig for your cause? She was only a beast, and yet she lies dead now because of your *cause*, dead like all the little villages trampled in the name of a *cause*. No animal would have done that—only humans!"

"What happened to leave you so bitter? Have you never known human kindness, then? Never mind," seeing Orlly's face tighten, "I don't wish to pry into your secrets. The forces of chance have hardened us in different ways, but we are not so very different, you and I."

Orlly stared down at her. "No," she said, "we are nothing alike." She touched So with her heels and felt his startled leap, loping ahead to scout the next stretch of trail.

Orlly signaled So to a halt where the trail narrowed along the barren heights. The peaks seemed nearer now, beneath their everlasting snow. She shook her feet free from the stirrups and slid to the ground.

"Damn her to hellsleet," she muttered, leaving So to nibble the few sprigs of hardy herbs between the rocks. "They can all go chop each other to bits! If only Sa hadn't been their first victim…" *If only I didn't have to remember.* The destruction of the village, viewed from afar by a frightened herder child, cowering amongst her father's selithi was one thing, dimmed with time and distance. But the fresher, more piercing loss could not be pushed aside so easily. She had thought she had found her home, only to have it wrenched from her.

…She had stood at the gate, trying to stem the hot, angry tears. The mountains had curved around her gently, protectively, even in farewell.

"My dear child," Ama the healer had said.

She had turned to see the familiar lined face, the eyes bright with compassion. "You cannot stay."

"I have no place to go."

"You have everywhere to go. To stay is to learn healing, to touch the core of life and let that energy flow through you. But your heart is filled to the brim with anger. How can there be room for anything else? How can your gift escape your hatred?"

"I can't help what I feel. I had nothing left when you took me in, and now this is my whole life. Besides, I'm good with animals. You said I had the touch for it."

"That I have never denied. You can heal a selith or a squirelle, but your heart is closed to your own kind. I cannot teach you."

"Tell me how to change. I'll do anything to stay." She had kept her eyes fixed on the far peaks, glistening in the sun, afraid to look back lest her control snap and she fall to her knees in pleading tears. After a long silence, she had realized she was alone.

They rode on through the rest of the day, stopping at the spring to let the selithi drink and to unpack warmer clothing. Orlly bundled herself in her new double-lined riding cape. The elthim donned her cloak, and Val and the men covered their armor with fitted jackets that permitted free movement. Val and Dev took turns walking to let the injured Taggart ride.

They reached the travelers' shelter well after dark. The ambush and forced slower pace had taken their toll of time, so that when they stumbled into the stone building they were all chilled.

Orlly helped Taggart to dismount and led the animals to the stable sheds. "Go on," she told Val, "get a fire going and warm up. I'll see to the selithi and join you later."

"Dev can do that. You're just as tired and in need of hot food as any of us."

"I'm fine," Orlly protested, forcing her cold-numbed fingers to manipulate the buckles of So's girth.

"Nonsense, the selithi carried all of us. You shouldn't have to care for them alone."

Orlly lowered So's saddle and turned to push the other woman aside. "I don't need your help."

Val looked at her, surprise and sudden understanding in her eyes. "No, I can see you don't." She went to join the others.

Orlly, stung by the bleak tone of Val's voice, unsaddled the selithi and rubbed them down. Her muscles warmed with the effort of stroking their long, powerful muscles as they began to bubble their pleasure. They thrust their muzzles at her, fodder trailing from their jaws, pleading for more and filling her with secret joy. Even the newcomer, Sey, rubbed against her. She smiled and murmured in the young female's ear, then went to attend to the demands of her own body.

Whoever had built the fire had made a competent, compact blaze. A cook pot hung from a hook. Dev, his fingers wrapped in a cloth and lifted the lid to stir the contents.

"Done. Are you hungry, lass?" He looked up at Orlly, his grizzled features reddened by the light of the flames. Without waiting for her reply, he took up one of the light trail dishes, filled it with jerky-laced porridge, and handed it to her.

Orlly took it and sat by herself in a corner, cupping her fingers around the warmth. She watched Val tending Taggart's wound, talking with the elthim, and her heart pulsed unevenly within her. She longed for the familiar comfort of the selithi. The young guard winced as Val snapped the ends of the bandage tight. Reluctantly, Orlly put down her meal and went over to them.

"No, not like that," she said curtly, telling herself that her only motive was that she despised incompetence.

"Look," Orlly said, smoothing and easing the fabric with her fingertips, "it's no good if you cut off the circulation and let gangrene set in." The knots beneath her touch felt wrong, so she unwrapped the whole bandage, peering at the deep slash. Even in the faltering light of the fire, she could see the edges of wound gape. Dark blood seeped out.

"That bleeding will continue draining his strength until I close the gap." She held Taggart's elbow and moved his arm backward and forward, watching the skin strain on the slash. She shook her head. "No, there's no position that doesn't open it further," she said, gently swabbing the blood. "I'll have to stitch it closed."

"With what?" Val asked.

"I've a sewing kit with silk thread. We'll have to boil it, but I've sutured selithi wounds with silk, and it works fine."

Orlly went back to her corner while Val sterilized the short metal needles and lengths of silk thread. She had not worked at healing a fellow human since her time of refuge and study with Ama. She did not want to remember what once had been hers and was no longer. Yet here it was, thrusting itself back into her life like a corpse that would not stay decently buried.

She laid out her materials and bathed the wound with boiled water. Val held a torch close by at her shoulder.

"That feels good," Taggart told her. With his tousled dark hair and his face shadowed in the uneven red light, he looked very young. "Will it hurt much?"

Orlly smiled. "You needn't be afraid. Close your eyes and feel my touch here," between his eyes, imagining her fingertip a tiny sun of warmth and life, "here," at the base of his throat, "here," on the inside of his elbow on the injured side, "here…"

Her voice settled smoothly into the cadence and inflection she used with the selithi. The lines of pain and tension in his face softened. Stroking the skin around the wound, she began to hum and watched his response, a deepening of the breath. She picked up the threaded needle, turning so that her hand would cast no shadow across the wound, and thrust the point through the edge of the skin. The boy did not flinch.

Orlly sutured the slash, matching the wound edges as closely as she could. Her hum rolled on, wending its own way through her movements. After she tied the last knot, she bathed the wound again and bandaged it lightly. "Let him sleep," she told Val. "He needs rest more than anything else, as do we all."

While the swordswoman tucked blankets around the young guard and made ready her own bed, Orlly washed and dried her needles and repacked her supplies. Without looking up, she knew that the elthim watched her through serene, alien eyes. She grabbed her bedroll and rose to carry it into the other room, preferring the comfort of her selithi.

The elthim stood before her, faintly luminous despite the near darkness. The fire had descended into embers. "You have a rare gift, child."

Orlly shrugged. "A lot of good it does me," she muttered. *Not enough to save gentle Sa, only to sew up some young idiot so he can go out and get slashed up all over again.* "I did little enough, just patch up a cut so we can move on tomorrow."

"You know that you did far more than 'patch up a cut.' Why do you hide behind old anger?"

Orlly pushed by her, breaking into a run to reach the selithi.

She awoke cold and stiff, with old Sy nuzzling her anxiously. Orlly forced her lids open to see his eyes, almost black with age. She stroked his chin and pulled herself upright. Something was bothering him.

In the other room, Elth'ua'lth stood at the door, holding it open a crack and staring into the swirling whiteness outside. Val, looking pale and tired, knelt by the fireplace, fumbling with her Flintstone and tinder.

Orlly went to the door and peered outside, shuddering as a blast of icy air met her cheeks. She could see only a few feet through the howling snow. "Blizzard," she commented, shivering. "Well, we can't travel in that. I don't understand it, for there's never snowfall this low at this season."

"This is no ordinary weather," the elthim said. "Valeria, come here and look at this."

Val put another stick of wood on the growing fire and stood up, wiping her hands. "I've never seen a storm like that."

"It is a fimbul-winter," Elth'ua'lth told her, "a storm of magic sent to bind us here." She shut the door firmly. "I cannot guess what might be sent to take us while we bide the storm, but we must not be here when it arrives. Let us dress as warmly as we can, for we must force our way through it."

"You're crazy!" Orlly exclaimed. "Even if my selithi could travel through that, we can't. I can't see three paces in front of my nose in that snow. We'd tumble down a mountain or lose our way, or get drifted in before midday and freeze to death.

Our only chance is to wait it out here."

"That is just what whoever sent the storm wishes us to do. I confess I am not overeager to plunge into it myself," the elthim said. "I know very well it may mean my death. But to stay here in the tempting comfort of the shelter will certainly be the end for all of us, even your beasts. Will you take my sworn word? Or would have you me describe the horrors that might come while we are pinned down here?"

The silvery eyes blazed with light, and the musical voice resonated with truth. Orlly felt it in her bones, felt the stir of the same certainly as when Ama had spoken to her of healing. She nodded and said grudgingly, "If we must, we must. I'll do my best to get us all through. But I still think that going out in that blizzard is daft."

They filled their bellies with hot porridge and fruit-meal, then used their bedrolls to fashion extra cloaks for themselves and blankets for the selithi. Orlly insisted that Val ride behind her on So.

"You'll only waste your strength fighting drifts on foot," she argued. "So's the only one strong enough to carry double, and I can't watch you and the trail at the same time. I want to know you're safe, not sliding into some crevasse."

So snorted as he stepped out into the thick swirls of white. His skin shuddered as the first flakes touched him, and he extended the spiny crest of his neck in alarm. Orlly sent him in the general direction of the trail, relying more on memory than vision. He sniffed the fallen snow and pawed at it, prancing.

"Elth'ua'lth once said that animals can smell evil magic," Val commented.

Orlly nodded, for once content to not argue.

So swiveled his ears forward, moving out slowly and carefully. The other selithi bunched closely around the elthim, as if trying to protect her from the wind with their bodies.

They inched forward with agonizing slowness. With each step the selith took, Orlly's heart pounded with fear that he would overstep the edge of the trail and carry her and Val to their deaths, or else plunge into a drift-filled hole and snap a leg. She was not sure she could survive another death such as Sa's. The cliff might be easier.

She found it better to close her eyes; she could barely see past an arm's length anyway, and any attempt at guidance would only undermine So's confidence in himself. She could feel him moving slowly but powerfully beneath her, the solid bulk of Val behind her. She imagined she could touch the selith's life-force like a steady, glowing sphere floating through honey. Behind her soared another, of a different hue: Sy bearing the injured Taggart. Then floated a shimmering silver disc spangled with jeweled facets that must represent the elthim. Finally came the fiery orb of young Sey. Her inner vision shifted as she focused on the balls of brilliant living light, Dev and Taggart and Val. They drifted together in a gossamer web of golden and platinum strands.

So's whicker brought her up short from her dreamy vision. The trail stretched before her, visible even in the clearing snowstorm. He pricked his ears and surged forward.

"I don't understand. We haven't been traveling that long. How could the storm just disappear?" Orlly asked in amazement.

"Longer than you know, child," came the elthim's sweet voice. "Whoever taught you did well."

They began to climb in earnest now, leaving behind the last flakes of enchanted snow. Val offered to dismount, but Orlly, seeing her pale face, insisted that she ride, and walked at So's head herself.

They stopped for a midday meal in the partial shelter of a stone face, a stark contrast to yesterday's nooning. Orlly nibbled at her meal as she checked the selithi, inspecting their feet and girths.

"Orlly, will you look at Taggart's arm?" Val asked. "It seems better to me, but I'm no healer." She had unwrapped the outer bandages to reveal the sutured cut, healing with only a trace of redness.

"What makes you think I'm one?"

Val opened her mouth in surprise, but did not reply.

Orlly gentled her tone. "What about the elthim? She's slogged it along with the selithi through worse than I'd care to walk through."

"I've been trying not to think about that," the swordswoman said in an uncertain voice. "She knows more about what we have to face than I do. If she says we dare not rest, I won't gainsay her."

"Let's be off, then. The hardest part of the Pass is still ahead. We must make it over before dark. It's too dangerous to travel without daylight, and there's no more shelter on this side. We'll be all right once we're on the far slope."

The selithi plodded on while Orlly and Dev took turns riding or scrambling over the rocks on foot. There were no more magical snowstorms or bands of assassins, only the barren loneliness of the heights. Orlly had often felt peace in the clean-swept stillness above the tree line, where the wind was the only other voice she heard. Now she sensed only emptiness, lifelessness, and the fatigue that had given Breakheart Pass its name.

They passed the crest of the pass just as the sun began to dip toward the horizon. With luck they would reach the next shelter at tree line before total darkness.

Making excellent time downhill, they came within sight of the plain rock structure of a shelter as the full moon rose, flooding the last stretch of trail with light. Orlly cried out in relief.

"Hold!" came from the elthim, her voice now rough and uneven. Orlly whipped her head around to see her halt on unsteady feet, her small hands raised in a warding gesture. "Gather behind me, all of you! Quickly!"

Orlly found her legs obeying the elthim's command. Val slid

her sword free and jumped from So's back, and Dev did the same, moving to her side. Instinctively Orlly reached one hand to touch So. *I'll die before I'll let them have another of mine*, she promised, thinking she meant only the selithi.

"Look!" Taggart, still astride Sy, pointed.

In the pool of moonlight before the shelter, an orange ember flickered and then ignited to a ragged ball of flame, throwing out arms of light. Val stepped forward, sword held at ready.

"No, get back," Elth'ua'lth commanded. "Your blade is useless here. You would only feed that thing."

Val obeyed reluctantly. "What do we face, then?"

"Were-dragon. Stay here, all of you. You can do nothing. If I fail…" Her voice faltered. "Die gladly if you must, but do not give it your fears."

She stepped forward as the orange mass elongated, projections spreading into wings, a distorted body, and a fang-toothed head. Blackness leered from its eyes. Orlly could smell its dank breath from where she stood.

The elthim held fast, her legs spread slightly, glimmering in the moonlight. The dragon-shape slithered hissing through the air and reared before the elthim, dwarfing her.

Elth'ua'lth spoke, her voice carrying in the night air, and the orange monster spun away as if struck, shrieking. It touched the edge of the shelter in an explosion of stench and sparks. The stone smoldered where the thing had touched it.

"I don't understand," Orlly whispered to Val. "She said she had no magic to fight the assassins. How can she now do this?"

"No magic to slay any living creature," the young swordswoman answered. "The were-dragon is not alive."

Orlly buried her face against So's muscled neck. The dragon's bellows drowned out Elth'ua'lth's lighter voice.

The elthim's pulse of light faltered. The strands of light linking her to the silver disc in Orlly's mind began to dim. Behind Orlly's closed eyes, the were-dragon loomed like a black pit, a maw spreading to engulf the elthim's shining sphere. Orlly lashed out in fury and denial, surprised to see a flash of white flame speed toward the dark. The black mass halted, its edges curling inward. The sparkling globe grew brighter.

Orlly opened her eyes to see a filmy shape coalesce above the standing elthim. It stretched upward, reflecting the light of the full moon, then solidified into a form bearing pair of extended wings, a noble head, and outstretched arms holding two slender daggers.

The dragon-thing coiled in on itself, its eyes rolling in distress. It shook its tail and rattled its wings. Then the blocky muscles of its haunches tensed for a leap. It sprang into the air, its whistle deafening to Orlly's ears.

With lightning speed, the moon-silver form rose to meet it, great wings fanning the air. Orlly caught a scent of sea-tang masking the dragon's stench for only an instant before the dagger points met its eyes. Then she fell to the rocky ground at Val's side, clutching her ears in a vain attempt to mask the horrendous din of the wounded were-creature. Even though the agony that filled her skull, she felt So brush against her, trembling, felt Val's strong body contract as she fought for control...felt the elthim stagger under the weight of the magic that fueled the dragon.

She looked up, eyes watering. Elth'ua'lth had fallen before the were-dragon, now a shapeless, writhing mass no larger than a newborn selith. It seemed to be struggling to reassert its form, vague gestures of wing or snout or tail emerging from the central lump, only to melt back at a gesture from the elthim.

The racket had died down, except for the whimpers of the selithi and whispered commands from the weakening elthim.

Val, kneeling at Orlly's side, raised her head and reached for her sword.

"You fool, you can't go out there!" Orlly grabbed the sleeve of Val's sword arm and pointed to the still-smoldering rock of the shelter where the were-dragon had touched it. "That thing'll burn your sword, and then you. Idiot!"

"I don't care," Val sobbed. "I've got to do *something*. Bakkar may be burnt out if the dragon is, but if Elth'ua'lth dies, there will be war anyway. Whatever you may think of me, I can't let that happen. I can't let all those people die. Don't you understand? Don't you care about *anything?*"

Orlly met her pale violet eyes. "Yes. But if you go out there, you won't be able to stop it, and you'll only waste your own life for nothing."

Val slid her sword back into its sheath, her shoulders shuddering with silent weeping. Without thinking, Orlly flung an arm around her. *I can't let that happen...I can't let all those people die.*

She watched the jeweled orb dim, sinking perceptibly into the darkness. A memory leapt to her vision—the network of interconnecting strands she had envisioned during their struggle through the fimbul-storm. Now she sensed only a few dying threads, and she tried to imagine what they had once looked like.

To her surprise, the threads pulsed brighter with a beat of life before subsiding. She searched her memories again, willing herself to see a growing web of iridescent fibers. More appeared, tenuous at first, then firming under her repeated mental insistence that they *did exist.* Rainbow hues, deepening to healer's green, spread outward from the focus, sliding along the glistening strands to reach the silver disc. To one side, she noticed a concentration of weaker colors, dancing like tiny stars from a triad of suns—the selithi were joining her. She caught at their unfocused atoms of light, imagining them woven into a steady flow, and then saw what she had evoked.

Emboldened now, she reached for the luminous globes that were Val and the two men, spun their light into a veil of living color, and tossed it like a fishing net along the web to Elth'ua'lth's strengthening gem.

The elthim's sphere regained its silvery radiance, set in a fireweb of light. Before her the darkness receded, curling in on itself, and shrank to a pinpoint and vanished.

Exultation shot through Orlly as she opened her eyes. Val huddled in the shelter of her arm, no longer sobbing. In the clearing before the shelter, Elth'ua'lth knelt before a blackened circle. Orlly scrambled to her feet and ran to the elthim.

She reached her just as Elth'ua'lth fell slowly to the bare earth, moving as if time itself were thickened. Orlly touched her side, now flat gray instead of luminous silver. Beneath her fingers, the elthim's ribs moved tremulously, drawing in a shallow breath.

"No!" cried Val, racing to Orlly's side and flinging her arms around the elthim's narrow shoulders. "She can be dead!"

"She isn't," Orlly said quietly. "She's still breathing."

"She isn't wounded. I don't see any blood," Val babbled, her words spilling over each other.

"I don't think it's that sort of wound." Orlly sank down, catching herself on both hands to keep from falling. "I don't know what's wrong with her." Then she steadied herself, closing her eyes once more for an inner vision. Nothing met her eyes but flat darkness and hot tears.

"Hellsleet," she whimpered, too exhausted to curse with imagination. "The first time I cared, and I couldn't do a damned thing. I couldn't save her."

"I wouldn't say that," said a stern, familiar voice.

Orlly lifted her head. Ama stood on a little knoll above the shelter, her carved staff in hand. She shook one gnarled finger at Orlly.

"You couldn't make that much psychic racket without my knowing. Come, child, wipe your tears. There's nothing wrong with you that a good night's sleep won't cure. I've waited years for you to be ready to continue your studies."

"But the elthim," Orlly said. "If she dies, there's a war."

"And that makes a difference to you?" The healer raised one grizzled eyebrow.

"Damned clear it does. Do you think I want to be responsible for other villages getting flattened as mine did?" she stormed. Then her words dried up. How could she describe the web of life linking her to the glory that was the elthim's spirit? To her selithi, giving love in return, and to her comrades? Warmth instead of perennial ice filled her heart.

127

Ama smiled, her seamed face crinkling into a dance of kindly light. She turned to the fallen elthim and touched her lightly on the forehead. "Nothing but a little back-shock from your enthusiasm. She'll recover in a few moments."

Val cried aloud as the elthim's eyelids twitched open. The elthim reached out a small hand to the young swordswoman and got to her feet.

As Elth'ua'lth looked down at her, Orlly felt herself bathed in the silvery radiance behind those gray eyes. The elthim took her hands and kissed her gently on the brow. The touch seared her with cool, crystalline light, reaching to her very heart. Beyond the elthim, she could see Val's tear-streaked, jubilant face.

"Say good-bye to your friends, child. It's time to go home," said the healer. "They don't need you any longer. Let them take the other two selithi; that boy can't walk down the mountain on his own legs, but So will answer only to you and ought to come back with us."

To Elth'ua'lth she said, "The trail is broad and clear. You'll not need a guide now. Good fortune attend you."

Val flung her arms around a started Orlly. "I don't know how you did it, but I thank you with all my heart. I promise, I'll care for your selithi as well as you would. When you've finished your training, come to Kasimire to get them...and visit me."

"Where?" blurted Orlly.

"To the Regent's palace—he's my father." Val brushed her tears away with the back of one sleeve, set her hand on sword hilt in a characteristic gesture, and marched back toward the shelter. "Come on, a good night's rest and then we've got a war to stop."

Orlly turned to the healer beside her. "I don't understand. I'm going back with you?" Hope and new understanding dawned within her, washing away the bitterness of old grief.

"Oh yes," said Ama. "You were much too clumsy with the life web. As you're a healer now, you must learn to be more skillful. I've a great deal to teach you now."

Under the Skin

It could have been a mugging, or some kid on dope roughing up a wino, but when she paused before the darkened alley on the humid July night, something in her guts went *zing!* and Jodie Marshall knew another woman was in trouble and needed her help. She stepped beyond the Hollywood streetlights and saw two bodies wrestling between the trash cans. Without thinking of the danger she might be putting herself in, Jodie dropped her sweat-soaked karate *gi* rolled in its black belt and sprinted towards them.

She could not see much more of the man than his back and a thatch of hair, but she did not need to in order to know what was going on. He hunched over his victim, pinning her legs a-part with his knees. The woman beneath him moaned, a hoarse, almost animal sound. Her white thighs shown in the darkness.

Jodie's first kick, a sweeping roundhouse with all the power her *kiai* could generate, caught the man across the back of his kidneys. Breath burst from him as his spine arched reflexively. His neck snapped back to meet her knife hand at the base of his skull.

The man's head thwacked against the cracked pavement, bounced, and then lolled from a limp body. Jodie clung to him like a limpet as he fell, and then slid her fingers around to the front of his neck, digging through the layers of muscle for his carotid arteries. The pulse under her fingers felt strong and vital.

She wondered what it would be like to press just a little harder...

It would be so easy, wouldn't it? No one would ever know it hadn't happened accidentally during the fight. Just a little more pressure, and the elastic walls of the blood vessels would bend inward, bend and finally collapse...

Temptation swept through Jodie like a wave of sexual heat. She sweated with wanting it.

The heart itself, now so arrogant in life, would begin to falter, beat by beat growing slower and less regular. Then the stillness, blessed peace, one less monster to prowl the darkness, giving women nightmares they would carry for the rest of their lives. His brain might cry out as it squandered the last of its precious oxygen supply, but it would be a silent cry. She would never hear it, not even in her dreams. Now she had the chance she'd longed for these past ten years, the chance to get back for what those bastards did to Sherry.

Just a few more moments...

The woman on the ground moaned again. She pushed herself up on her elbows, her face hidden beneath a tangle of darkness.

"C'mon, we've got to get out of here." Jodie lifted the other woman by one slender wrist. The skin was marble cool under Jodie's fingers, the bones light and fragile as a bird's.

"I'll take you to the hospital—you might be hurt and not realize it. Adrenaline does that to you—" Jodie hurried her out of the alley, pausing only to scoop up her *gi*.

"No hospital. No police," the woman said in a low, heavily accented voice. She sounded Russian or Polish, not Hispanic, but Jodie could not place her origin.

"You can't let that creep walk away, not after what he tried to do. The next woman he jumps might not be so lucky—she might end up dead."

Jodie realized that she was talking too fast and her fingertips ached from pressing against the woman's arm. With an effort, she released her grip. It wasn't the woman's fault that she had been brainwashed into taking whatever shit this sexist society dumped on her. Or maybe there was another reason.

"You don't want the authorities to know about you? Are you an illegal or something?"

The woman's face glimmered in the artificial light—huge shadowed eyes, pointed chin, wine-dark lips. "I need only a place to rest."

"I can't just leave you here." Jodie pointed to her battered Honda at the curbside. "You can stay with me for a few days."

The woman slid into the front passenger seat. "I shall not overstay my welcome. A few days, as you say."

Jodie unlocked both locks to her one-bedroom apartment. "C'mon in, sit anywhere. What's your name, by the way?"

"Mary Smith."

"Look, I don't care who you really are or why you want to stay hidden—" Jodie flicked on the lights. "And if you're dealing, I don't want to know about it, but we've got to call the cops on this."

Mary Smith sat on the battered sofa covered with an old chenille bedspread. "What good would that do?"

"For one thing, the creep could still be lying there and they'll pick him up. Even if you don't press charges, he'll spend the night locked up instead of assaulting the next woman he comes across. Also for the record, so the cops start believing us about the frequency of rape around here. Every unreported attack puts us that much further from decent protection."

"As you wish, but it will do no good."

She was right. The duty officer sniggered, "You did *what* to him and left him *how?*" And refused to take the report without Jodie's name.

Christ, another bozo who doesn't believe women can fight back, Jodie thought as she hung up.

The next morning Mary Smith was gone. After Jodie dressed for work at the women's bookstore, she headed for her favorite coffee shop. She was low on funds, as usual, but after last night she deserved a meal she didn't have to cook herself.

"Hi, Stell." Jodie slid onto a stool at the counter and picked up the copy of the *Los Angeles Times* that the last customer had abandoned. "How's life in the old roach coach?"

"And to you too, Jo. The usual?"

"Yeah, and the coffee up front, please. I had the strangest night—Holy shit."

The waitress craned her neck around to read the page Jodie laid flat on the counter.

"Some creep got bumped off in an alley. Since when is that news in Hollywood? They figure he was a rapist because his dong was out. Serves the bastard right."

But he was alive when I left him. I swear he was! Maybe some doper rolled him for his wallet and it had nothing to do with me. But if I hadn't left him there...

Christ, Jodie, he had it coming. One less macho shit pig in the universe.

He deserved prison, he didn't deserve to die...

Jodie bent over her coffee, feeling the warmth seep through fingers grown suddenly cold. She had wanted him dead in the height of her fury. But she'd stopped herself from acting on it.

Or had she?

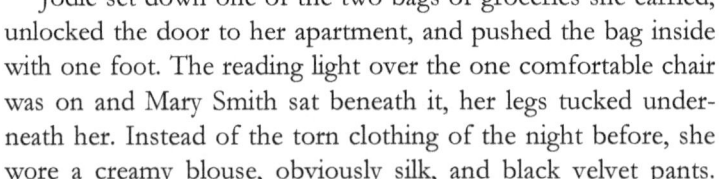

Jodie set down one of the two bags of groceries she carried, unlocked the door to her apartment, and pushed the bag inside with one foot. The reading light over the one comfortable chair was on and Mary Smith sat beneath it, her legs tucked underneath her. Instead of the torn clothing of the night before, she wore a creamy blouse, obviously silk, and black velvet pants. Two expensive-looking suitcases lay in the corner beside the orange-crate bookshelves.

Mary looked up from the book she was reading. "My friend! How glad I am to see you!" she exclaimed.

"Can you give me a hand with these groceries?" Jodie mumbled. "I'm sorry, I've only shopped for one."

Mary got up from the chair in a movement that would stir envy in a dancer. As she took the bag, Jodie smelled her perfume, a dry spicy scent, unfamiliar and disturbing. Mary laughed. "I did not expect you to feed me too! I will put these things away for you—no, let me do just this little thing. You have done so much for me already."

In the bathroom Jodie pulled off her clothes and stepped into the shower. The hot water beating on her shoulders help to relax the iron tension of the day. She lost track of time, for when she had dried and dressed, she found the living room empty. She wolfed down a frozen dinner, flipped the TV on and off a few times, and finally tumbled into bed.

The dream began as an ordinary residue of the day's events, but soon Jodie found herself walking down a deserted hallway, peering into one doorway after another. As the light faded into shadow, colors took on a strange new richness and all her senses grew sharper. The cold air brought her waves of intoxicating scents; her own heartbeat and the gentle whisper of air in her lungs seemed more compelling than an ocean storm. Finally she reached the last doorway and stopped. She looked down at her hands, to find them spattered with fresh blood. But instead of being horrified, the sight and smell filled her with an almost orgasmic ecstasy, a pleasure so deep that it sent her reeling into terror and she woke up in a cold sweat.

The next day Jodie awakened feeling as if she'd been on a three-day drunk, her body sodden and unresponsive as she lurched out of bed. She ran cold water down the back of her neck and scrubbed her teeth while she stared in the mirror. *You*

did want to kill him, she thought despondently. *That's what your subconscious was trying to tell you last night. What are you going to do now? How are you going to live with this?*

Jodie decided to make the morning karate workout even if it meant losing a few hours of work. Her boss wouldn't object, and she badly needed the mind-clearing exercise. She dug out a fresh *gi* and her belt. The stitched black fabric had gone gray with wear along the sides.

We are taught to revere life and never to use our art for aggression, but only the preservation of that life. But how could I have turned away from everything I believe in for one moment of insanity?

The class was small, and Jodie was the only woman present. Normally this didn't bother her, although she had gotten some harsh comments from friends who felt that a woman of her rank owed it to her sisters to work out only with other women. Some of the men had an ego problem about a woman who was their rank superior, and she'd had to "accidentally" bloody a few noses during sparring. As *sensei* led them through the solo exercises, Jodie worked out next to a barrel-chested man named Steve Azusa. Although he smiled hello as usual, white teeth shining in his dark-complected face, she did not return his greeting with her usual glare, *What do you think I am, some second-class plaything?* She remembered he was a cop, a detective sergeant with the LAPD.

There is no scarlet letter on your forehead, no token of what you've done, Jodie told herself, clinging desperately to her concentration. *It's only your own conscience that says he can see right through you. And why should you care what he thinks? He's probably an arrogant s.o.b. like the rest of them.*

Jodie finished the workout with a long round of sparring with Steve Azusa. She forgot her doubts, forgot the misery of not knowing if she was really a killer. All she saw was his face, as closed and set as her own, but with a hint of good nature in the lift of his eyebrows. With a mind like ice she blocked his moves, spinning to counterattack. Her hands and feet were not bone and flesh, but hammers, knives, claws, as bereft of emotion as the tools they resembled. Finally *sensei* drew the class together for closing meditation. Jodie sat on her knees, *seiza*, and felt her heart beat calm, her thoughts grow still. *Sensei* clapped three times to end the class.

Got to air this place out, Jodie thought as she unlocked the door. She'd worked late that night to make up for the morning's karate practice. The air in the apartment tasted flat, as if all the life had gone out of it.

Mary Smith sat on the sofa in a pool of light from the reading lamp. "Ah, my friend, you are so late tonight. You work too hard. I shall treat you to a concert—Holly Near, at the Pavilion—that would please you?"

Jodie shook her head with genuine regret. "I'd love to, but I'm so grubby, and it's too late for dinner—"

"Not a problem. You dress, and I'll make you something you can eat on the way. Please let me do this for you, it's the least I can offer in return for the refuge you've given me."

They sat in the best orchestra seats, waiting for the concert hall lights to dim. Jodie said uncomfortably, "You're spending rather a lot of money—"

"I would rather not speak of it. Do you intend to tell me—"

"No, I'm just used to paying my own way, usually the cheapest." *I wonder if she uses her money for dope, too. That would explain why she bounced back so quickly after that first night—maybe be the new designer crack...* "I don't understand why you don't have a place to stay," she continued somewhat snappishly. "Surely you can afford a hotel."

"Do you understand that I would rather not be identifiable by the authorities?"

"You're an illegal alien, then?" *And not a dealer?*

"Something like that."

"You should be getting legal help through the Sanctuary movement or the ACLU—"

Mary sighed and laid one hand on Jodie's. She lowered her voice to a disturbing intimacy. "I have found through the years that there is a certain loyalty that only one woman can give to another."

"Are you making a pass at me?" asked Jodie, suddenly skittish. She wasn't turned on by other women, but there was something about Mary....

Mary smiled and withdrew her hand. "I speak of sisterhood, not a sexual bonding. Why else would you risk yourself to save a strange woman? Why else do you run a women's bookstore for a pittance when your skills could bring you much more from a corporation?"

"I didn't run down that alley because of some politically correct concept of sisterhood," Jodie answered hotly. "I knew in my guts what was happening, and then I had to help you. I've never had the chance to jump a rapist before, but I can't tell you how many times I've wished I did. Not enough to take stupid chances, hoping something would happen, but ever since I was sixteen and my very best friend was gang-raped—"

"My dear, you don't have to tell me this."

Jodie said through her sudden tears, "I want you to know, to understand why saving you was so important to me. She fought back—and they took after her with chains—and she died. Those incredible bastards—I saw what they did to her. Thinking about it—I don't believe I'll ever be free of it. I had nightmares for years, that it was that it was me being raped and murdered, me instead of Sherry. That's how I got into karate, to stay sane. I would have given anything to save her, but there wasn't a damn thing I could do. But this time—this time—"

"Hush. More than you can know, I understand the passion of your anger. It is a mirror to my own. Once I was as you, struggling with the brutality of what men had done to the women I loved. My hatred was all that kept me alive. See, the lights grow dim. Day's judgments fade into shadow and the truth emerges, pure as the virgin moon."

Jodie turned to stare at her companion before the concert

made further conversation impossible. Whatever else she might be, this woman she had saved from rate had an extraordinary and disturbing presence.

Put the whole thing behind you now, she told herself. *Mary is safe, there's one for Sherry, and that's the end to it.*

For the next month she believed it. Then came another dream of hunting down a darkened corridor, a dream in which the blood on her hands touched a chord of hunger within her. Restlessly she paced the hallway, always stopping before the final door. There was the same smell in the air, a perfume of fear. She drank it in, and it mixed with the smell of the blood and flooded through her, searing her with pleasure.

I'm going crazy, Jodie thought, staring at the newspaper story. *How could I kill a second time, and without any conscious memory of it? The first one I could put down to the fury of the moment, getting carried away. It was an accident. But this time—Mary and I were at the ballet— ABT at the Shrine—we came home—I went to bed, I got up this morning—I don't remember anything in between! Could I have walked— and killed—in my sleep?*

The tough evening karate class brought Jodie only a parody of calm. One moment she remained convinced of her own guilt, the next she knew with equal certainty that she had not, *could not* have done such a thing. After the workout, she wiped the sweat from her face with the towel that she kept by the drinking fountain and leaned against the wall, delaying the trip home.

"How about a cup of coffee, on me?"

Jodie scowled reflexively and started to snap back that she didn't date men, but Steve Azusa continued quickly, "This isn't a pass, you just look like you could use a friend."

I can't keep on like this, she thought. *Hiding and lying, I have to find out the truth, and it might as well be from someone I already know.*

Over coffee, amplified by doughnuts, Jodie blurted out her story. Steve listened intently, without interrupting her. When she finished by saying, "…and I honestly don't know if I killed them or not," he shook his head.

"It's not my case, but I can tell you this: those men didn't die of a blow to the back of the head. I don't disbelieve you hit the first one hard enough to knock him out, but what actually killed him was some blood disease. The coroners had to call in Public Health, and they're going nuts trying to figure it out."

Steve swallowed the last of his coffee. "But what if those guys had died from trauma? You'd have made a confession without your Miranda rights."

"And you'd have to take me in. I guess that's what I was hoping for, if I'd really done it."

"Feeling a little guilty?"

"Steve, I *wanted* to kill that first creep. I was so bone-deep angry there was nothing I would stop at. I know I'm not rational on the subject of rape, but I didn't know just how far I'd go. I still don't and that—that frightens me. I can't go back to thinking I'm a civilized person, not after the way I felt."

"I won't jolly you along with speeches about how many normal people feel that way, too. A pat on the head won't make you feel any better. But it's no crime to want it, only to actually *do* it, Jo. So get off your own case. If it's any consolation, I feel the same way about rapists."

"What could you, or any man, *possibly* know about how I feel about rape?" *And why am I telling him all this? Am I so weak I have to go running to a man for reassurance… Or confession?*

"I haven't been raped, if that's what you mean. But I've laid my life on the line to bring in some crack pusher or a wiseass pimp that keeps his girls hooked and beats them to a pulp if they squeak back. I've seen the smirks on their faces, knowing they'd be back on the street just as soon as their bondsman can hop to it. I've thought of all the decent people they are going to hurt, and that one day they might get trigger-happy and blow my ass away. I think how much better this town would be without them. I think, I'm the one with the gun, and there's no one else looking…"

Jodie held her breath, seized by the fire and darkness in his eyes.

"You know what I feel," he said. "Don't tell me it isn't the same. Nobody, not cops or women's libbers or nobody, has a monopoly on righteous anger. But the bottom line is—my hands are clean, and yours are too, lady. The rest is nobody's business."

Jodie could not rebut his argument, but she had yet to find a way of forgiving herself for wanting to kill, for the blood lust now that ran like an unbreakable thread through her dreams. She clung to her relationship with Mary as the one good thing that had come out of the whole incident, refusing to discuss her moving out. As the weeks passed, she became increasingly worried that she might have saved her from rape, only to lose her in another way.

"Mary, I'm going to level with you," Jodie said. "I said I didn't want to know it if you were dealing, but whatever you're using is killing you. You've got to get help."

Mary Smith lay on the sofa, her eyes flat, trapping all the light that entered them. It was two months later, three months since she had come to live with Jodie, and her once rosy skin lay over her cheekbones like parchment over driftwood.

"It is nothing. I will be better soon."

"Soon! You mean when you get your next fix! Mary, that's not *better*, it's only making you worse."

Jodie sat on the sofa and laid a firm hand on her friend's shoulder, feeling the bones as fragile as eggshells. "I see what you're doing to yourself. You look great, hyped up on super-crack or whatever you're doing, we have a good time, and then you get wasted. Two, three weeks at most, and you're a basket case. Look at you, you can barely sit up by yourself. How much longer do you think your body can handle that shit?"

"Do you want me to move out?"

"No, I just don't like what you're doing to yourself. I care about you."

"As I for you. We have much in common, two sisters in a

world of hostile men."

Jodie backed off, realizing that there was nothing to be gained by further argument. Mary disappeared again while she was in the kitchen fixing dinner and she felt strangely bereft.

It's none of your business anyway, she thought as she drank her second glass of wine. *At least she's got some way to keep her going, which is more than you can say for yourself. You're a damned hypocrite, Jodie Marshall, getting so worked up about Mary doing dope when you just bumped off two men.* Morosely, she finished the bottle. *I don't care what Steve says, I wouldn't feel this way... And a dream this way, unless I'd done it.*

That night the dreams came again, dreams of blood and darkness, dreams of terror and hunger. The shadows welcomed her, the hallway as familiar as her childhood home. Again she halted before the last door, her hands slick with blood. Pleasure coiled around her, and she did not shrink from it. Only as she bent forward with a hot red blood, almost touching her lips to it, almost feeling it slip down her throat to ignite the core of her ecstasy, did she awaken, terrified.

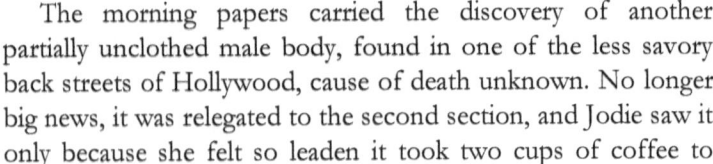

The morning papers carried the discovery of another partially unclothed male body, found in one of the less savory back streets of Hollywood, cause of death unknown. No longer big news, it was relegated to the second section, and Jodie saw it only because she felt so leaden it took two cups of coffee to fully wake up.

Steve agreed to meet her in his office. He'd been up most of the night, working on a child disappearance case, and his eyes were red-shot, his face ashen under the stubble of his beard. He said, by way of greeting, "You look even worse than I do."

"Don't joke, Steve. There's been another body found."

He nodded. "I saw the bulletin. Why are you so upset?"

"I don't remember what I did last night."

"So? Neither can half the city, but they don't come charging up here to tell me so."

"Steve, I don't know how, but somehow I'm tied in with these murders—"

"Not murders."

"All right," Jodie agreed. "Maybe I didn't throttle them. But I could have killed the first guy, and on both the other nights I can't remember what I did. Doesn't that suggest something to you?"

"What, that you're somehow poisoning them in your sleep? They died of some weird kind of anemia, Jodie—not arsenic, not strangulation. And certainly not a bop on the head."

"Maybe I—"

"We've already had three nutcases call in, claiming to be vampires. Forget it, you had nothing to do with them."

"I want to believe that—and if I could only remember—or see those men's faces and know that I had never seen them before—"

"You mean look at them down at the morgue?"

Jodie's stomach turned cold. "I hadn't thought—" she began. "But then I would know, wouldn't I? Steve, I swear I'll never ask again—" *And I also swore I'd never depend on a man for anything!*

Steve brushed her words aside. "All right, I'll get you in to view the one from yesterday. Then I'll hold you to your promise. Not another word about this thing."

The room was colder than she'd expected and had a strange chemical smell. A board-looking technician pulled the refrigerated drawer from its slot in the far wall. *It's a goddamned filing cabinet for bodies*, she thought, suppressing a shiver. Steve unzipped the thick plastic bag.

Jodie took a breath and bent over the drawer. The corpse was a Chicano in his 20s, black hair curling around the base of the skull. The body seemed to be made out of rubber instead of flesh, its expressionless face a flat uncompromising gray. The hair and eyebrows stood out like stiff, artificial bristles, and through the drawn-back lips, a fringe of yellowed teeth glinted.

I don't know this man at all, Jodie thought with some astonishment. *And somehow I'd know if I'd seen him before. Even in my dreams.* She looked up at Steve.

"You're no killer, Jodie," he said, and recovered the corpse.

I can't be—I know I'd remember a man I'd killed, she thought as they climbed the stairs back to daylight. *There would be some shock of recognition, something...* "I suppose I should feel relieved."

Steve said, "I knew you hadn't done it, but I think you're using these deaths to cover up something else. You act as if you feel guilty, of what you don't know."

"Guilty—for how much I wanted to kill that bastard with my own hands, for how close I came to it? Maybe. Even if I didn't kill those men, I put myself on the line when I jump to that first guy. Something good did come out of it, but now... No wonder I can't let go of this thing, watching what's happening to her."

"Who?"

"Mary, the woman I saved."

"She's still staying with you?"

Jodie shrugged at his implied criticism. "We only run into each other a few nights a week, and she has nowhere else to go. She is using, I'm not sure what—coke or super-crack may be. I think she's got the cash for it. I've tried to get her into a treatment program, but she won't listen."

"So you saved her from rape, only to lose her to dope? Do you know who she buys from?"

Jodie shook her head, knowing what he'd say next.

"We have to have more than that to make an arrest, especially if we want to push her."

"I could follow her. If I saw the deal, I could identify—"

"Don't you go taking stupid risks!" he said, his voice hard. "If she won't turn him in herself, if she's not ready to get help, then kick her out and let her take her own chances. You can't save the world, Jodie. Not even the female half of it, and especially if she doesn't want your help."

"Don't patronize me!"

They paused at the top of the stairwell, Steve's hand unmoving on the knob of the door that led to the ground-floor lobby. He said, "I don't want you getting mixed up with stuff you can't handle. Leave it to the pros."

"You have no right—"

"I'd like to have the right," he said quietly, still keeping the door closed. Jodie felt his nearness and the half-lit space like a tingling all over her skin.

"I like you very much, Jodie, or I wouldn't have gotten you into the morgue. I'd like to see more of you—" He reached out to caress her cheek.

"Keep your goddamned hands to yourself! You're no better than the rest of them!" She wrestled the door open and plunged into the open space, trembling with anger and adrenaline.

The next evening Jodie lay in bed, feigning sleep, remembering other nights when Mary had "gone out." *This time I'm going to find out who she buys from and put the sucker out of business, no matter what Steve Azusa says.*

Jodie held herself rigid as she heard the sound of cloth brushing against the door frame, followed by light footsteps. She kicked off the covers, pulled on her sneakers, and slowly opened the front door. The hallway was empty. Cautiously she went downstairs and through the foyer.

Mary was halfway down the block, heading north. She walked straight, never swerving, without any apparent suspicion that she might be followed. It was easy to follow her through the garishly lit streets.

Gradually Mary slowed, losing the directedness of her walk. She seemed by degrees lost and vulnerable. A couple of men stopped, obviously looking for a trick. Mary shook her head, her dark hair rippling about her face like a child's mop. She made her way farther from the main streets to others less brilliantly lit, less traveled.

This is a hell of a neighborhood to get lost in, Jodie thought, seeing the gun poorly hidden in the jacket of the pushers look out on the corner. *You go wandering around, looking like you don't know what you're doing, you're going to get jumped, or worse.*

With a sudden chill, she remembered the alley where she had first met Mary. *Damn that woman, she's asking for it*—And then she realized, *She's been here before, she knows what it's like. If she comes here regularly for dope, she should know how to walk to get left alone. But she's an open invitation...*

Jodie stepped back into the shadow of a phone booth and watched as Mary waited by herself at the bus stop. A man strolled up, wearing jeans and a work shirt. Jodie could read menace in his every movement. Mary nodded and hugged her hands to her sides, a perfect victim. The man moved in closer and she shrank from him but did not move away, even when he put one arm around her shoulder.

It was all Jodie could do to force herself to stay hidden. Mary was breaking every rule in the self-defense book. It was only the knowledge that whatever Mary's game, she had played it many times before, that kept Jodie from interfering.

The man leaned closer, edging Mary away from the bus stop and toward the darkness of a side street. Mary made no sound as he shoved her back along the deserted side street. There was no point in calling out for help here, not in this neighborhood.

Jodie found herself at the edge of a boarded-up building, clearly the haunt of more than one illicit operation. She heard scuffling, and approached with caution. Light from a passing car reflected off one crumbling wall.

It was like a flashback to the first time she had seen Mary, pinned underneath the first rapist. The arch of this man's back was the same, and the pale gleam of Mary's thighs underneath her rucked-up skirt. *Why doesn't she cry out? Why is she doing this to herself?*

Jodie's hands tightened into claws. *This time I won't stop*, she thought, and stepped soundlessly toward the rising pair.

The man was heaving back and forth, but not, as Jodie had first thought, in the reflexive thrusts of rape. Again and again, each time weaker than the last, he threw himself backward ...*away* from his victim. With a gasp he collapsed, rolling to one side. Mary rolled with him as if they were glued together, her mouth pressed to the side of his neck.

"Mary...?" Jodie realized that it was not the shadows that made her lips look so dark, but the blood that glistened on them.

Mary sat up, shifting into the light so that Jodie could not miss the radiance blooming in her skin.

"... Is he—"

"He's still alive," Mary said with an odd lisp.

"What are you?"

Mary pushed the body to one side and got to her feet, walking toward Jodie with her arms outstretched. The blood spattered on her hands was in the exact pattern from Jodie's first dream.

"Join with me now," Mary whispered. "Together we can put an end to this creature's miserable existence—together feast, together live. For the sake of justice, for the sake of all women. All the women he's already destroyed, all the women who will be safe from him now. It's what you've longed for all these years..."

She drew Jodie to her in a lover's embrace. Her perfume enhanced the smell of the blood, that dry spicy scent that was like no other. Jodie revealed in it, felt it flood her veins with fire.

"It is simple, really. A sip of my blood, and you will be one with me. You can have anything you want, forever, be anything you want. An avenging angel, slowly cleansing Mother Earth. Long have I searched for a companion to share this holy work, long—"

"But to kill—" Jodie blurted, her voice a harsh parody of Mary's silken whisper. "To kill is wrong."

"Wrong? Oh, my dear, these creatures are not worthy of your compassion. No honorable man need fear us, only those who have of their own free will chosen the bloody path. We nearly complete what they have created for themselves."

"I don't believe that—prison, yes, but—" Weak, too weak compared to the bringing power in Mary's voice, to the memories that rose up in Jodie's mind.

"Let us not speak lies to one another, lies about beliefs and political correctness. You know what I am and why I have come to you. In the silken darkness of the night I heard you call to me, even as I called out so many years ago. The fires that burn your soul were my beacon. It was your anger that drew me to you, your thirst for vengeance. I am what you've dreamed of, a woman's weapon aimed against all mankind. And now, you will be too."

Jodie shook her head helplessly. Whatever kept her from that last doorway in her dream kept her back now, and she clung to it for her very soul.

"Do you still deny the truth, my friend, my mirror? In everything but this single last step, we are already one."

No wonder the body at the morgue confused me, Jodie thought in anguish. *It was my hatred, not my hands, that killed him.*

A flickering movement behind Mary brought Jodie from torment into panic. "No!" she screamed and thrust her to one side.

Mary whirled with the sinuous power of a leopard, but the man was too close, the jagged wooden splinter that he thrust at her too fast. She staggered under the impact as he stumbled to his knees. Jodie caught her in her arms and they both fell heavily into the dust.

The blood that spurted from where the length of wood protruded from Mary's chest was thick and black, rank with the scent of her perfume. The man heaved himself to his feet and staggered from the building.

"I'm going for help—" Jodie began.

A pale slender hand waved briefly. "A stake... through the

heart… too late…"

"There must be something I can do."

"Remember…" came a gossamer whisper, and then there was silence, deep and final. Slowly the form of the woman who called herself Mary Smith collapsed in on itself. Without her artificially sustained life, gravity pulled the graceful structure into dust. Her perfume swirled in Jodie's nostrils, a last moment of sweetness before it faded forever.

In Jodie's mind the last door began to swing slowly shut. She knew if she could hold on another moment, the dreams would vanish along with the woman in her arms. She had only to keep still and the nightmare of guilt and recrimination would fade.

No, she realized, it was more than that. Another Mary would come into her life, drawn to what Jodie had made of herself. And then more dreams of blood, more deaths, the choice recurring again and again until she finally decided—to become fully who she was, or to give up her hatred forever.

The last motes of dust clung to Jodie's fingers. She wiped them off on her jeans, got to her feet, and headed back to her apartment, walking a little unsteadily. For in that final instant she had touched her lips to the dark unnatural blood, and already she could feel the chill fires of the grave creeping toward her human heart.

Our Lady of the Toads

In Gideon's dream, the walls of the steamer trunk pressed in on him. The lining had a pungent, musty smell. His ears echoed with the sound of the lock clicking shut and footsteps retreating, fainter and fainter until he was alone in the airless dark, alone with the beating of his heart.

Then came the first clammy touch on his hand, hesitant, as he knew it would be, only this time he couldn't move away, couldn't scream, couldn't breathe. Could only lie there under the tiny paws, the soft amphibian belly, one lurching step and then another, up his arm and over his sleeve. In their wake, he felt the faint tingling where warts would soon begin, then only a lingering pressure through the fabric of his shirt.

Breath seeped from his lungs. It wasn't over yet, he tried to tell his dream-self, his child-self. But his body was already melting into relief as he thought of the bar of lye soap his mother kept underneath the kitchen sink. In a little while it would be morning, safe sweet morning.

Plop! A squirming mass landed on his face, then another low on his throat where the collar gaped. Raw, unfocused sound poured from his mouth. His body bucked, thrashed, elbows and feet pummeling the bitter hardness of the walls. Fingers scrabbled against the arching lid and bits of lining shredded away, powdering his face.

His throat swelled shut with aching and his nose ran watery snot down the sides of his cheeks and still the screams kept coming. He clamped one hand over his mouth, screaming silently now, screaming inside—

———•◦⟆≥◦•———

Gideon Eldridge sat bolt upright in bed, a sweat-drenched sheet twisted around his legs. Despite the sultry Ohio summer heat, goose bumps peppered his bare arms. He ran his hands over his stubbled cheeks, raked back his hair.

Jesus! He hadn't had that dream in years, not since he was a kid. It had felt so real, so like a memory.

He wasn't seven years old any longer, Gideon told himself as he disentangled the sheet. He was thirty-seven, he'd been through State College, Army Reserves, two divorces and a decade in New York City. By rights, nothing should have the power to frighten him any longer.

Why this dream, why now? He'd returned to the house on Maple Street after his father had finally drunk himself to death, and then only long enough to sell it.

Wearing only his briefs, Gideon padded to the window of the second story bedroom, the guest room, not the one he'd had as a boy. Below, the drowsing town shimmered in the light of a moon gone watery and green. The houses, each with its square of lawn and fungus-shaped clumps of hydrangea and lilac, had faded to gray. Nothing moved except the rippling shadow of a cat.

Twelve o'clock and all's well, he thought and turned back to bed. But his eyes, gliding over the motionless streets, caught a flash of light, a bar of yellow where none should be, quickly snuffed as if someone had jerked a curtain closed.

He strained to make out the house it had come from, elevated above the rest. His sweat turned cold as he recognized it—the house on the hill. The house his friends had taunted him to enter alone after dark when he was seven years old, although he could never quite remember what he'd seen there. The house reputed to have its own garden of nightshade and hemlock, as well as its own basement cemetery, its own pond of piranhas. The house on the hills was vacant no longer.

The phone rang as he was finishing his third cup of coffee and looking over the latest pile of manuscripts. It was the real estate agent handling his father's house.

"I've got a prospective buyer coming by to look at the property at one o'clock," she said, meaning he should make himself absent.

"Okay." His father's house had been for sale for three weeks without an offer. Why now? he thought again, and felt a sudden electrifying *zing!* in his guts. "Listen," he said suddenly, "do you know who bought the house on the hill, the one that's been empty so long?"

"The old Newbury house? Why, were you interested in it?"

"Just curious." He forced a laugh.

Papers rustled over the phone lines. "Here it is. Hmmm, it was never for sale, only lease. The owner—a Miss Lily Newbury—has been out of the country. Seems she's changed her mind and decided to live in it herself."

Gideon shivered as he replaced the receiver. The thought came to him that the owner's reappearance was no coincidence. The house on the hill, dormant for all these years, had only been waiting for him to return.

The house looked much as he remembered it, with its brooding cobwebbed gables and paint bleached to a pale fungus color. It stood by itself, surrounded by a weathered board fence, with streets on three sides and a vacant lot on the fourth. Gideon circled around to the lot and squinted through a gap between the planks. He couldn't make out anything like his father's yard, with its close-shaven lawn, kettle barbecue and sagging plastic lawn chairs. Weeds rioted in every corner and something splashed in the depths of the pond at the far end.

"If you find my garden so interesting," said a low-pitched female voice at his shoulder, "why don't you come in for a closer look?"

Startled, he spun around. The woman behind him was thin and tall, horse-faced. She wore a billowy black dress with red and yellow embroidery at the neck.

"Well, I—"

"You can tell the others all about me so they don't have to go peeking through the fence, too." Slipping one hand through the crook of his elbow, she led him around to the gate.

Gideon's muscles obeyed her, as if by meeting her gaze for that single moment he had allowed her to gain some kind of preternatural control over him. He started sweating.

"People are naturally curious," he stammered. "Where you come from, what you do."

"If I'm married, they mean. Who my friends are."

She led him around the yard, pointed out the various plants, *Matricaria, Symphytum, Cycades, Equisetum, Artemisia*. He didn't recognize the Latin names; they all looked like overgrown weeds to him, vines and bushes and plants that were part fern and part palm. Unseen creatures rustled in the flower-tipped grasses and leaves rippled in the breeze like flirting dancers, showing their silvery undersides. The longer he stayed, the deeper his sense of unease. The place had a pungent, untamed smell. A dangerous smell, it stirred uncomfortable memories.

"Well," he said, "I'll see you around."

He felt her eyes on him until he was almost through the gate, and only then did he turn back for a last fleeting glance. He saw her crouch in the tangled grass, black skirts spread around her, whispering to something small and brown that she held in her hands, cradled as if it were precious.

Gideon's nerve broke and he rushed down the hill. He knew that warted hide, those bulging eyes. And to hold it so close, almost tenderly, to remember—

—mountains of jade and onyx, whales singing in the depths of crystalline oceans, forests of deepest green, mammoths trumpeting as they danced beneath the moon, a circle of standing stones—

Yowl! Gideon tripped over a cat, scrambled to catch his balance on the sloping street. The cat hissed at him, tail twitching, and bounded toward the house on the hill, a ripple of sleek black fur. Heart hammering in his chest, he watched it go. He could not have remembered those things. He must have been bewitched.

Black cat—unmarried woman—hard unfeeling bitch of a woman—a toad for, what was it called? a familiar...

Gideon thought of running back to the relative safety of New York City. But he knew instantly he would not, could not. The witch, like the dream itself, had come to him for a reason.

Weeks crept on. Gideon took the house on Maple Street off the market and made arrangements to do his copy-editing from there. He spent hours in the public library, looking up everything he could find about witches, their powers and weaknesses. The books didn't agree, being part history and the rest superstition, but he was able to sift out the most potent-sounding weapons and protections.

As the harvest season approached and the first tinge of frost crept into the evening air, the children returned to school and the town made ready for its annual Pumpkin Festival. Gideon noticed the Newbury woman's first visitors. Two women arrived in a taxi from the airport in New Athens.

Gideon couldn't work, couldn't sleep. He drank too much and wrote snide remarks on the manuscripts he was editing. He forced himself to clean out the attic, but found no trunks among the bags of old clothes, the broken furniture, the boxes of yellowed photographs.

Then a fourth arrived, and a fifth. *More will come*, he realized with sickening certainty. *Thirteen in all to make a coven.* And Halloween was drawing near, the night when their powers would be at their greatest.

He stopped counting and started gathering the supplies he would need.

———·◦❧◦·———

Gideon waited in the shadows at the base of the hill, watching the last of the trick-or-treaters make their way down the sidewalk. He clicked his pencil flashlight on and checked the time. Ten o'clock. Two hours left. The night around him lay still and shivery as the voices of the children faded into silence.

He patted the pockets of his fisherman's vest, where he'd hidden his supplies—a cross, a blue bead on a string, a bag of salt that had been consecrated on Palm Sunday, a vial of holy water and an automatic pistol loaded with the silver-plated bullets he'd gone all the way back to New York to find, although he wasn't positive they'd work on witches.

Gideon crept up the hill and around to the side of the house, his ears straining for any sound. Lights flickered through the cracks of the board fence. He caught the sound of women's voices in some sort of chanting. His hackles rose and his mouth went dry. He took out the cross.

There, perched in front of the gate as if on sentry duty, was the largest, ugliest toad Gideon had ever laid eyes on, truly worthy of being a witch's familiar. In the flashlight's glare, its unblinking eyes gleamed like polished obsidian. Eyes, he thought, that had watched the empires of men and dinosaurs rise and then crumble into dust. Eyes that beheld the slow circling dance of galaxies and the most insignificant microbe. Eyes that looked right through him. Then, in an instant, the creature was gone.

Gideon's hand shook as he took hold of the latch. The gate creaked on its hinges, but the muted singing did not waver. With a silent prayer, he clutched the cross, put his shoulder to the gate, and shoved.

He stumbled into a clearing aglow in the brilliance of a bonfire. Surely, he thought dazedly, the blaze should have been visible from outside. And surely the yard could not be so big. The fence had disappeared behind waving grasses and silver-boled trees, wild and arching under the sweep of stars. Shadowy figures stood in a circle, thirteen in all.

The singing stopped. Gideon thrust the cross in the direction of the nearest witch. "Stop!"

The figure turned, a plain, gray-haired woman in an old-fashioned costume. She was sopping wet. Something moved at the corner of his vision and he turned to see a young girl, hair cropped short and wearing the charred tatters of some white garment over armor. She reached up, touched the cross, and gently brought it to her lips. The cross burst into light, casting an unearthly radiance across the girl's face. She murmured something in French and the light subsided to a clear glow.

"What dis mon doin' here? Here, where we work deep magic?" A black woman, tall and strong-looking, stepped forward. She wore a homespun dress, a rag wrapped around her head.

"He has come seeking witches, though he knows not what they are," another woman said in a heavy accent. Her dark hair was caught up in shining ringlets, her dress a glimmer in the shadows. Gold encircled her neck and bare arms. "Shall we show him what *real* witches do?"

Gideon's heart hammered against his ribs. He fumbled in his pockets. His fingers met the cold steel of the automatic. He drew it out. "Stay back!"

The Newbury woman stepped into the light. She wore a long robe that seemed one moment to be flowing water, the next, a cascade of petals or the milky tails of comets. "This man has come into our midst uninvited, that much is true. He may be ignorant and frightened, but I do not think him evil."

"You always were too generous, Lilith," said a plump, English-accented woman who would have looked grandmotherly except for the livid bruises around her throat.

"Consider the harm he has already done, intruding here. The juncture cannot hold much longer and we have work yet to do."

"I'm not afraid of you!" Gideon cried, but his voice came out in a terrified squeak.

"No?" said the Greek woman, moving closer. "Perhaps you should be."

"Turning him into a pig is too good for him!" A dark-eyed girl stepped forward. She wore full, tiered skirts, a patterned shawl over her shoulders. When she pointed an accusing finger, Gideon noticed the numbers tattooed along her forearm. "An eye for an eye, that's what his book says. Let us have justice!"

"Silence!" Lilith held up one ivory hand and the clearing fell silent. Shadows stirred behind her eyes, waking Gideon's memory. The black terror of the steamer trunk, no longer securely anchored in the past, flooded through him. His fingers tightened on the trigger of the automatic, but nothing happened. The safety catch had somehow been left on. He hurled the gun away and pulled out the pouch of consecrated salt. When he threw it in her face, she laughed and the crystals drifted glittering to the earth.

"You have followed those who sinned against us," Lilith said, "those who tried, in their ignorance, to rend the very magic with which we bind the fragile threads of time."

"I don't believe you! I don't believe any of you!"

"Why think you we gather here?" the drowned woman said in a kindly voice. "Why think you we died?"

Slowly, Gideon lowered the cross. How could he fight them, these witches who were already dead? In the back of his mind, a child's voice pleaded, "*Please don't*—"

Gideon felt his body shrivel around him. His vision went bleary and the room receded to a blur. When he raised his hands to his face, he felt the huge, hairy warts. They had always been there, all those years, but had never been visible before.

Gently Lilith took his hands and placed the toad in them. His fingers curled around the fragile body. He felt the intricate pattern of the creature's hide, a silken tent over the miniature cathedral of its bones, the jewel-like glands along its throat. For a moment, he felt himself falling into the fertile darkness of its eyes. Then he blinked and the eyes turned into mirrors, only it was not his own face he saw reflected there.

Gideon's flesh turned cold. He knew now who had locked him in the steamer trunk. He knew why.

On a dare, a seven-year-old boy had penetrated into the center of a magical garden, had seen places that no longer existed and things that might never come to be. A warted toad had been his guide to wonders beyond reason. And a terrified, drunken father had locked him all night in a steamer trunk with a half-dozen of the creatures to cure him of such nonsense.

Gideon understood why witches were seen as evil, these women caught forever in fragments of time, pursuing their own mysterious goals. They were as dangerous to the world of human cruelty as the unblinking stare of the toad in his hands.

"Talk to her." Lilith's voice came in a sweet, silvery whisper. "Tell her your fears and your dreams. Let her wisdom cleanse your memories."

Around him, Gideon heard murmurs of approval, even though he could no longer see the other witches. The clearing had gone misty, replaced by the outlines of his own garden. But a garden changed, the manicured beds sprouting into a tangle of exuberant growth. A gap opened in the middle of the tight-clipped lawn and a spring bubbled forth. The toad gave a convulsive kick and jumped to the ground, heading for the burgeoning grass. Gideon hurried after the toad as if his soul depended upon it.

Pearl of Fire

I traveled by river barge as far as I could, as the forested hills I had known all my life fell away into rocky pastures and then fields of barley and millet. When my path led me south I joined one trader's caravan and then another. A decrepit camel brought me across the broken, withered lands, and at last, I reached Ixtalpi, refuge of thieves and outlaws and all manner of desperate souls, huddled in the shadow of the black, volcanic Viridian Mountains.

I never expected to become the guardian of the Pearl. It had always passed from father to son, a closely-guarded family secret. True, I wondered why, with so few men to defend Sharaya, we had never fallen, why the dregs of the Duke's armies never harried us, why we had always been able to fend off Eaglehurst, with whom we had long maintained blood feud.

The Pearl had been intended for my brother. Devron was fourteen when Great-grandfather fell ill. No one knew exactly how many winters the old man had survived, but this one would be his last. He called us to him one blustery morning, when the clouds were more black than gray and sleet rattled against every loose-paned window.

As usual, Devron could not be found. He was probably

hiding in the stables. My mother and father and uncles stood around Great-grandfather's bed, the headboard carved with the scene of a hunt, the stag at bay, yet fighting on, the dogs lying dead at its feet. The rows of candles from the night before had almost burned out. I remember watching one and then another gutter into curls of smoke, still tinged with the honey scent of beeswax. I was, I suppose, a little afraid of Great-grandfather, who was wrinkled and gruff and had never so much as patted me on the head in all my ten years.

I could hear Great-grandfather's rattling breaths in between the gusts of wind outside. As the soft golden light of the candles died away, his skin turned whiter. I had the fanciful thought that when the last one had burned itself to ash, his life would end.

A feeling welled up in my child's breast, of loss and tenderness and a great yearning to speak before it was too late. I had been standing beside my mother, the way I did when I was little and hid myself in her full skirts. Something drew me forward. Only two candles remained, and one flickered, leaping and struggling as if the storm outside had penetrated the room.

Great-grandfather had closed his eyes, but now the lids jerked open. His eyes were full of lightning and clouds and things I could not name. His lips—so withered, so dry!—moved. I thought I heard him speak a name, but whether it was Devron's or my father's or that of someone dead long before I was born, I could not tell.

The next to the last candle went out. The stone walls shivered and grew still, expectant. My father and uncles waited, motionless, hardly breathing. I felt the pressure of my mother's fingers on my shoulder.

Again, the old man struggled to speak. Tears sprang to the corners of his eyes. A pain shot through the center of my own chest.

Great-grandfather lifted one hand, one poor bony hand that quivered like a twig in a gale. The skin was all dried out and mottled with huge liver-colored spots.

No one moved.

Suddenly, I could bear it no longer, that he should be calling out, reaching out, and no one would answer him. No one held him in loving arms. He had never been kind to me, but he was hurt and lost and alone.

I broke away from my mother's grasp and rushed to him. What did I know? I took his hand between both of my own.

"Great-grandpapa!" I cried out in my child's voice. "I am here!"

At first, he did not seem to know me, but when I pressed my lips against his shriveled cheek, he roused. "Is it you? Is it time at last?"

"Yes, it's me."

"Rayzel, no!" My mother's voice seemed to come from far away.

Before anyone could stop him, Great-grandfather shifted on the bed, raising up enough to slip a long silvery chain over his head. I had seen the chain before, glinting through the opened neckline of his shirt, and assumed it was some sort of priest's medallion, such as those old people wore for protection against joint-bane and fever. What dangled from it, however, was no slip of metal, but a glowing marble set in a cage of silver wire. I caught a flash of bronze in its depths, red like fire.

Then, with a grip so fast and hard it left me breathless, Great-grandfather pulled me close and looped the chain around my neck. Heat flared though the layers of my dress and shawl, as if the pendant, whatever it was, had been plucked from a fire.

One of the men—my second oldest uncle, I thought—shouted something, but I could not understand. All I could hear, above the pounding of my heart, was the whispered sigh that came from Great-grandfather.

"It is done, then."

The last candle went out.

Devron burst through the door and everyone started shouting at once, except for my mother, who was screaming, and me. I felt numb and on fire and shaken to my bones, unable to grasp what had just happened.

"It's his!" my father yelled, meaning Devron. "Give it—"

"You fool! It's *been* given! To her!"

"But he didn't mean—he thought she was the boy—

"Oh, that I should live to this day!" my mother wailed. "My own daughter!"

"Then take it back!"

"How can we? Until she dies…"

"Doom! Doom has come upon us all!"

"Oh, my poor sweet child!"

I slumped to the floor. I could not understand anything beyond Great-grandfather being dead. Of that, I was certain. His life had gone out of him, and I had held his hand, and surely that was not a bad thing. Why did the room seem filled with curling bronze-red smoke? Why did my chest burn as if someone had placed a live ember there? Why was my mother weeping as if I had been the one who died?

At first, I was overcome by a great weariness. My mother brought me milk and bread, and tucked me into bed. I slept for three days, and when I awoke, I felt strong and clear and hungry. My father looked grim as he told me that from this day forward, I must be like a son to him. I must ride a warhorse instead of my gentle pony, and fight with a sword, and study the plans of ancient battles, and learn how to command men. I was young enough to consider it a great adventure.

The days and weeks and years went by in a blur. I grew tall and strong from the strenuous exercise. How had all of this happened? Why was I set apart? Why did animals, even the house cat, shy away from my touch? Few of the horses would carry me, sweating and white-eyed, for more than a few minutes. Why did my brother suddenly cease his old taunting, bullying ways?

Why was I never cut or bruised, even when my knife slipped at table or the blade of my sparring partner slashed through my guard?

Why must I always wear the Pearl, but never openly, tucked safely between my new breasts?

Sometimes, when the moon was rising, swelling towards fullness, and I stood in the darkening practice field, weary and aching, searching for the strength to lift my wooden sword one more time, I caught a glimpse of the faces of my uncles. I did not know how to read what I saw there. Pity and sorrow, I thought, and grudging respect...

They left it to my mother to explain. On one of those nights, after practice, she came down from the house. My oldest uncle, who had taken charge of my sword training, gestured a halt, and my brother and the other men retreated gratefully into the twilight.

My mother beckoned for me to come with her. We sat on the fallen log beside the horse trough, talking quietly about daily events. The house cat had returned from her rambles, and we would have kittens soon. The cook had burned the bread. The goose girl was to marry a farm hand.

The men finished tending the horses, and for a long time, silence hung over us, except for the animals tearing at the hay and the distant sound of chickens clucking, the clink of pans in the kitchen. I had been sweating hard, and now shivered in the cooling night. An owl swooped soundlessly from the top of the barn across the shadowed fields.

My mother lifted her face to the moon. It turned her into a stranger, a woman of silver.

"You want answers, Rayzel? You must see them for yourself, what the Pearl of Fire has made of you."

She led me to the trough. The water was very still. I could see the moon reflected there, glorious and shining and pure. I stepped closer, into the place my mother indicated. The cold bright light touched me, too.

"Look."

I bent over, expecting to see my own face, streaked with dust and sweat, a smear of dried mud over one cheek bone, my hair disheveled and tied back with a bit of string.

My breath froze in my throat. I shied away, unable to absorb what I saw in the water's smooth surface. An illusion born of moonlight? A fragment of a forgotten nightmare?

My mother's strong hands held me fast. Where could I run to, anyway? Slowly, slowly, I looked again.

A dragon glowered back at me, every curved metal scale and jagged spinal ridge, each fang like a curving dagger, limned in sharpest clarity. Bronze tinted the moon-silver reflection. Molten crimson lurked behind the opaque eyes.

"What magic is this?" I breathed.

Why did I feel no fear, only a sense of fatality, of resignation?

"You see?" My mother's voice belonged to someone else, harsh as a crow's. "You see what cannot be undone? Why you cannot be harmed by sword or lance or dagger?"

The Pearl had done this to me...but what could be done, could also be undone. I fumbled for the chain around my neck. It stuck to my skin as if it had melded to my body. I could not budge it. My mother stilled my hand with a touch. She shook her head. "Are you so ready to die, my daughter?"

"No, to live!"

"The Pearl of Fire passes only from the hands of one who has surrendered any hope of living." Her voice trembled with inexpressible sadness. I had never before felt so loved, or so alone.

"Who would you pass it on to? Who else will use its power to defend us? Your father, with his bad heart? His brothers, who think of nothing but their own pride? Devron? He is my son and I love him, but I know what he is."

A coward and a bully.

I left the chain around my neck. I bent to my lessons, pushing myself ever harder, hastening the day when I would stand between my family and the dangerous world. Every year, since Great-grandfather's death, the Eaglehurst raiders had grown bolder. Soon, I would go up against them, I with my hide of dragon's bronze, I who could not be harmed.

Just past my fourteenth birthday, I went on my first foray against our old enemy. Eaglehurst had been raiding the long green valleys, burning villages and looting. We lay in wait for them, my youngest uncle in command, for my father had been laid up with chest pains. Under the stark midday sun, we hid behind the ramshackle communal barn, so that the smell of hay and barley overlaid that of fear.

The village was laid out in a series of open yards bounded by thatch-roofed cottages, storage sheds, livestock pens. Chickens scratched in the dust and a few sheep, too stupid to run for safety, bleated as they stood in the opened gates. Not a child ventured forth to greet us.

I held my breath and caught the jangled rhythm of hoof beats, the clang of bridle rings, men shouting.

"Wait until they pass," my uncle said, holding up his hand.

The rangy, leather-mouthed dun mare, one of the few horses who tolerated me, pranced beneath me.

My uncle pointed at me. "Go."

My sword slipped free. I clapped my heels to my horse's sides. With my uncle and his men at my heels, I burst from cover.

The dun mare leaped forward like a loosed arrow, racing toward the Eaglehurst men. They had slowed, searching for resistance. There were so many—twice our own numbers. Some carried lighted torches, a few of them, crossbows. The sun glinted off their swords, their eagle-headed helmets of leather and steel. Their captain was shouting orders, pointing at which cottages were to be burned first.

I bore down on the nearest raider. He wheeled his horse, but too slowly. I could not see his face. His own sword came up. The momentum of my charge drove my sword deep into his body beneath the arch of his ribs. The impact shivered through my whole body, almost jerking my sword out of my hands. My mare kept going and it was all I could do to hold on to it as we swept past.

My vision clouded, crimson. The taste of fire and red sulfur and blood filled my mouth. Men and horses swept past me, stumbling, bleeding. Wildfires raged behind my eyes. My skin, where the Pearl lay cradled between my breasts, burned with exquisite desire. I gulped deep breaths of air and spewed forth a charnel wind.

The hunger of the Pearl raged through me. My sword smoked with blood and more blood.

I hardly noticed when a terrible stillness fell on the common. A few riderless horses skittered away from the fallen bodies. My uncle directed his men to put out the single fire. Two of our own men were down, one unmoving, the other struggling to his feet, clutching a slashed thigh.

The dun mare came to a halt, trembling, her hide hot and wet. The fire died within me. The sky shifted from red to shivering gray. I swayed in my saddle. My sword fell from my limp hand. I felt utterly empty, used-up, bereft.

Dimly, I felt my uncle's hands catch me as I toppled. Later, one of the men told me that he had carried me home in his arms.

Some years later, we enjoyed a glorious golden summer. I had been leading our men along the borders for enough seasons now that Eaglehurst had pulled back, licking its wounds. For once, the Duke was at peace with his neighbors; no mercenaries or refugees wandered our mountains. I rode watch with my uncles, but with much less urgency than before.

I also rode alone. The forest that bordered our lands and Eaglehurst, once too dangerous for even armed travelers, had now become a series of abandoned sunlit glades. The last of the spring wildflowers still lingered in the moist pockets beneath the largest trees. The very air smelled of growing things, of rich earth, of the dust that gently settled along shafts of brightness.

I swung down, loosened the girths, and tied my horse by a halter so that she could browse. The air was still and warm, the only sounds the faint whisper of a breeze and a far-off bird. Leaving my sword tied to my saddle, I dug into my saddlebags, beneath the packet of food, the whetstone and cloth for cleaning steel. My fingers brushed finely woven wool. I pulled it free, took one last look around, and skinned out of my men's tunic and breeches. The boots I could do nothing about, as my feet were too tender to run barefoot.

The dress fell around me in lamb-soft folds, emerald trimmed with lace-flower and daisies. I'd found it in a cedar chest last winter. It was probably my grandmother's, and a bit too short. I spun in circles, relishing the feel of the skirts as they swirled outward. I pulled my hair free, combed it with my fingers. For an hour, a blessed hour, I might pretend the Pearl was a love token given to me by a gray-eyed stranger. I might be just an ordinary girl.

The hour passed too quickly, leaving me wanting more. I folded the dress, tied back my hair, tightened the girths, and went home. But I came back as the wildflowers were drying and bees buzzed around the burgeoning queen's-lace and painter-brush. I came, and danced, and wept when it was time to go.

All too soon, the summer neared its end, and the faint scent of must and honey hung in the air. The leaves had turned that intense, almost fiery green, when he first came.

I was dancing and singing, some mindless tune I learned from the horse boys. My feet were bare now, having toughened over the months. Although I heard nothing, I knew I was not alone. With a sense that was half-human, half-dragon, I *felt* his presence. A man, yes, I knew that, and young as I was young. Unsure and cocksure and enthralled as if by magic, drawn to my voice, yearning for something magical, beyond the ordinary. Even before I saw him, I loved him.

He stepped from the shadows. My eyes noted his ordinary hunter's clothing, vest and shirt and pants in shades of green and brown, wide leather belt around slim hips, russet hair tumbling over muscled shoulders. My heart saw only the light in those gray eyes, the catch of wonder in his breath, the way he looked at me as if I were the most wonderful, most tender thing he had ever seen.

I paused in my dance, and the green skirts fell still around me. We stood in a pool of slanting light. We talked. We danced to the music that rose, wordless, in my throat. When he reached to take my hand, a shadow passed over me. I drew back and he, taking it for maidenly modesty, plucked a strawflower, kissed it, and then held it out to me.

It was impossible, our love. Perhaps I was intoxicated. Certainly, I was heedless. I kept on, as the leaves turned orange and then crimson and then brown. He laid his cloak on the crisp leaves and we lay on it, murmuring secrets to one another.

In my madness, I kept meeting him, even when the forest was no longer safe. The Eaglehurst raiders had struck again. He never failed me, my sweet, gray-eyed lover. The hidden part of my heart, the part I thought dead forever when I accepted the Pearl, the part that was mine alone, came alive in his presence.

Of course, I did not tell him who I was. Nor did I ask. He was a younger son from one of the bordering families, it did not matter from which side.

As winter lowered over the forested hills, Eaglehurst pressed us hard, seeking revenge for their past defeats. One gray afternoon, we met them at the river where the slate-dark water frothed and pitched between steep, rocky banks. Here we held fast, skirmishing back and forth. As usual, I placed myself in front. I urged my horse half-way across the river, blocking the narrow ford. The air reeked of wet rocks, horse sweat, and blood.

The Eaglehurst charged at me, shouting their battle-cries. Their helmets gave them the aspect of raptors, not human men. They came at me in twos and threes, trying to slash through my guard. I had no need of defense. My body reeled under the force of their blows, but I felt nothing. Wherever I struck, they fell.

The clang of steel against steel, or perhaps against bronze, filled my head. The Pearl roused at the sound of their death screams, the blood, the terror. I felt its exultation shivering through me, consuming me.

I swung my sword again. Again. Again. Sliced air, leather, flesh, all the same. The rushing water ran red around my horse's legs.

At last, a horn sounded from the Eaglehurst side. *Fall back. Retreat. Save yourselves while you can.*

They scrambled back across the muddied banks. Their captain shouted something about not leaving any of their fellows behind. Bare-headed, he plunged into the river, on foot now, struggling to reach one who had fallen to my sword. I caught a glimpse of a gray beard, white-rimmed eyes, and then I was moving again, screaming curses, sword high. They turned and fled.

I pulled my mare to a halt. She fought me, half crazed with fight and rushing water and the dragon-stench rising from my skin. I could not let her win or she would never carry me again, and few horses could tolerate the Pearl. She dipped her head in surrender and picked her way through foam and rock.

The rider, whose body they had tried to retrieve, lay pinned by the water against the rocks. As I rode by, the current tumbled him over, so that he shifted on to his back. His helmet came free.

Russet hair, tangled like rust-stained riverweed. Eyes gray as a storm, staring and empty. One hand, palm up as if grasping the water that slipped through those strong, graceful fingers.

I should have known. I should have known.

And if I had, would I have chosen differently? Would I have denied us those brief hours for the pain of what came afterward?

The mare heaved herself up the slope, happy to be out of the surging water. I hunched over, trying to breathe. My lungs had turned to bronze.

"My lady?" someone said. "Are you well?"

"Of course, she is well." My brother's voice. "She can't be hurt, can she?"

No, not hurt. Not ever.

"Take up their fallen," someone said with my voice, harsh as a bell and distant. "Do not leave them for the river, or to be eaten by scavengers. Send a messenger under truce to Eaglehurst. Offer to return them, so that they may bury their own."

"In exchange for what?" one of the men asked.

I touched the mare with my heels and she moved off. Blood still gleamed on my sword. When I arrived home, I cleaned it, as always. I rubbed down my own horse, as always. A servant took away my muddy, blood-stained clothing. As always.

I lay in my bed, eyes staring and empty.

In exchange for what?

I moved through the days, eating and dressing and talking, each in its proper time. I beat back the Eaglehurst time and again, across the river and further each time, until I stood in the smoking ruins of their great manor house. Their scattered remnants harried us like rats. They learned to fear the red-bronze fire of my sword.

Then my father died.

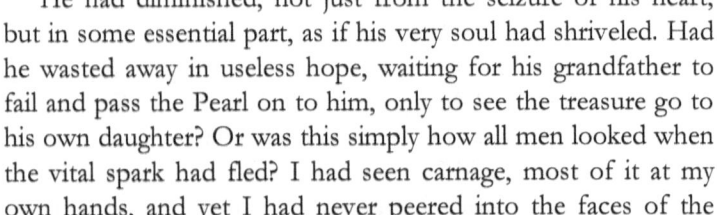

He had diminished, not just from the seizure of his heart, but in some essential part, as if his very soul had shriveled. Had he wasted away in useless hope, waiting for his grandfather to fail and pass the Pearl on to him, only to see the treasure go to his own daughter? Or was this simply how all men looked when the vital spark had fled? I had seen carnage, most of it at my own hands, and yet I had never peered into the faces of the dead as I did my father's. For the first time, I was not afraid to see death. I saw it as a release, as a benediction.

My own life stretched before me, seasons of killing and more killing, and soul-devouring loneliness. There would never be another lover for me. I would not dare.

"The Pearl of Fire passes only from the hands of one who has surrendered any hope of living," my mother had said.

The Pearl had taught me patience, so I waited. I waited to see my father buried. I waited until my mother had set aside the black veil of mourning. I waited until my brother had taken up rulership of Sharaya, now Greater Sharaya. I waited until we were alone, not in the great hall adorned with plunder from Eaglehurst and other conquests, but a moment of quiet in the stables, after riding the borders as his bodyguard.

"I will leave you now," I said.

It took him a moment to realize I meant more than returning to the manor house. "I don't understand. You can't leave. The Pearl cannot leave Sharaya."

Cannot? I looked at him slantwise, raising one eyebrow. The Pearl had also taught me silence. Then I shrugged. I had never found any difficulty in crossing the borders. He spoke from his own fears. He could lose half of what I had brought to him, and still have more than any one man needed.

I resolved, as well, that no more men would bleed away their lives for greed. Not my brother's, not mine. Not the Pearl's.

I turned and walked away, out of the stables redolent with sweet hay and the warmth of horses, into the pooling dusk.

"Where will you go? What will you do?" he shouted after me. *Without us,* he meant. *Without family or home or name?*

I traveled by river barge as far as I could, as the forested hills I had known all my life fell away, and at last, I reached Ixtalpi, refuge of desperate souls...

Once I had left the mountains, I attracted considerably less notice. Here, in the wide lands of the world, a woman with a sword, even one traveling alone, was not so unusual. Several times, fellow travelers approached me with offers of employment or simple companionship. I turned them all away.

I took a room at an insignificant inn and went walking.

Beyond the city walls, the slopes of the volcanic peaks rose gently at first, then stark and steep and black. Red light flickered near the blunted peaks. Several times, the ground rumbled and shook, a vast and rancorous underground beast. Ash blackened the sky and turned the sunset a lurid crimson.

In a strange, fey mood, I took my supper in the common room of the inn. The air was close and smoky. Greasy soot coated the rough wooden walls. I found a place at the end of the long trestle table. A scrawny lad brought me a bowl of some kind of stew and a mug of ale. The ale was warm but surprisingly good, and the stew too spicy for my taste, most likely to encourage customers to order more ale and to disguise the odd flavors of the meat. I ate the stew, called for more ale, and sipped it slowly. The blend of astringent and mellow flavors slid down my throat like a memory of summer.

The ale softened my mood enough so that when my neighbors at the table struck up a conversation, I did not turn away. Across from me sat a grizzled, balding drover. The man and woman on either side of the table wore leather vests, faded and rubbed shiny along the seams, decorated with strings of shell, horn-bead and bone. They looked young and hungry, with hawk-keen eyes and skins tinged with copper. Neither bore any visible weapon, not like the knife prominently strapped to the drover's thigh, but I had no doubt they were armed. Mercenaries, perhaps. I did not recognize their accents, but the drover made a joke about their being from Raë on the Western Sea, and not to be trusted.

Soon a game of dice and castles was proposed and accepted. Having no better way to pass the evening, I ordered more ale and joined in.

Six of us made up the opening game, with the addition of two locals. The locals dropped out after the first hour and left the inn, supporting one another in their vacillating homeward path. The game went on, the stakes gradually rising. Winnings passed back and forth across the table. Ale flowed. A sense of wellbeing settled over me. I derived as much enjoyment from losing as from winning.

After losing three rounds in a row, the drover pushed himself away from the table. That left the two Raë and myself. The woman, Juthe, pulled out and stood, looking over her man's shoulder, one hand resting there with deceptive ease. I saw the edge of desperation, ale-tempered, in their eyes, the quick glances, the readiness to raise the stakes once again. They were gambling with assets they could not afford to lose. I thought to let them win, but the cards would not oblige me.

The man, Culliy, and I faced each other over the table. The pile of bets went back and forth, growing larger in leaps, never settling long with either of us. Having already lost my sword, I added a small knife from my boot, on to the pile.

The cards went against me. I grinned as he raked in the pile and started to leave.

"Wait," Juthe said, quick as a serpent. "Stay."

"I have nothing more to wager," I pointed out.

She jerked her chin toward my chest. The bones dangling from her vest clinked softly. "That?"

In the heat of the close dark room and the excitement of the game, I had loosened the ties of my shirt. The chain that carried the Pearl gleamed dully, crossing my sweat-bright skin and disappearing over my heart. I sat back, drew out the Pearl. It glowed like banked embers.

Culliy let out a long whistle. Juthe licked her lips.

The ale spoke to me, *Why not?*

Something stirred behind my mind, restive. If I would never use it again, why not let it pass to those who might derive some advantage from it?

Why not let the Pearl itself decide?

I slipped the chain over my head, and, to my astonishment, it came away easily. I dropped it in the center of the table, half-expecting the wood to burst into flames. It landed with a thump and a clatter of metallic links. The skin over my breastbone, where the Pearl had lain so many years, felt tender, new. My ribs ached. I drew a breath, deeper and freer than I could remember.

Culliy pushed forward the entire pile of winnings. We drew cards, one and then another, building our hands. I did not look at mine, for what did it matter? The ale and the wild mood owned me. Culliy glanced down at his cards. I saw the little signs, the tightening at the corners of his eyes, the faint pressure of Juthe's hand on his shoulder, the slightly slower movement as he sat back, his movements too controlled for true ease.

There was nothing more to bet. One hand would take all.

Culliy's face stayed stony as he laid out his cards. A good hand, but not unbeatable. I let my gaze rest on the painted designs. Then, without looking at my own cards, I slapped them down on the pile of discards.

With a shrug and a grin, I pushed myself to my feet. "That's a night, then. Good fortune to you both."

I did not look back until I had reached the far end of the common room, the narrow stairs leading to the sleeping chambers. Culliy had lifted the chain, about to drop it around Juthe's neck. The Pearl flashed iridescent, reflected in her eyes. Until that moment, I had not been certain that it would let me go.

I slept that night like one dead. If I dreamed, I had no memory when I woke. The room had only a straw pallet on a wooden frame and a table with pitcher and bowl for washing, pegs on the wall for cloak, a single rickety chair. Nothing like a mirror. If I looked in one by moonlight, what would I see? If I shattered the mirror and drew one of the pieces of glass across my skin, would I bleed? I could not remember the color of my own blood, or the taste of my tears.

I left Ixtalpi the next morning. The innkeeper, having watched last night's game from the bar, gave me a free bowl of gruel for breakfast. It was last night's stew, watered down and simmered into mush, but it filled my belly. I had no idea where I would go or how I would earn my bread. I could not go home, that much was sure. I had some skill with a sword, but only for attack, not defense. In all likelihood, I would not survive the first skirmish. I found, to my surprise, that I disliked the notion.

Heading down slope, out of the shadowed Viridian Mountains, I paused at a crossroads. East or west? I had never traveled in either direction. It came to me that for the first time in my life, I had no ties to any land or lord, nothing to keep me from going wherever my two strong legs took me. I took the less traveled road, and then, whenever it branched, the way that seemed wilder.

The road narrowed to a trail wide enough for a single line of baggage animals. Here and there, a pile of droppings, still moist underneath, gave evidence of recent travelers. I was no tracker, but I thought there might be three or four small horses, one of them unshod, as many more men on foot, and a narrow-wheeled cart. In my mind, I spun out a story about the party, who they were, where they were going, and the songs they would sing to one another around the evening's fire.

The trail wound upward through scrub forest, skirted running streams, and dipped into sunlit glades. A pleasant passage, I thought as I stretched out under a tree in one of these meadows for a midday nap. As I allowed myself to be lulled by the hum of insects, I thought of my gray-eyed lover, remembering now not the anguish of loss but the golden afternoons we had spent together, the joy and comfort we had of each other. In my dreams, I wandered through the great house of Sharaya, but the halls and corridors lay dark and empty. The windows were open and dead leaves skirled across the floor in the chill breeze.

I jerked awake, sweating, to glimpse the last crescent of brilliance as the sun sank below the western hills. Shadows had already begun their slow reach, dimming the meadow. The open space no longer felt safe. I found the trail and hurried along it.

The trail climbed higher, and the feeling of unease lessened. I began to look for a place to spend the night, some sturdy branch, overhang, or shallow cave. The moon rose, full and bright enough to cast shadows. I went on with the vague thought that my fellow travelers must surely have made camp by now, and might allow me to join them.

Even as I was trying to convince myself of the folly of continuing on, the risk of a fall, broken bones or worse, I heard voices ahead. I could not see any lights at first, for the trail followed the twisting contour of the hillside. The voices sounded distant, oddly distorted, and they did not seem friendly. I hurried as fast as I dared, stumbling here and there over unexpected stones.

The raised voices escalated into screaming, fell away into a moment of silence, and then wild, anguished keening.

I rounded the bend and saw the campsite, limned in orange firelight. The cart stood in a little flat place just off the trail, cradled between two arms of rock. For an instant, the place looked deserted. Nothing moved. Then my fighter's vision picked out the pattern of fallen bodies from the scattered rubble. I had seen enough dead men to know them now.

The sobbing came from the far side of the camp, beside the picket line. The ponies shifted, white-eyed at the reek of blood. A woman knelt there, cradling a man's body. Rocking, weeping. Juthe, it had to be her, even with her voice distorted, stretched to the breaking point around her horror and pain.

Fools, to take on so many. Unless…unless the Pearl itself had urged her to it.

Unless the Pearl wanted fresh blood. I had thought to pass on a gift. Instead, I had burdened them with a curse.

Soft as shadow, I moved through the camp. I need not have taken any pains to be cautious, for she had no awareness of me, or of anything but the body in her arms. I knelt an arm's-length away, empty of words.

Her shirt was torn, ripped by a dozen blades in a dozen killing strokes. Through the rent fabric, her skin shone, untouched. The Pearl rested between her breasts, glowering, sated.

She turned to me, her eyes all tears. Had I wept like that? I supposed I had. Tears had not brought my lover back, either. The thought came to me that she might do herself harm, that she had neither kin nor oath to bind her to life. I reached out my hands. She let me take him and lay him out.

I folded Culliy's hands across his chest and smoothed his eyes closed. His body was still warm, his muscles pliable. He would stiffen in an attitude of grace.

As for Juthe, she would have nothing of comfort. Her grief burrowed inward like a canker worm. In time, she would grow numb, inured, even as I had. In time. But not yet.

She stumbled through a chant in a language I could not understand, Raëth most likely. At first, I thought it was a prayer for the dead, a requiem. But there was no sorrow in it, only a wild, consuming rage.

Her eyes changed as she reached for a knife fallen on the ground. She lifted it, pressed the flat to her forehead, then to her lips. Smoothly, she placed the point over her belly, both hands holding the hilt. She thrust again and again, grunting with the effort. The tip would not pierce her skin. Her knuckles turned white. Sweat slicked her skin.

Juthe tossed away the knife and glared at me. "Can kill— cannot die." She clawed at the Pearl where it hung between her breasts. "Curse, is this thing! You…you knew?"

I looked away.

Then she was on me, her hands on my shoulders, shaking me. Her shirt was slick with the blood of the men she'd slaughtered; the smell sickened me.

"Must die!" she shrieked. "Die in honor! Tell me how!"

A light burned in her eyes, fire and blood and madness, reflections of the inferno within the Pearl.

"Give it back to me," I said.

She whipped the chain over her neck and shoved it at me. The Pearl swung back and forth. "Take! Evil bargain!"

My fingers closed around the Pearl, stilling its motion, imprisoning it. The bronze-red globe flared, implacable. I shivered at the prospect of what I must do, to endure. It would never tire, the dragon within me, never cease to thirst. I could never use it, that much was certain. It would taint every purpose.

I could not use it…but I could keep it from using anyone else.

Juthe reeled away from me. I thought she fled into the night, for I heard no sound from her as I went about the camp, straightening the fallen bodies, seeing to the weapons and the animals. I ate the burned food, banked the fire, and wrapped myself in a borrowed blanket.

The next morning, I found a spade in the cart. A little ways from the camp, I found a grassy slope, not too steep, and dug a shallow pit. I would rather have made separate graves, but I had not the strength. As it was, by the time I had dragged the first two to their resting place, I was sweating hard.

Wordless, Juthe picked up the feet of the next corpse, and together we carried him to the common grave. We worked without stopping until the camp was cleared and the earth smoothed over. Juthe returned my sword, but I buried it with the dead.

I found a small barrel of ale in the cart and we sipped it together, sitting with our legs sprawled in the dust and our backs against one of the cart wheels.

"Give you back evil thing," she said. "Now, tell me how to die!"

"You—" I stopped myself, thinking hard. "You must wait a year and a day for the spell to wear off. Then…" I shrugged, praying that I had given her grief enough time to subside.

After a time, when she made no move to get up, I asked, "What will you do now? Will you find employ with some company of mercenaries?"

She shook her head. "Culliy say quit, keep safe."

Yes, and when the money ran out, they gambled, then turned raider. How could I condemn her, I who had slain so many?

If we were together, I might be able to keep an eye on her, prevent her from getting into a situation that might test her year-and-a-day immortality. "Can you manage that cart?"

"Farm daughter." Her gaze flickered to where the Pearl lay, hidden beneath my shirt. "That?"

Who will keep us safe from that?

I saw what a few hours of exposure to the Pearl had done to her. What decades had done to my Great-Grandfather. What the desire for it had done to my father, my brother.

I will keep us safe, I thought. I must and would...because only I could.

The bronze dragon could never be beaten, never smashed, never destroyed. The mailed fist and the prideful spirit would yield at last to the lust for carnage, the seductive lure of invulnerability.

But the Pearl had no power over the open heart of a child rushing to comfort a loveless, dying old man, nor the tender heart of a young girl dancing in a sunlit glade.

Only a bruised and broken heart, a heart once filled with anguish and now turning toward hope, could tame the Pearl of Fire, could transform it into something else. What that might be, I could not imagine, only sense the possibility.

I lifted my face to the day, and felt the breeze cool against the wetness on my cheeks, now certain of my course.

My heart would guide me.

Pearl of Tears

My brother was slain by a woman without a soul.

I had loved him above my other kin, for our mother died at my birthing and Father—the Lord of Eaglehurst—had no use for a mewling, sickly daughter. When I was older, my nurse told me that my brother had looked down at me in my cradle—even now, I can picture those gray eyes so like my own, that hint of a smile at one corner of his mouth—and I had ceased my fitful wailing. "She's beautiful," he had whispered. And so I was, in those rainwater eyes, if in no others.

When our soldiers returned from that bleak winter battle, I went running down the steps from the great manor house, half-tripping on my skirts. What was left of our defense force filled the stone-paved courtyard. Father had already gone down to them, his azure cloak bright against the mud of their forest gear. Half our horses were gone and those remaining bore oozing gashes. The men were worse off, exhausted, slashed and battered, their eyes hollow.

"Where is Joram? Where is my brother?" I ran from one to the other. The first soldier I asked gave no sign he'd heard me, nor did the next. Father ignored me, bent deep in discussion with the captains. I caught a phrase, *the Dragon of Sharaya*, and the very sound turned my bones to jelly.

The sky opened and the clouds bore down upon us,

shrouding the house and all the fields around. I went among the wounded, washing and bandaging, spooning cups of broth, and holding hands as they grew cold and still. I tried not to think about Joram, wounded or dead, with no one to comfort him. I felt nothing but emptiness, and so I filled it with work. Father shut himself up in his war room, which had once been Mother's solarium, and plotted retaliation. I sensed his anger like a rumbling through the stones beneath my feet, growing and gnawing.

The next morning, when the rain had lifted, a Sharayan rider approached under a banner of truce. Unbidden, I slipped into room where Father received him, praying for news of Joram. Perhaps if I knew with certainty that he was dead, I might be able to grieve. I might be able to hate. The message startled all of us, Father and captains and me, for it was an offer to return of the bodies of our fallen.

For a long moment, no one spoke. Such a thing had never been done, or if it had, it was long ago and not by our old enemy. Sharaya was ruthless and without mercy, everyone knew that. It must be a ruse, a trap. My father did not believe the Duke would keep a truce, and so would not agree to let any enemy force approach us unhindered. After what I had seen, I did not think we could stand against the Dragon, not even if every last one of us were to band together.

In the end, however, the messenger convinced Father to set his own conditions as to time and place and who might be present. Father accepted, although the entire offer now appeared to be the prelude to a demand for total surrender. The only choice was to refuse, and not even Father at his most furious would throw away the chance to give proper rites to our own dead. So that very day, he rode out with a company of picked men to bring my brother home. I was left yet once again, not knowing what to feel or how to hope. I filled my hours with nursing and thoughts that *they could not return, not soon, surely now, what could have befallen them, what must I do if-if-if,* until finally, finally, came the signal from the lookouts and the sound of hooves clattering on the courtyard stones. I rushed to the window of the infirmary chamber and threw it open.

Below, I spied two men easing a body down from where it had been slung facedown over the saddle of Joram's horse. I could not make out the face, only the soaked clothing and the water-stained leather. The russet hair, drenched and tangled like riverweed, dripped on to the courtyard stones. In life, it had been the color of mine, or perhaps brighter.

I clenched my fingers around the window sash until my joints creaked and breath came like fire in my throat. It would have been better if I had fainted or shrieked or raged.

She'd done this, the Dragon of Sharaya. And now I had nothing to live for except to see her suffer.

The words were said, the rites performed, and the bodies were covered by new-dug soil. The priest recited words of peace, that Joram and the others were now beyond all pain, all sorrow. I thought, *Funerals are not for the dead but the living,* and did not know which I was.

Sharaya kept their word to leave us unmolested, but the armistice did not last. We'd been sore hurt in the last year, and those who came to take the place of the trained warriors were unseasoned or unsound in body. A few women, accustomed to defending their flocks and strong from hard labor, joined them. They were not swordswomen but archers and pike-wielders, sling-throwers and sentries. I pleaded with Father to let me join them, so that I might learn to defend our home. And, although I did not say so to him, that I might have a chance, no matter how remote, to put an end to the Dragon.

He said no. Of course, he said no. He had never counted me of any worth, the daughter who had cost the life of his lady and any future sons she might bear, and he did not do so now. *Stay out of the way,* he meant. *Keep to women's work. Maybe the Dragon will spare you if she sees you are of no account.*

I cut my hair, bound my breasts, and combed through the attic until I found a chest with Joram's outgrown, discarded clothing. The shirt was too broad across the shoulders and the pants too long, but I had some skill with a needle and managed to alter them so that they would not attract undue attention. The fabric still bore the faint smell of wild herbs, and a few dried flower petals clung to the threads. I wondered when he'd last worn it, where he'd gone on those days when he'd come home smiling, if he'd lain on his back in a meadow dotted with blossoms, if some country girl or smallholder's daughter had made him smile.

When I presented myself at the first training session, no one challenged me. I roughened my voice and affected an accent similar to that of the forest folk. The only one who looked at me with any suspicion, and even that was but a moment's, was one of our few remaining officers. Herel he was named, for the small swift falcons of the highlands, and his family had served mine for generations. In peaceful times, he would already have retired to enjoy his grandchildren. He watched as each of us displayed our skill—or lack of it—with sword, bow, spear, hammer, and staff. I was too small to handle a weapon that required strength, but he could not afford to discard any resource.

There wasn't much time for training, only for fighting one delaying action after another as best we could. Very soon, I discovered that although I had little skill, I had no fear. I didn't care what happened to me as long as I had an enemy in front of me. It wasn't fury that drove me on, or desperation, but something far colder. That very fearlessness kept me alive until I attained a measure of competence at arms. I still couldn't hold my own against a trained swordsman, but I was quick and light, more an assassin or a cutthroat thief than an honest duelist. To everyone's surprise, I developed a talent for tracking, for moving so quietly that my presence often went unknown until I was almost upon my quarry. Such a gift served us poorly, however, for there was no need to stalk the Sharaya Dragon.

She led her forces against us again and again, bold and relentless, and each time there were fewer of us left to stand against her. She always rode in front, mounted on a horse that looked as if it had been ridden through hell. We lost more territory, and more, until we battled before the smoking ruin that had been the great house.

Herel still led us, although he had not recovered from a festering leg wound some weeks back. He sat astride one of the few good horses left to us, shouting out encouragement. In the past, I had been assigned to a party of lightly-armed fighters who fought together, harrying and skirmishing rather than engaging head-on, but as my comrades fell, I snatched up a spear from its fallen bearer and joined the others defending our captain. All the while, I searched for the figure that haunted my nightmares.

Come to me, come to me...

It seemed to me then that the tumult of fighting quieted and a path opened in the enemy forces.

I could not mistake the Dragon. Who else disdained helmet and shield? Who else raised her sword in salute even as the blood of the slain—*our* slain—dripped from it?

Come to me... I tightened my grasp on the my spear. Likely I would have only a single chance.

Just then, just at the moment when surely she must have seen the hatred on my face and known that she was mine and I was hers, she paused. Did she sense a threat from the side? One of our best remaining fighters hurled himself forward and thrust the point of his sword under the edge of her breastplate. The stroke would have felled a raging bear, but the blade slid away, as if her very flesh was adamantine. She twisted in the saddle and beheaded him with a single stroke. His body remained upright for a terrible moment, and then toppled like an uprooted tree.

I felt the life go out of his body as if from my very own. Was this how Joram had died, with so little effort, such casual slaughter?

Then, as if shaken from a stupor or suddenly disenchanted, the Sharayans took up the fight again. The heart had gone out of our own forces. I knew what they were thinking, because the same despair howled through my own mind: The great house was lost. Even without the Dragon, we faced overwhelming opposition. Our deaths would serve nothing.

"Retreat!" Herel shouted, gesturing with his sword. *Retreat while we still can.*

As for myself, I was glad enough to leave that place. I would have the revenge I craved, I swore to my brother's memory, but not now. Not here.

We ran like rabbits with the hounds of Sharaya on our tails, in a frenzied scramble. I heard a scream behind us but did not risk a glance to see who it was. Sooner than I hoped, the pursuit fell away. They could have had us all if they had been determined, but the habit of following the Dragon was too strong. I imagined their exultation, their certainty that in time, they would trap us all.

Some hours later, Herel brought us to a stumbling, panting halt. Men and horses trembled on the brink of exhaustion. He'd taken us north, toward the mountains, but we had not yet traveled beyond familiar lands. Some of us knew these woods and the paths through them, the meadows and ravines, the caves. We sheltered in one of caves, not deep but well-hidden.

I set to work ordering the camp, checking who was wounded and how badly, making an inventory of what little we had managed to carry away. Nobody questioned my orders; they were all too numb to think clearly, and I needed to be doing something.

Dusk fell quickly in the forest and a chill arose from the surrounding rock. A couple of the men who'd somehow escaped injury found enough fallen wood for a fire. I decided to risk it. The wounded would benefit from the warmth and the light would comfort the dying.

Gradually the others drifted off to sleep, if their snores were any indication. I shifted closer to the fire, now an occasional flicker of light against the embers. I folded my arms around my knees and tried to make sense of what I had witnessed on this day. Everything I had been told about the Dragon of Sharaya— and disbelieved as superstition or battlefield exaggeration—was true. She could not be slain by ordinary means. The sword had struck true and yet had not touched her. Was she then a demon, a thing of supernatural power? A dragon in the shape of a woman?

What hope had I of avenging my brother's death, I who was not even a mediocre sword fighter?

Clothing rustled, drawing my attention. Herel, who lay nearby and close to the fire, propped himself on one elbow. "It is not defeat, my lady, for we will fight another day."

With what weapons—against a dragon? I thought bitterly. And then, *"my lady"*?

He must have seen the surprise on my face, for he continued, still keeping his voice low, "Your brother did not have a twin, and you are as like to him. Yet in this you are unalike. Hatred, not love of home and lord, drives you."

I did not waste my breath with false denials. "You think I should have stayed at home, embroidering holiday shirts? Should I throw down my knife and crawl to whatever lord will give me sanctuary?"

"I think you will not rest until you stand before the Dragon of Sharaya, no matter what I say."

I sat up straighter. Here was a man who would tell me the truth. "What is she, this Dragon? Is she even human?"

Herel studied me for a long moment, perhaps weighing the guilt of sending me to certain death. "Her name is Rayzel, daughter of the Duke of Sharaya. It is said she bears a magical talisman, a proof against all bodily harm. If that is true, it is a miracle we resisted her this long. My own father told stories of the old Duke, her grandfather. Or maybe her great-grandfather, who can tell? No foe could stand against him, but he sought only to protect his own lands. Lady Rayzel..."

I had seen her face, so lacking in human emotion. Perhaps

the talisman granted her invulnerability of the heart as well as the flesh. "She would see the entire world in flames."

He nodded, as if I had spoken his thought. I tried to remember when the war had changed from traditional raiding to this campaign of annihilation. Before Joram was killed, it had seemed far away and happening to someone else. Certainly, he had been able to spare an afternoon now and again for his secret courtship.

My only chance would be to take the talisman from her, most likely by trickery or stealth. My size, which had served me poorly in combat, might yet be my greatest asset. Few swordsmen took me seriously, but I could move quickly and silently. I'd make an excellent thief.

"Tell me about this talisman," I said to Herel. "What does it look like? Where does she carry it?"

"It is said to be a Pearl of surpassing beauty, in appearance like none other. When roused by blood, it glows like fire-licked bronze. Or so it is said," he added, his voice made hoarse by weariness.

"*So it is said,*" I repeated. "Have you yourself seen it?"

He looked away, into the shadows. I regretted stirring sorrowful memories, but I needed to know. "I have seen...something. I am not sure what. But Rayzel of Sharaya does wear a silver chain about her neck. That much I have seen with my own eyes."

Hope flared, the first I'd known since the day Joram died. This Pearl might render its wearer invulnerable to sword and spear, but it was a physical item, a bauble. And once it hung around my own neck, Sharaya would pay.

Those few of us who survived the fall of Eaglehurst lived as outlaws in the remote areas of brush and forest, never staying long in any campsite, always looking over our shoulders for fear we would see the Dragon, her sword gleaming like red-gold, coming after us. Herel died the first winter of a lung fever, and some looked to me as the next leader. I wanted no obligation, no loyalty to anything but my own vengeance. By this time, even the few veterans acknowledged my skill. I had earned a place with them not by bloodline—for none of them knew who I truly was—but by blood.

I still wore Joram's clothing, although with each passing season, it became more worn and less like the garb of a nobly-born youth. I suppose I became tattered and weathered as well. Certainly, it seemed that the men treated me as one of them, as my brother would have been. Sometimes I felt as if I were carrying on with his life and not my own, fighting and fleeing, speaking the names of the dead around the evening fires. I would remember why I was here instead of him, and what quarry I hunted, and why I must never rest.

After a time, we gained a measure of respite from Sharayan patrols. I took this as a sign that I might now resume my own hunt. We dared to emerge from the broken lands and scrub forests where we had hidden ourselves. The others were weary of constant vigilance and poverty, of cold and poor food and rarely a song. So we made our way back towards Eaglehurst, to the lands we once had known. We went warily, not only out of fear of discovery but because we did not want to bring retribution on any village that aided us.

At one of these places, the largest and most prosperous we'd visited, we ventured into the single inn and traded our few coins for ale and new-baked bread. The villagers and a few travelers regarded us with mild interest and, when they were satisfied we offered neither threat nor the promise of exciting tales, went back to their own business. I settled on a table next to the least taciturn of the travelers. He was of Herel's age, grizzled but not mean-eyed, a trader in small metal items like pans and sewing needles.

"What news from the road?" I asked. "We've been a-forest so long, there's much we've not heard."

His gaze swept over me, but lightly. He took me for an

unbearded youth, and I did not disabuse him of that notion. "Like there'll be peace for a time."

"Why is that? Has Sharaya run out of enemies to pick a quarrel with?"

The traveler shook his head. "It's called Greater Sharaya now, and any man fool enough to go up against her is long since food for worms. Seems the new Duke's got no stomach for campaigns and prefers to sit home, toasting his toes."

One of my company, overhearing our talk, moved closer. "Might as well, with the Dragon on guard." He looked as if he'd like to spit the bitterness out of his mouth from speaking the name.

"Word is," and here the trader lowered his voice and leaned close, "the Dragon's gone as well."

"Gone?" I echoed.

"Gone?" the Eaglehurst man said. "What happened to her? How can she just disappear?"

She wasn't dead, that much I was certain, because *I* was destined to kill her. For the first time in my exile, I felt afraid that she might now have gone beyond my reach.

Where? Where? The thought rampaged through my skull. The trader drew back, and I realized I'd been glaring at him, as if I could wrest the answer by the force of my will.

"If Sharaya is appeased and the Dragon is gone..." my comrade said, clearly turning over the notion in his mind, "then we can go home again."

Home, someone else repeated, or perhaps I heard it only in my heart. "Go home," I told my company. "Be at rest."

Where would she have gone, and why? The reason did not interest me, only the direction, and I sat long in the inn's room, gazing into my half-drunk tankard, wondering where to begin.

I ventured into Sharaya itself, working when I could and picking pockets when I must. I used the money to buy ale for anyone who would gossip, and after a time, I put together bits of stories. A woman fitting Rayzel's description had been seen bargaining for fare on one of the boats that followed the river down out of the mountains. As I followed her path, I puzzled over what could have brought her to leave behind family, home, safety, the privilege of a noble birth. These things had been taken from me, but she had *chosen* to walk away. There was no current threat to Sharaya, nor was there likely to be. Was this a sort of expiation, a penance? The very idea was so beyond all reason as to be laughable. And yet, I saw a bizarre justice in her wanderings. Everything I had wished for her, a redoubling of my own exile and suffering, she now took upon herself.

But it was not enough. It would never be enough.

The mountains fell away into sloping pastures and then fields of millet and barley. At every town, every crossroads, I asked after her, always dreading the discovery that I had either lost the trail or my quarry would turn out to be someone besides Rayzel, some poor woman driven from her home, perhaps a mercenary looking for employment. So far, my luck held.

The way led south, across the withered, rock-strewn badlands. I stood on the outskirts of the last trading town, little more than a collection of tents clustered around an ancient well, and looked out over the caravan route. This far, I had trusted to my own sturdy feet, with an occasional ride on a farmer's cart. Hot wind stirred the sand that had blown up from the desert. My lips were already parched. I had a little money, but not enough to buy a camel, and no horse could cross such an arid, desolate place. This same wind would scour soon my corpse. For a moment, the image of dry bones half-buried in sand rose up in my mind, only they were not mine. They were *hers*, and yet I felt no exultation, no relief that the desert had been my executioner.

As I turned back toward the town, I reminded myself that such thoughts were fruitless, not to mention self-indulgent. I would have to find a means of earning money or a caravan willing to hire me. Tracking and petty theft would undoubtedly not be in high demand, but I wasn't afraid of hard work.

Now and again I'd seen women on the road, tall and strong, swords slung over their backs, but I'd been traveling as a youth for so long now, no one questioned my disguise, and I felt it safer to continue. As I looked for employment, I gave my name as Joram, in part to keep my own purpose alive. Because I had experience with horses, I found a position at one of the stable yards, with room and one meal a day in addition to my trivial pay. Best of all, I had a good reason to strike up conversations with the caravaneers, if not the masters then their assistants. We talked about the roads, the weather, the state of their beasts, where they were going, and all the best gossip from afar. Sooner or later, I would casually ask whether a swordswoman had taken passage with them across the sands.

No, no, and *no* were the responses as the moon changed in her phases and one day became much like the others. One day, when the question had become wearisome in its repletion, *Yes.*

A camel-boy and I were sitting on the worn step behind the kitchen of the adjacent inn, sipping warm ale as the sun dipped toward the west. *Yes,* they'd sold a camel to a woman of such a description. I must have just missed her departure, so the time was right.

"Where did she go?" I asked.

"Only one place to go, 'cross the sands—Ixtalpi, it's called, the city where madmen and demons mingle on the streets. And gamblers. It sits at the foot of the Viridian Mountains, that spew forth fire and ash, or so it is said." As he said this, the boy spat into the dust.

It sounded like the perfect place for the Dragon of Sharaya.

"*It is said?*" I repeated, an idea nudging my mind. "You have not seen these marvels for yourself?"

The boy shook his head, and I saw that he was even younger than I'd first thought. Young, and far from his own home.

Carefully, lest I disturb the luck that at last seemed to be coming my way, I gave him to understand that I very much wished to see such sights, if only there might be some other to take my place here, with its warm bed and daily meal. Before we'd finished our ale, we'd struck a bargain to swap places. The caravan-master was only too happy to exchange a frightened, homesick boy for the strapping youth I appeared to be.

The mountains were everything the boy had intimated, dark and jagged. Black mists curled about their peaks, but whether they were natural fog or some demonic vapors, I could not tell. Ixtalpi itself was a warren, its buildings huddled at the base of the slopes. The afternoon was wearing into dusk when we arrived, and already a lurid red light tinged the western horizon.

I collected my wages and ventured into the town. Not wanting to squander my meager purse, I selected an inn that was neither ostentatiously luxurious nor overly dilapidated. The price of a single room was more than I expected, but I dared not share one with half a dozen men, all of us jammed into one bed and the floor, and likely a few of them interested in a closer intimacy with a beardless youth. The inn keeper might have thought my modesty laughable, but he accepted my coin. I had come too far to risk failure from something as simple as being exposed as a woman, and yet I could not bring myself to discard my disguise. In some way I barely understood, I had become Joram, and to set that aside now felt like a betrayal.

The overpriced room came with a meal, so I settled in the common room, pretending to focus on the trencher of surprisingly spicy shredded meat, pickled vegetables, and a grain I did not recognize. All the while, I listened to the conversations around me, trying to sense the temper of the town and the best way to inquire after another traveler. That first night, I heard nothing of any value, except that my quarry was evidently not the only woman with a sword in this part of the world. What she might do if she suspected someone was on her track, I could not imagine. All the way, I'd been far enough behind her and so well-disguised, it was hard to imagine she'd detected me.

And why should she? Eaglehurst was destroyed, any man capable of standing up to Sharaya long dead.

By day, I strolled through the markets and stockyards. I didn't expect to hear anything of value, and therefore was not disappointed. My real work took place at night, when I drifted from one tavern to another. As often as not, a round of cheap ale would yield an hour's gossip, tales from the road and far-off places, and also not a few stories of doings within Ixtalpi itself. I dispensed my coin slowly, for I had no idea how long I must make it last. I heard stories of horse races, knife fights, snake-wrestling contests, and the birth of a two-headed camel calf. Most of the reports of gambling were either so exaggerated or so dull I paid them little attention. Then, on the third night, I heard something that piqued my interest.

A game of castles and dice...a young couple from Raë on the Western Sea, mercenaries by the sound of them...a woman with a sword, "a hard one, that"...

Bets rose as one by one the other players dropped out, and the couple won and won. The woman with the sword played as if she cared nothing for winning, as if she had nothing worth losing.

Then, when it seemed the game was over, one final bet: a gem bound in silver wire, hanging on a chain around the swordswoman's neck.

"Glowed like a bed of coals, it did," my storyteller said.

"Aye," said his companion. "I'd not touch the thing, for all I've seen it with my own eyes." As he said this, he made a sign to ward off evil.

"What happened?" I asked in the silence that followed. "Who won?"

"Why them young couple, of course. Took off the next day to who knows where, proud as peacocks. Up to no good, but so long as they keep their trouble to themselves, what do I care?"

"Just as well," his friend agreed.

I stared into my half-empty tankard, unable to believe what I'd just heard. She'd *lost* the Pearl? In a *game?* What kind of madwoman was she? Or maybe she wasn't mad at all, but so sickened by what she'd done, she no longer cared for living?

Had she, after all these years and so much bloodshed, developed a conscience?

Or was I the fool to think that was possible?

"Where…" I began, my throat suddenly dry, "where did she go?"

My two informants exchanged shrugs and glances, as if to say that anyone mad enough to follow that woman deserved whatever ill fortune they brought upon themselves. The friendlier of the two unbent enough to suggest that if it had been him who lost such a pretty bauble, he'd be on his way to get it back, one way or another. This made as much sense to me as any other aspect of the whole fantastical story. I paid for another round for the two of them and returned to my own inn, where I settled my account and told the owner I would be departing before dawn. I might have a long way to go, but some instinct told me that at last I was nearing my quarry.

The trail led me down slope, out of the Viridian Mountains and through a crossroads. I'd heard it said that the doors to the lands of the dead swing open at such places during certain times of the year, and as I searched the dry ground for a sign of her passage, I felt a breath, a whisper on my face. It felt as if Joram urged me toward the less-traveled road. His guidance proved good, for before long, I spotted the print of a boot I now knew to be hers. She'd stepped out of the center of the trail, and so the track had not been overlain by others.

There had been little enough traffic on this road as it narrowed, soon only wide enough for a single line of mules or a small cart. I followed slowly, attending to the story left in scuffed dust, bent leaves, the moisture remaining in the animal dung, the occasional depression left by a boot when the wearer had strayed into the looser soil to either side. I knew this game well, and I was very good at it. I read what had gone before, not only the beasts and men but the order in which they had passed.

First had come the narrow-wheeled cart and three ponies, one of them unshod, and as many men. They traveled at a pace so as to not overtax the animals: a trading party, about their ordinary business. Two sets of footprints overlay those of the cart and ponies, one smaller and lighter than the other. They paused behind brush at turns where they might be seen by the traders. As they went on, their pace hastened, as shown by the depth of the heel strikes in the dirt. They became bolder, less wary.

At first, I wondered if one of them were Rayzel of Sharaya, until I saw a third set of prints. They were clearly made by a tall, strong woman…and she was following the couple, who in their turn were on the trail of the trading party. Their lead was two days but no more.

I straightened up from where I had squatted, examining the overlapping prints. In a fair game or a crooked one, she'd lost the Pearl. Now she wanted it back. She was stalking the young couple even as they hurried after the traders. To the west, the sun was rapidly slipping behind the forested hills. Dusk would come early in this place. Although it galled me to think that Rayzel might even now be lengthening the distance between us, I found a place to rest for the night. I had waited this long. I could wait a time longer.

Anticipation woke me well before dawn. I broke my fast, drank from my small supply of water, scrubbed my teeth with a frayed stick, and returned to the chase. The morning air was clear, still cool from the night. Once, a long time ago, I would have said this was a wonderful day to be alive, with the sun bright on the leaves and the scent of wild herbs on the breeze. I wished Joram might have lived to enjoy it with me, and I supposed he was, in the sense I carried him with me.

Once my muscles were warm, I picked up my pace, running when the trail permitted it. It wound along the contours of the hillside, so that often what lay ahead was hidden until the last moment. Around one such twist in the trail, I came upon the remains of a campsite. Here the cart had been placed between two arms of rock. Here, the campfire. Here, the picketed ponies.

From one end of the site to the other, I marked the traces of a struggle. I touched my fingertips to the darkened splotches in the earth, knowing before I smelled the reside that it was blood, and not old blood, either. Four men had died here, the three traders and one more. They'd been laid out on the dirt and then dragged to a grassy slope, where a shallow pit marked their common grave. The earth was still moist under a thin crust.

How could Rayzel have done this? I demanded of the empty sky. Then I remembered, *Of course. She is not a mortal woman, with a heart to care for travelers. She is a dragon, the Dragon of Sharaya.*

The cart was missing, as were the ponies, and I assumed she had taken them as booty, along with the trade goods. Why not? Ever since I'd known of her, she'd taken whatever she wanted, lands, flocks, men's lives. To my surprise, she was not alone. The woman from the couple traveled with her, and clearly this woman did not stumble or lag as a captive would. The idea she went freely startled me. Even more surprising was the evidence that these two had sat together, as close as comrades, as trail-sisters. This was not the behavior of a victor and her spoils.

For the first time in my long quest, I felt a tremor of doubt. I had thought the powers of this Pearl were of the body only. I had not dreamt that it might also enslave the mind. How could I fight such evil? I could not slit its throat in the night. Not only might I fail, I might become subject to what I most hated.

On the other hand, what was there for me, besides this chase? Who would I be if I turned back now? The last, defeated heir to once-great Eaglehurst? A traitor to my brother's memory, and now to my very self?

Slowly I wrestled my way back to an approximation of courage. I hadn't thought the end of my long search would be easy. I admitted to myself that I'd had no thought of what would become of me once I confronted the Dragon of Sharaya. Perhaps that meant I would not survive, that I intended to finish her at the cost of my own paltry life. That must be why I had carried Joram's ghost, his very appearance, all these years—because I myself had no separate existence.

The trail crested the hills and then dipped into the valley beyond. I had no knowledge of these lands, but I could feel the vitality rising from the meadows. Birds nested in the surrounding groves, and rabbits darted away at my approach. Two heavily-pregnant does looked up from their browsing before bounding into the shadowed forest. Occasionally I glimpsed rolling pastures below and once, distantly, a herd of red-brown cattle.

Because I kept to a more rapid pace than my quarry and because the two women had lingered at the first campsite for the better part of a day, I gained on them rapidly. Now a new worry came to me, that they might reach a town or other settlement before I caught up with them, a place where they might gain allies. The last thing I wanted when I stood before Rayzel and demanded her life in payment for her crimes was an audience. So I hurried throughout that afternoon, sometimes scrambling down slopes and over rocks, risking injury and pushing myself for more speed.

My efforts paid off, for as twilight drew close, I saw that they had set up camp in a little grove that bordered the pastureland. I didn't know the type of tree, short and spreading, leaves massing dark in the gathering night, but suspected there was a water source there as well. I made out the cart, the women tending to the ponies, and then the flare and warm orange light of a fire.

In the forests of Eaglehurst, I had learned to move like a whisper through the underbrush, so softly that not even a hunting owl marked my passage. Now I drew my stealth around me like a cloak. I became a shadow against shadow, a flicker in the gloaming. I had no reason to think the two suspected my presence, but with a little care and skill, I would make sure that did not happen.

I breathed so softly and stepped so silently that I heard their voices long before I got an unobstructed view of their camp. Two women, of course. Of that I had already been certain. But as I paused to listen, I heard something that I did not expect.

One of them was weeping, long shuddering sobs that surely arose from the very pit of despair, that place bereft of hope, of thought, of words. That in itself was not surprising, for who would not weep in the company of the Dragon of Sharaya?

No, what brought me up short were the soft murmurs of the other woman, the gentle phrases, the tone of voice that rose and fell as a mother might sing to a fretful child.

Rayzel, the Dragon of Sharaya, was *comforting* the other woman.

How could this be? Had the world so disarranged itself, that the sky and earth had lost all reason?

Heart yammering in my ears, I stumbled forward. Only by long habit and fortune did I keep hold of my dagger. A moment later, I was glad I hadn't dropped it. The Dragon lived by her own law, but she was not beyond mine.

Only a thin screen of lacy branches stood between me and the campsite, a veil scarcely worth the effort of brushing it aside. In the light of the fire and what remained in the western sky, I could see the women clearly. I had not erred, for there was Rayzel, wearing the trail-worn garb of a sword-soldier. There was no mistaking that strong build, that hair, that line of brow and cheek. The other woman, the one curled into a ball, half on Rayzel's lap, wrapped in Rayzel's arms, she must be the one from Raë. Her body shuddered with the force of her sobs, and Rayzel rocked her, held her tight.

"Hush now," Rayzel said softly. "You did not kill those men of your own choice, but that is over now…"

"…never be free of it…"

"You must go on. That's what your lover would have wanted for you, is it not? Would he not forgive you for what was not your fault?"

The light shifted on Rayzel's body and I saw it then, hanging from a chain around her neck.

The Pearl.

The thing that had made her invincible, that had brought

DEBORAH J. ROSS

about the destruction of everything I loved—my home, my own hopes, my brother's life.

Before I had made a conscious choice, I darted into the camp. Rayzel was vulnerable at this moment, her arms encumbered by the other woman. Even with magically-enhanced reflexes, it would take her a moment to get to her feet and draw her sword.

She noticed me, her head coming up. Her gaze met mine. I moved to close the distance, but she didn't shove the other woman aside. It was as if she had no care to defend herself. Something in her posture, a stillness that bordered on surrender, made me pause when nothing else would have. I stood for an instant, dagger clenched low beside my knee where it could not be easily spotted, muscles primed for a lunge and a quick upward strike.

Now the other woman reacted, pulling away from Rayzel with a whimper. She scuttled away from the fire to hide herself in the shadows. It was just the two of us, the Dragon of Sharaya and me. I tightened my grip on the dagger, drew a breath like fire into my lungs, and—

—and before I could take that next step, the step that would commit me to the attack, her expression changed. The hardness fell away, and I looked into the face of a young girl, the girl she had once been, not beautiful, but radiant and open of heart. Even as my brother had been. Even as I had been.

"Joram?"

The astonishment in her voice held me fast, and I realized then that my brother and I had so resembled one another, and I had so assiduously taken on his manner and appearance, that she saw him instead of me. Yet I heard not a trace of fear in her cry, as would arise from confronting the ghost of a man she had slain. No, what I heard so clearly was wonder, wonder and joy. I might have brought her death—that was yet to be decided—but I had also brought her the thing her heart desired more than any other—to see her beloved one last time.

For there was not the slightest doubt in my mind that she

had known Joram and had loved him with the fervent innocence of first love. No matter what came afterwards, he had left
an indelible imprint on her heart.

Rayzel blinked, and the young girl she had been faded into
the battle-hardened woman. She made no effort to rise, as if
granting me leave to do what I would. Try as I might, however,
I could find no trace of the implacable Dragon, the one who
had looked down on the destruction of Eaglehurst. I discerned
endurance and sorrows as deep as my own, and I also saw compassion.

"You are not Joram," she said, and it seemed to me that she
would a thousand times have preferred to meet his ghost,
vengeful or not, than any living person.

I straightened slightly. "His sister."

"Sister? I did not know he had a sister. Might I know your
name?"

I told her, although I had not spoken it for so long, my
tongue did not recognize it.

She hesitated, which surprised me even more deeply. "I
suppose you have come to avenge him. And that you will not
believe me if I say that I would give anything to exchange places
with him."

"Fine words."

She smiled a little, but sadly, and shifted so that she knelt
before me. Her hands were empty. If she had a weapon about
her, she made no attempt to draw it. Moving slowly, she slipped
the chain over her head and let the Pearl fall to the earth. It
glowed as if it bore a living ember at its heart, but the light was
uneasy, as if a subtle intelligence, a *hunger*, burned there also.

What had she said to the other woman? *Not your choice, not
your fault…*

"Now I am as mortal as you," she said. "My life is yours to
take, as recompense for what you have lost. I ask only one
thing—that you bury the Pearl with me. That you make no
claim on it for yourself. I have done enough harm to your
family. I would not have you carry the curse as well."

What kind of trick is this? I wondered, and realized there was no deception in her voice, no falsehood. What would it cost me to grant her this one thing? I wanted justice for my brother, for Eaglehurst and its people. For all my life as a bandit and thief, I had no interest in turning into the one who had brought so much harm to so many.

When I agreed, she smiled again, like the sun emerging from behind a cloud. "You are indeed Joram's sister, to have such kindness in you."

If I had had any doubt that she had known him, known the heart and core of who he'd been, it vanished. "How could you do it—how could you," the words stumbled over one another, "knowing him?"

In answer, she looked down at the smoldering red light of the Pearl. If everything I had learned was true, the gem had made her invincible, immortal. I had not imagined what else it might have brought—or driven—her to become. I could almost hear her wish that Sharaya and not Eaglehurst had burned, that she had led an ordinary woman's life, that her own death at my hands might in the smallest way compensate for all the grief she'd caused.

My legs threatened to give way beneath me. I understood then that she had not killed Joram and all the others. This *thing* had. Now it was about to take her life as well, using me as its instrument.

I let my dagger fall. The blade landed on the links of the chain with a hollow, clashing sound. The camp was empty except for the two of us. The Raë woman had fled.

I lowered myself beside Rayzel. I had thought that getting close enough to slip my blade between her ribs would be the hardest part. I'd had no idea, no idea at all, what she'd endured all these years.

"If I bury that," I said, pointing, "it might not stay buried." Someone might dig it up. I'd heard enough tales about cursed objects to know they had ways of becoming found. I didn't think it was possible to destroy this one, or Rayzel would long since have done it.

She nodded in a friendly way, as if in that moment we had shifted from being bitter enemies to allies. "I thought to carry it, in time to…to tame it."

"How can you tame something like that?"

"Not with sword or whip," she replied, and again I heard such sadness in her voice, my own throat threatened to close up. She looked at me again, and her eyes were bright. "With memories. With tears."

Tears for Joram? Tears for the loss of her home, her own kin? Tears for the sweet young girl she had once been?

Tears for me?

I had seen that she'd loved him. What I had not realized until that moment was that *he* had loved *her*. But he hadn't been able to save her.

I could.

I could…if I would.

And if I chose not to, if I turned my back on the girl my brother had loved, who then would be the victor?

Not Eaglehurst, in ashes.

Not Joram.

Not me.

The Pearl would win, and the hunger I'd sensed would claim even more lives.

Together, Rayzel and Joram had found a moment of joy. I could either snuff out its very memory or I could set it free.

I picked up the Pearl, handling it by the chain only, and let the gem come to rest on her opened hand. There it pulsed once, twice, as if it had a heart of its own. A hungering heart. A dragon heart.

With both hands, I closed Rayzel's fingers around the Pearl. "Then I will help you tame the Pearl."

She drew back in surprise. Clearly, she'd expected death, a slow one of revenge or a quick one of mercy. "Why would you offer to do such a thing?"

"Because," I said, leaning forward to kiss her as a sister,

"surely we have enough tears between us."

"Enough tears, yes," she repeated, and kissed me in turn. "Enough tears to quench even a Pearl of Fire."

Dragon-amber

Merren woke gasping, her dawn dream shattered. The dying night lay unnaturally still around her, the air heavy with dew. She lifted her head cautiously. The wards she had set the evening before had not been activated, nor was there any sign of physical violation of the sanctuary.

Merren gathered her legs beneath her, glad that she had slept in her breeches with no heavy forest robes to slow her movements, and reached for her staff. The ritually carved bronze-wood felt cool and reassuring beneath her fingers. She stood alone in the clearing, a stocky young woman with a cloud of unruly curls dark against her russet skin.

From the south, her ears caught a puff of air cascading into a rumbling breath. She focused on its source, a velvet black eddy in the auric fields. No ordinary prowler would create such an imprint, and the wards would have alerted her to the supernatural.

The growl came again, and a tug at her inner senses. A beast stepped from the shadowy forest to the clearing, its outlines visible in the strengthening light.

A dragon—neither natural nor supernatural, but born of a fusion of mortality and magic from the deep times before Light had twisted into Form. They possessed wisdom without language and an honor so convoluted that humans could only guess at its elements. Generally they avoided humans, even nature-wizards like Merren's folk, keeping to their mountain retreats.

A dragon—sighing at her threshold! It was dull black in stillness, but the iridescent linings of its scales gleamed in rainbow glory with the slightest movement. She could see the outlines of its dorsal crest and the complicated knobs of its vestigial wings. It fixed her with its pale amber eyes and rumbled again.

I must not fear. It is a child of the Light like any of us, Merren told herself. She held out one hand, fingers outstretched and palm toward the dragon as if it were a creature of magic and not mere flesh.

I greet you, O-Brother-Dragonkind!

The dragon rustled its scaled in a profusion of prismatic light. Its deep thrumming escalated to a musical cry. A spasm of urgency reached Merren, clawing at her guts.

She said aloud, "What is it?" and stepped closer to the barrier established by the wards. The dragon had made no move to enter the protected zone, and she was not sure whether that was because it could not, or for some reason would not. She knew so little of dragon lore. Perhaps its present behavior was a lure to draw her forth to her doom.

But Merren did not believe so. She suspected that if the dragon had intended to harm her, it would already have done so. She spoke the rune to dissipate the wards. It was a risk, yet the texture of the dragon's plea urged her to it.

The dragon shook its heavy head and dropped, belly to the grass. Merren tightened her grip on her staff and approached it. She had not appreciated before how massive it was. Prone, the beast reached to the middle of her thighs. Even as a purely natural beast, its power would be formidable.

The dragon reared up, balancing its bulk upon its hind legs. The exposed scales of its belly glistened like honey, like watered silk. Gleaming talons arched above her head, then subsided.

"Cooommm," came a ragged sound from the beast's throat. Layers of nictitating membranes flickered across its glowing eyes like rare gems—amber, ruby, emerald. Merren felt herself half-ensorcelled by the sheer beauty of the creature.

Whatever has driven you to me, O-Brother-Dragonkind? It must be a worthy cause. *But what challenge can I meet that a dragon could not?*

The dragon turned, a swirl of darkness and sparkling color, and strode into the forest. It led her south and a little west, angling through the airy groves toward the ancient heart of the forest. Merren trotted along, tapping the familiar maytrees and bronzewoods with the tip of her staff. Their branches quivered with her passing.

The forest thickened as they turned west, climbing above the sunlit bowl of Merren's sanctuary to crazy hillocks where angry old trees shouldered their neighbors aside.

It needs taming, this wood; love and taming.

Merren did not realize she had used thought-speech until she felt the dragon's flash of agreement. Neither of them liked this territory, where the bones of the land jutted out like half-formed weapons, ungentled by sun or blossom. The underbrush forced them to a walk.

She knew they were near their destination when the dragon surged forward, heading toward the densest twist of forest. Until then she had felt the spirits of the trees neutral at best, but now she could sense an eerie miasma streaming from the tangle before her. The wood was not actually evil, only degenerate toward the alien, the tree-spirits drifting further and further along their own strange dreams. Merren shied away from prolonged contact with them, fearing to carry their taint to her own familiar trees.

Overlaid on the burgeoning separateness of the grove was a residue that was in no way innocuous. Fear, shock...a violent warping of natural energies.

Merren slammed her mind-senses closed, grasping her staff in both white-knuckled hands. The dragon had nearly disappeared in the thick growth. She ran to catch up with it.

The residue of wrongness peaked sharply in the little

clearing. A man lay face down, sprawled like a child's poppet over the root of a huge ashleaf. He wore leather vest and pants, laced woodsman-style above soft boots. Even in the dim light, his tousled hair gleamed like fine gold.

The dragon padded to the man's side and nudged him gently. Merren knelt by his head and touched his shoulder cautiously, relieved to find it warm and resilient. The left side of the vest was stained deep blue.

Merren checked the man's scalp and back, but could detect no other wounds. He might still have a fracture or internal bleeding, which could kill him if she moved him. For a moment she paused, trapped between her own ignorance and the demanding need emanating from the dragon.

The dragon thrummed a command and bent his nose against the man's hips, lifting as Merren turned his head and shoulders. Finally he rested against the slope of the tree roots, head and torso slightly elevated. Merren's eyes went first to the livid bruises around his eyes, then to the seeping indigo stain on his right side. It stank of sorcery.

She studied his face for a moment before inspecting the oozing burn, curious to know what manner of man had entangled himself with such evil. He was well-built, graceful rather than overly muscular, his features a shade too generous for regularity. The bone structure was clean, the flesh overlying it firm despite a hint of sensuality in his mouth. On a heavy silver chain round his neck he wore an amulet of carved amber. A twist of dark light deep in the heart of the gem reminded her of the dragon.

Merren bent over the wound, drawing back the crisped edges of the vest for better exposure. Fumes swirled with the auric residues of the attack, blurring her vision. She picked up her staff and used its tip to trace a safe-field:

"North to the pine,
West to the palm,
South to maytree,
East to bronzewood,

Sun and stars, moon and dew,
Be cleansed, be cleansed…"

The fumes dissipated with each ritual phrase, leaving a fading corona of green light—green for forest, green for healing. The dragon, relaxing, stretched at her side. The blue exudates shimmered, darkening to near black. Beneath it, the man's ribs moved softly.

Merren sighed in relief. The glancing blow had scorched skin and muscle without shattering internal structures. She touched the pulse point at his neck and felt his heart beat, slow by steady. No shock, then, but he might remain unconscious for hours, even days.

"I'll need my water pack and remedies," she said aloud, as much for herself as for the great beast. *Guard him well, O-Brother-Dragonkind. I shall return.*

Merren found her camp undisturbed, the serenity of her familiar trees like a wellspring of strength. She leaned against the ancient bronzewood that had been the focus of her meditations. Her heartbeat altered, coming into subtle harmony with the tree. Bronzewood was her own, the touchstone of her wizardry. Her staff was not a piece of dead wood, but a tangible link between her physical manifestation and her spiritual growth. She drew away from the tree, still restless.

Mother-of-Trees, why have You set this task on me? I never sought power or fame, hearthside or human companionship. All I asked was to learn Your children and their wisdom. And how do I even know this is a quest, an ordinary man alone and injured in a patch of weirding forest?

Merren closed her eyes, leaning her forehead once more against the bronzewood's solid comfort.

He is no ordinary man, not guarded by a dragon and reeking of sorcerous assault. It cannot be anything but a quest.

The dragon's cry reached her before the clearing was in sight, a brazen howl that rattled her bones. Merren felt the bronzewood staff quiver in resonance as she dropped her pack and plunged forward.

She was nearly thrown on her back as she entered the space between the deviant trees. The man still lay as she had left him, but the dragon was now a blur, whirling to attack—

Green... Not the color of life and growth, but the sickly hue of putrescence—a ball of livid light, it threw out tentacles that stank of evil. It whipped through the molten air, reaching past the dragon for the man. The dragon shrieked again and leapt to intercept the streamers. A tip of green touched its shoulder and disappeared in a shock of thunder. Merren's nostrils filled with the smell of sulfur and decay.

She had never battled sorcery before. As a natural wizard, Merren was pledged to harmony with all living things. Even the leather of her boots and belt came from animals that had died without violence. What had she to do with creatures of death and artifice?

And then she saw the trees, the alien-dreaming trees of the twisted grove. Their spirits dipped toward the green light, curious and...hungry.

"No! The Mother gave me guardianship of all trees when She took my oath! You too are my children, strange though you may be—and that thing shall not have you!"

Fire pulsed through her veins as she hurled herself toward the ball of green light. Fire met the answering throb from the bronzewood staff, catalyzing Merren's fury into a point of focused power. She swung her staff at the ball and felt the node of righteous anger arc out, clipping the glowing sphere.

Sparks burst from the green ball, fading into sulfurous ashes. Merren staggered under the impact, her shoulders arching in protest. A tentacle of deadly light whipped toward her. She raised the staff to deflect it as the dragon leapt to protect her.

The ball swerved, avoiding contact with the bronzewood.

Thunder boomed again as the dragon intercepted it and fell back to guard the man. The sphere began to rotate, throwing off sparks of poison-green light. The dragon cried out and jumped again, but the ball, spinning wildly now, evaded it easily.

Merren choked back her own sense of failure. She might swing at the sorcerous device, might even stun it with her bronzewood, but neither of them could destroy the thing now. It was too fast, too powerful for them. It feared the staff, true, but she could not get close enough to it, not by herself.

Together! Together now!

The dragon swung into action as if it were an extension of Merren's spirit and will. It swept alongside the ball, intercepting its path, diverting its attention…until the crucial moment when Merren leapt at the sphere and plunged the tip of her staff into its heart.

The thing died in silence, a faint, nauseating hiss through the auric fields and then hot ashes falling amid a horrendous stench. Merren dropped to her knees at the dragon's side, their brief partnership fading into calm. The trees leaned toward them, shaken into a semblance of awareness, strange but no longer alien.

Merren set up her camp in the little clearing while the dragon lay vigilant by the man's side. She sang to the trees as she worked, feeling them grow gentler under her care. The familiar chores helped dissipate the echoes of turmoil from her mind. She had not chosen this quest, it had been chosen for her. She had no time for anger now, nor any energy to waste on useless yearnings.

The man regained consciousness the next day, although his strength still seemed fragile. Merren nursed him with herbs and her own vegetable foods. The dragon disappeared into the forest from time to time, and she assumed it was hunting.

She called the man Ahr, the first letter of the mystical alphabet, because he had no memory of his own name. Nor could he recall why he was companioned by a dragon, or how he had fallen afoul of black enemies.

"You're clearly important," she insisted, keeping her eyes carefully from his. She found his intensely masculine energy disturbing. "Somebody wants you dead or captive, somebody very powerful."

Ahr nodded, sipping Merren's tisane. "I remember a little—the dragon fighting at my side. And a face, carved like a mask of gray ice. Black pits for eyes. As far as I know, I myself have no magic..."

"Mine does not deal with such things," Merren said. "You've described a rune-face, and there's no question of the source of your burn. If you're asking for advice on such matters, I can't give you any. I deal with living things and the natural order, not the obscenity that attacked you."

"I'm grateful for your help, tree-maid."

"Merren. My name is Merren."

"Merren, then. Perhaps my memories will return to me in time. I'll be well enough to travel in a few days. I can go south and seek work in Chi-y."

Merren thought of Ahr stumbling about the countryside, ignorant and unprepared. The dragon, catching her mental image, rumbled and lashed its tail in protest.

"No," she said, her voice breaking. "I can't let you do that. If I cannot help you myself, I must guide you to someone who can. You see, the dragon agrees with me."

"I won't permit you to risk yourself for me."

"Ahr." Merren laid one hand upon his shoulder. "Even with a dragon at your side, you cannot go blindly on your way. You are too vulnerable—"

"Then that is my own business. You need not involve yourself."

"I have already become involved by powers greater than either of us. I am not indifferent to you, I...must find my own way through this quest, just as you must. You've been placed in my care and I would not serve you with any less than my best."

"No prince could ask for greater," Ahr replied, smiling.

"You say that as if—"

"I were one? Who knows? I don't feel particularly princely, just aching sore."

"I'll change the poultice on your burn. You could be a monarch's son, you know, stripped of your memory and sent to wander. Our village bard sings of such things. That would explain the dragon."

"Yes, the dragon. I feel it bound to me as if by magic, yet you seem able to communicate with it much better than I."

Merren bent over Ahr's healing wound to hide her blush of pleasure.

Rauch, the Elder of Merren's clan site, looked at Ahr's hair and said, "This young one needs help. *Beware, O-Daughter-Spirit* No true magic is this wound, but sorcery born."

"I know that," Merren murmured, restless even in the familiar protection of the living shelters. "He ought to go to his own land-sage, but he has no memory of where he was born. The dragon serves him—that must mean something."

The old wizard stroked the feathery edge of his beard. "You've gotten yourself in a fine tangle here, meddling with artificial magic instead of sticking to your own trees. There's nothing we can do for him, and we can't send him to an ordinary charlatan. Much as I dislike the idea, you'll have to take him to Heävyth and see the Mage."

Merren stared at him. Outside, the dragon resonated with her emotions and rumbled a protest. Ahr asked, "What's the matter?"

"The Mage will never see me, Rauch! She has never had friendly dealings with us nor we with her. She abhors natural wizardry!"

Yet for Ahr's sake she will see thee. Whatever attacked him belongs to her realm of sorcery, not ours. I have heard of late that she wishes nothing greater than to fuse natural and synthetic magic. To do that, she needs one of us under her control. Were it not for the dragon, I would suspect a trap.

Merren nodded and withdrew from Rauch's shelter, bringing Ahr with her. Outside in the dappled sunlight, the younger clan children stared at them shyly, murmuring and pointing to Ahr's bright hair. Most of the adults and older children were hidden, more comfortable with their trees than with human strangers.

She cleared her throat. "I must go to my foster father's tree and visit my kin. I haven't seen them since I began my journey-man's foresting, nor have I sat in the Motherhall. You and the dragon will be comfortable enough at the questing house while supplies are gathered and forest ponies caught for us."

"We're going to Heävyth, then. Do you think it holds the key --?"

"To your past? Perhaps one who lives there does, if she will tell us. The Mage...Elyng."

He looked at her, capturing her with the intensity of his eyes. "You don't approve?"

"There are old quarrels between the trees and the Mage."

Ahr nodded, respecting her reluctance to give further details. "Heävyth. How long a journey?"

"On foot, ten days. Less, of course, with the ponies. Rauch will also see that we have food and a few coins for the city. With any luck we won't be there long..." She paused, frowning. "But we cannot take the dragon. Here at the clan site, he's a wonder to the children and we have no need of secrecy. Once on the road, or in the city...we could draw no greater attention to ourselves."

"And you think we need to stay hidden?"

"What do you think? You've had your name, your past, your purpose ripped from you by some unspeakable sorcerer who found you even in the depths of the forest! Do you think he's going to let you march up to Elyng's door without another attempt? Until we find out who you are and why he wants to destroy you, we dare not risk it."

"I—I cannot leave him. Any more than he could leave me."

Merren heard the ring of truth in Ahr's stammer and lowered her eyes, saying nothing.

They saddled the restive, newly caught forest ponies at dawn, fingers clumsy with cold on the complicated knots. Merren had not ridden in years and Ahr, although he sat his mount with assurance, was unfamiliar with the gear. Rauch and the others of the village had given their road blessings the night before. They rode easily for the first few days, letting their muscles become accustomed to the stresses of riding hour after hour.

"I haven't seen the dragon," Merren said. They sat by the ashes of their small cook fire at the edge of the thinning forest.

"Not since yesterday, no." Ahr touched the amber at his throat. "I can't understand—I suppose I took it for granted, thought it would be with me all along."

"Not like me."

He smiled, looking up. "You I couldn't drive away, but I don't—hold you in the same way. Merren, I would not take you from your forest unwilling."

"I'm not unwilling."

"So you said before. Your words say one thing and your spirit another. No, Merren, look at me. Whoever I am, you must do this for me, not my name or title. I may be the Lost Son of Chi-y that your village bard sang of. It may be my father who battles at the Last Door, holding the shreds of life lest the land pass leaderless into chaos. Or I may be none of these things. I would have a deeper bond with you than mere speculation."

"I serve the Mother in all things. Her roots are my roots, Her sap my heart's blood. Whom do you serve, Ahr of no name?"

"I do not know what gods I used to call upon. By my will, I am now of the Light."

215

"We cannot face the Mage with any division in our hearts. I've held you from me, true, because I did not seek this quest. If I have been harsh or unkind, I ask your pardon. I would not leave Her groves for any man's name or rank, but—" she cupped his chin in one hand so that his eyes met hers, "—I would be your friend and ally for your own sake."

"Does your wizardry bind you to celibacy also?" He laid his hands over hers, surrounding her with warmth.

"No." She smiled. "Nothing that partakes of joy and life is foreign to my craft. And it has been a long time since I had a lover to warm my bed."

———·✦·———

They rode south as they passed through the placid farmland surrounding Heävyth, the forest ponies growing fatter and less wild. Merren felt uneasy in the open spaces with their few trees fettered, almost comatose. Even the lush hedgerows were mute and docile. As they went on, Ahr grew more confident, as if his identity were returning with the change of countryside and the healing of his wound.

Merren could not be sure exactly when she knew they were being followed; the subtle clues, a twist of shadow just beyond her sight, a tugging at her inner senses, all gnawed at her. She could not detect any threat, nor did she ever see any actual physical evidence of their trailer. She set her wards at night, as usual, and the only intruders were natural vermin, harmless and easily deflected. She did not speak of it to Ahr, to add to his fears when they stood before the Mage.

———·✦·———

Heävyth at last. The city assaulted Merren's senses, acrid stone dust clawing at her throat. She stood in the marketplace just inside the heavy gates, feeling like a child ripped from her homeland forests. *Mother-of-Trees, be with me now!*

216

"A room, a bath, and then to our mission." Ahr's voice was buoyant.

"No, first we go to the Mage. That's her tower, there on the white hill."

"We can't present ourselves to her covered in trail dirt," he protested.

Merren smiled. Her worn clothing and gear smelled healthy and familiar against the odors of the city. "We are not seeking her approval, to come before her ornamented and perfumed. The day is yet young, our strength good and purpose firm. Why should we wait and give her extra time to plan a counterattack?"

"I thought we were asking for her help."

"Ahr. Listen carefully, for both our sakes. There is no path for you that is not laced with peril, certainly not the road to Elyng's door. If she gives us aid, it will be for reasons of her own, not from fascination with your bright hair. She may tell us true, or lie to us. Or she may refuse to listen and attack me as her enemy. We must not bend our wills in a vain effort to please her before we have even tested her temper."

"Merren." And she felt her heart move at the sound of her name. "You risk that danger for my sake, and I am blundering fool in your care. I don't know that I deserve—"

"The dragon thought so."

"Dragons can be bound," he replied.

"You take much upon yourself, dryad," Elyng hissed. Her long black hair gleamed next to her pale skin. Pale skin, pale eyes, shining against the pale stone of the tower's highest chamber.

"I do not come for myself, Domina," Merren answered politely. She held her bronzewood staff in both hands so that it did not rest upon the cold floor. "I ask you to set aside our old differences and look upon me only as a neutral agent. Wrong has been done this man, wrong by sorcery. Unless you have turned from the Light…"

Elyng hissed again, tossing her head in a river of jet.

"…you cannot let it go unrighted, not such evil perpetrated by one of your own."

"You are so righteous, you tree-people, always telling others what to do, always thinking you have the right of it! Why should I believe you? Why should I not drain your essence right now and discard the husk?"

"Because," Merren said steadily, "I bear the Mother's blessing, and am no trifling plaything. Nor would you say these things to me if I were."

"This cannot go on," Ahr interrupted. He stepped forward, facing the Mage, dwarfing her slender height. "The tree-wizard does not ask this of you. I do. If she has put herself in jeopardy, it is for my sake. I must be the one to bear the risk."

"You?" Elyng moved toward him, her hips swaying under the folds of her silken gown. "And who are you to say such things to the Mage of Heävyth?"

"I do not know who I am. That is why I stand here before you."

The Mage touched his face with one pale finger, her eyes on his golden hair. She reached for the amber that hung at his neck, then drew her hand back as Ahr reflexively avoided her touch.

"But I do know who you are, or I can find out easily enough. You say it is your affair, not the dryad's. Very well, what will *you* give me for this knowledge?"

Ahr paused, confused for the first time. "I have nothing of any value to offer you."

"Nothing?" She sweetened her voice. "You have the amber."

"No!" Merren thrust her staff forward like a weapon. "You must not—"

"Silence, dryad! He has renounced your aid! The choice must be his!"

"He doesn't know what it means!" Merren retorted. "An unfair bargain, without knowledge of its worth!"

Elyng smiled, her lips curving in a poisonous arch. "Fairness and justice are two different things. Which do you seek, O man of no name?"

"I seek what is mine by right."

"No matter what the cost?" The Mage's eyes glittered in the tower's gray light.

"I do not know what you offer. Would you tempt me from the Light for the sake of a kingdom not justly mine?"

Elyng threw her head back and laughed. "Well said, stranger. Keep your dragon-amber for now. I shall give you your name and the price I ask. You can judge for yourself whether it is worth the cost. Your father named you Dyveth."

Ahr gasped, trembling suddenly. His face washed ashen.

"And the price?" Merren demanded, watching the smile on the Mage's lips.

"A night with me. A small price for such a lusty lad."

Ahr shook his head as if to clear his senses. "Dyveth. I am Dyveth of Chi-y. She does not lie, Merren. I know not what has happened since my abduction, but Chi-y is mine on my father's death."

"To find out you are a king's son and heir to a great realm," purred Elyng, "is that not worth a small moment of pleasure for a lonely woman? A little companionship for a single night?"

Dyveth looked toward Merren, who kept her eyes carefully shielded and said nothing. "I am not free to do so, nor do I trust your motives."

"Is the dryad your mistress to chain you to her laces? But she is of no account, and a man need not be scrupulous about such things."

"But a king must be," Dyveth declared. "Truth for truth, loyalty for loyalty. It is the only way."

Elyng raised both arms above her head, her loose sleeves billowing like a daemon cloak. "You have had your chance, king's-son. Now I will take *mine!*"

The room filled with pungent smoke, and flames lapped at the walls. Merren drew Dyveth to her side and thrust her staff aloft.

"North to the pine! South to the palm!" Dew, sweet and cool, wet her skin. The fires hissed as they died.

The Mage's howl of anger distorted into an inhuman shriek. Her body began to elongate, her nails and teeth glowing metallic in the darkening room. The shadowy bulk loomed over them, bloated and reptilian.

Merren shouted again and pointed her staff at the transforming sorceress. "South to maytree! East to bronzewood!"

With a clap of silver sound, the staff was torn from Merren's grasp. She went spinning to the floor. Her sight cleared to show Dyveth kneeling above her, his face flushed. Her knees were two bonfires of pain where she had fallen on them. "Don't risk yourself, prince. Not for my sake."

"No." He straightened up to face the Mage, his hand closing on the amber token. The golden gem flashed, sun-blinding Merren's eyes as Dyveth cried aloud, "Dragon, come!"

The dragon bounded from dimensionless space just as the creature that had been Elyng reached talons toward Merren's heart. It roared, shouldering the attack aside. Blue flames replaced the red ones. The dragon swiped at the Mage with one massive paw, and suddenly the room lay silent.

Merren coughed as she rose, clearing the lingering smell from her lungs. Gladness rose in her as she beheld the dragon, shimmering in strata of iridescent splendor. It had followed them, faithful even in its invisibility, and on the trail had sensed its shadowy presence. The bundle between its forefeet stirred, moaning.

"Elyng..." Merren touched the hair, now dull brown instead of jet, sweeping it back from the Mage's pale face. The sorceress curled into Merren's arms, sobbing weakly.

Dyveth touched Merren's shoulder. "Don't trust her tears."

"No, they're real enough. If there had been more contact between her and my clan I would have realized at once. But as it was, I could only suspect. I didn't think she had voluntarily forsaken the Light. See, the dragon has broken the geas upon her; its ancient power runs deeper than magic."

"You mean she was being controlled by another, that she did not attack us of her own free will?"

"I think that when we discover who, we will also find your enemy. Elyng, open your eyes. Look at me."

The Mage stirred, responding like a child to Merren's words. Her eyes were faded blue, her face soft and bewildered. She no longer wore silvery silk, but plain gray wool, tied with a knotted belt of her own hair. There were no traces left of the polished siren, only a pale-skinned, youngish woman with unkempt hair.

She whispered, "The tree-maid...and the dragon." There was no fear in her as she looked at the great beast, only wonder and bone-deep fatigue. "Then it was not all a dream..."

"Would that it had been," Merren said, helping her to sit upright. "What do you remember?"

A spasm contorted the Mage's face. She hid her face in her hands, her unbound hair falling forward like a tangled curtain.

Merren seized her by both shoulders and said sternly, "Then you owe us, Elyng of Heävyth, you owe us dearly for your unlawful assault. You have been an instrument—"

"I know! The stars above bear witness that I know!"

"I demand payment now! Who did this thing?"

"I dare not tell you—it would bring doom crashing down on all of us!" The Mage threw her head back, white ringing her eyes, but she could not tear free from Merren's hold.

"The name, Elyng! The name—or shall I have the dragon rip it from you?"

"Merren, you are so harsh with her," Dyveth said. "If she did this thing against her will—"

Elyng shook her head. "No, the tree-maid has the right of it. The only way I can redeem myself is by undoing the wrong I have aided. Evil does not come into our lives unasked; the weakness is mine and I must bear the payment for it." She turned, trembling, to look Dyveth in the face. "Your enemy is Zyborn."

"Zyborn Rainbow-hand!" Dyveth exclaimed. "He has always lusted for power, true, but my father banished him from Chi-y after the magician Cathlamet discovered him dabbling in the darker arts."

"He has mastered those arts and is Zyborn Black-hand now," said Elyng, getting slowly to her feet. "As I have discovered to my sorrow. A wily one he, full of false words and broken promises."

"And my father? And Cathlamet?"

"I do not know. Were your father dead, the loyal Cathlamet would hold Chi-y in regency for you. He would not betray you with a futile search, for he knows that if the dragon cannot defend you, then surely no mere mortal can."

"I remember. It was Cathlamet who bound the dragon-amber to me. He must have guessed—"

Merren silenced him. "The dragon's power protects you now, and that is enough. We must go to Zyborn and end his menace without delay. He will seek new allies, perhaps ones even our combined strength cannot withstand. When you summoned the dragon and freed Elyng, we lost any hope of secrecy. Best to finish the thing quickly."

"I don't know where he is," said Dyveth. "After he fled Chi-y, he could have gone anywhere."

The Mage said, "He is here in Heävyth. The black onyx palace on the Amorath Hills just south of the river. It was the home of a rich man once, with gardens all around and many servants. Now it's a shell of stone, beautiful but sterile. They say that even the bronzewood house-tree in the courtyard is dead."

She paused as Merren cried aloud. "I would go with you, if you will have me. My powers may be somewhat diminished, but Zyborn will not take me lightly again."

Dyveth said, "Should we trust her?"

Elyng had drawn herself up in simple dignity and patted her hair back from her face. Merren realized that the Mage was not much older than she, a slight woman with traces of prettiness and fever-bright eyes. She remembered Rauch's warning and said, "You have not shown us any great friendship…"

"I will swear by your staff!"

Merren touched Elyng's forehead with the tip of the bronze-wood staff and felt the quiet pulse of clean power. She nodded as Elyng whispered, "I was not long under Zyborn's influence."

"Have we any hope of defeating him?" Dyveth asked.

The Mage replied, "If would not, not alone, But remember this, king's-son. It takes greater strength to conquer with mercy, as you and the tree-maid have shown me, than to destroy utterly. And Zyborn would not lust after dragon-amber so fiercely if it did not have the power to defeat him."

They are alike, these two, prince of one city and mage of another. I belong with my trees, not in even the finest palace. It is one thing to share my bed with Ahr the nameless wanderer, and quite another with Dyveth King's-son. Merren suppressed a sigh, feeling small and cold in the belly of the stone tower with no green anywhere, no earthy tang of life singing in her bones.

The dragon rumbled, its voice laced with heartsick yearning. Merren touched the fiery hide of the creature and felt it tremble. It had sensed her own homesickness for the forest and responded with its own profound longing. She could feel its memory of wild icy mountains, crystalline air, and freedom.

Elyng brought food and drink for them, fish cured with peppers, deer-tongues in aspic, and a cold casserole of tubers and mushrooms. Dyveth downed it all with relish, even the sour fruit wine, but Merren would not touch the flesh dishes and drank only water.

"You have scruples about such things, tree-maid," the Mage observed. "Does your discipline prevent you from enjoying other good things the world has to offer?"

"None so good as what I gain by it. No one who dines on the misery of other creatures can hear the rapture of the trees."

"Or you the sighing of the spheres. A truce, then, for a common cause cannot heal our differences so easily," said Elyng.

Dyveth added, "I have never heard of either—"

The sudden, choking darkness ate the last of his words. Merren, her vision blurring under the impact, grabbed her staff and felt the pulse of heat within it. Her eyes steadied enough to make out Elyng huddled on her knees and the dragon in one corner, its eyes gleaming palely in a well of velvet black.

Heat and ice ran together in lightning flashes down the stone walls, filling Merren's nostrils with the smell of ozone and something unnamable, far less clean. Above them, in the exact architectural center of the tower, simmered a ghostly parody of a human face. Flat silver were its cheeks, fleshless lips curling in a sneer, its eyes smoldering green fire. Merren recognized the deathly hue of the ball of light that she had battled in the weirding grove.

Dyveth scrambled to his feet and stood, legs wide apart for balance, fists raised. His words came tight and ragged, as if torn from his throat. "Black-hand! Zyborn Black-hand! This time you have met your match!"

The metallic grin widened further, eyes narrowing into slits of amusement as Dyveth, maddened, leapt for the image. His hands passed through it and he fell heavily, his breath coming in a sob. The dragon swept to his side.

Elyng looked up, her face ashen behind her twisted hair, and cried. "it's his rune-face! You can't touch him."

"Then none of his essence is here?" Merren asked.

The Mage shook her head.

"Can he be brought here?" Merren asked, gesturing with her staff to the leering visage. "Focused in that?"

"I—I think so. Anyone of master rank can use a projection as an anchor for far-traveling. You do not mean to lure him to us?"

"Shall I let him stay safe in his palace while he toys with us, until fatigue or luck finish the battle? He tried that once, but he will not get a third chance," Merren said. "We will drive him to us with magic his death-sorcery cannot withstand, and then we will be able to deal with him."

The lightning, now glowing silver and green, sparked from

the walls, lashing out at the three humans. As they drew into the center, Elyng began a protective chant. Merren watched her, sensing the pattern of the Mage's craft. It was not so unlike her own, except that it drew power from changes and differences, not harmonies as did natural wizardry.

"Elyng…Domina, do you know the art of parallels?"

"Parallels? We do not use that word. Ach! That bolt was close. I do not know how long my barrier can hold."

"As above, so it is below. As in summer, mirrored in winter…"

"Yes, I can partner you in that. Do you need me as anchor here or—"

"As it is here, so be it there? In the courtyard of the onyx palace…facing the house-tree."

Elyng nodded, her expression grim.

Merren held her staff before her like a sword. The bolts of greenish light were coming even closer now, sparking off the edges of the Mage's safe-field. She could feel the walls of protective power shudder and knew they would crumple under a determined attack. It did not matter, for they would buy her the time she needed.

"Dyveth, get between us. Elyng and I are going to—to work some magic together. Do not look at the rune-face; the more successful our counterattack, the more threatening it will seem. Keep your temper under rein and trust in the dragon." She felt rather than saw his nod of agreement.

The bronzewood between Merren's fingers pulsated as she focused her concentration upon it like lens. She felt the vibrations as a choir of voices, wordless and blending like branches in sunlight, like running water. Interwoven in that harmony came a light tinkling of bells, as delicate as birdsong or the petals of a solitary wildflower. The Mage made a formidable ally, with the power of such control.

A deeper rhythm joined them, a beat like the planet herself, forcing the two humans down, down into their roots. The dragon's hide rippled, wave after iridescent wave.

Even as Elyng freed them from the dissolving safe-field, the earth beneath the tower reached up to them, cradling their spirits through the stone. The echoes of Elyng's song told Merren that a similar process was happening in the onyx palace on the Amorath Hills, living joy as an antidote to the searing green poison of Zyborn's art.

Merren remembered then, remembered the chant begun during her brief battle with Zyborn-in-Elyng, and not yet completed. She had called to her the four dimensions of the forest, had gathered their energies but had not yet released them.

North, pine… West, palm… South, maytree… East to bronzewood, east to my own!

The dormant spirit of the massive house-tree at the Amorath palace stirred in response.

Stamp! Merren brought the staff down on the pale stone floor. "Sun and stars!"

The rune-face howled in agony. Dyveth cried out and pointed to it, where a single bead of white light shone in the twisting green of the mask. It glowed, hotter and fiercer, a spear point of fire to ignite the coolest forest, to singe metal and vaporize living flesh.

The dragon shrieked, but Merren heard its battle cry only as deepening of its song, the bass rhythm now surging into exultation. The white beam tore through the last traces of Elyng's safe-field, but Merren smiled as she lifted her staff again. "Moon and dew!"

Bronzewood touched stone, stone linked to earth and the seed of life. Merren's inner eye captured the myriad tendrils of healthy green as they enveloped the mage-tower. The white beam crackled into a shower of stars. In the distant onyx courtyard, the aged house-tree burst into bloom.

"Be healed! Be healed!"

The scent of flowers filled the air, wild and heady. The rune-face wavered, failing. When it touched the stone floor it disappeared, leaving the shrunken husk of an elderly man robed in green. He lifted his ravaged face toward them, lips drawing back from yellowed teeth, and muttered, "Never!" He looked toward to dragon with avarice and loathing as the forest power stripped the evil from him. Then he collapsed in on himself until only a tracery of dust and tattered cloth remained.

The three-fold song in Merren's heart faded as her vision cleared. New green adorned every crack and seam of the stone tower. Dyveth, breathing heavily, went over to the pile of ash and prodded it with one boot. Elyng clasped her hands before her, laughing.

The dragon curled in on itself, dead black, a well of sadness.

"I will not go with you to Chi-y, Dyveth King's-son," Merren repeated. "You speak from the gratitude of the moment, not from sense or rightness. Once back in your city, you would find me was strange as lost as you were in my forest. You are not longer my woodsman lover Ahr, nor could I abandon my trees to be your court lady. If you seek an ally in magic, look to the fair Mage…"

Elyng, sitting across from them, her hair dressed with moonstones and turquoise, bit into another grape and smiled. "You are as generous as ever, tree-maid. But I have much to do in my own tower. You've left me with a formidable housekeeping task, tending all that green."

Dyveth said, "You ought to claim a reward. It's not fair to leave us with that kind of debt." He reached down absently to stroke the dragon's hide. The beast, its eyes almost lifeless, did not respond.

"I have already said I want nothing," Merren said wearily. The rapidly burgeoning green of Elyng's tower only intensified her longing for her trees. "Domina, you have given us the grace of your good will; there is no greater gift I can return to my village."

"But for yourself, Merren, for all we've been through together," Dyveth protested. He shook his head in the soft morning sunlight, the gold of his hair like a nature-given crown. "Please. Let me give you something."

She met his eyes for a moment, measuring, and then dropped her gaze to the dragon. *He won't accept my answer. He wants to tie me to his memory with gifts of gold or gems, like the dragon-amber.* She found her voice: "Release the dragon."

"What?" Dyveth said, and Elyng's head shot up.

"The dragon. Its freedom. That's what I ask for."

"But I can't. Cathlamet promised there was no way it could leave me as long as I held the amber. It is bound to me."

"As was I, by the will of the Mother. Your magician captured its spirit within the amber. Zyborn knew it, and wanted control of the dragon as much as he wanted your death. With his destruction, you no longer need the dragon's protection, or mine. Return to amber to its source, and we shall both go free…or are you, prince, no more than a pale shade of Zyborn's tyranny?"

"No, I…" he began, visibly shaken. "I would be just with you, Merren, and honorable. I would have you remember me as a man and not a figurehead." He fumbled at his throat for the silver clasp.

The dragon, which had been lying like a lump of carbon at his side, sprang to its feet, vestigial wings spread wide and flaming like a cascade of rainbows. Dyveth laughed and tossed the amber into the air. The dragon, singing, leapt to meet it, and Merren knew that not for worlds of glory would she have missed that moment of elemental joy.

O-Brother-Dragonkind!

The Casket of Brass

A breathless spring twilight crept across the palace on the hill. Even the twin rivers that nourished Kharazand, City of a Thousand Gardens, flowed gently, imbued with an eerie, somber calm. The twin domes of the royal palace glimmered in shades of pearl and silver.

Hoof beats fractured the approaching night. Iron sparked on paving stones. Five riders, one fleet and light, raced from the city gates toward the palace. The leading horse shone like marble, its tail a river of cloud. Its rider was small and wiry beneath a flowing hooded cloak. Four stouter animals followed, lathered, their breathing hoarse. They pounded up the tree-lined avenue beside the long, slender mirrored pools. Guards barred their path, scimitars drawn. At the sight of the lead rider, they bowed and stepped back.

The riders clattered to a halt before the formal entrance to the palace, spiral columns framing marble stairs. Gravel scattered under the hooves of the horses. The lead rider jumped lightly to the ground. Grooms and servants, a dozen at least, rushed forward. The rider shoved back the hood of the cloak, revealing a woman's delicate features, tilted eyes beneath sweeping brows set in honey-gold skin. Her blue-black hair had been twisted back into a simple knot, and over her riding trousers, she wore a scholar's robe of thick undyed cotton. Her sole weapon was a dagger in a leather sheath at her belt.

She handed the reins of the gray horse to the most senior of the grooms. "Give him a little water now, only a few sips." Her voice was throaty with the strain of a long, exhausting ride. "Then see to it yourself that he's walked until he's dry."

She glanced back at the other riders. "Malik, go with them. Make sure all the horses are cared for. On your head be it if one of them founders."

"It shall be done." The captain of the escort swung down, shifting his own cloak away from the scimitar at his hip.

The young woman rushed up the stairs, the other guards at her heels. Her riding boots rang on the smooth stone of the stairs. She burst through the elaborately-carved double doors before the attendants could open them for her. A senior steward rushed forward, trailing a handful of assistants. She remembered him, an honest man who had perhaps not risen as high as his merit and industry deserved. In the years of her absence, his beard had gone white and wispy, and the body beneath the modestly ornamented robe was gaunt with age.

"Lady—"

"My grandmother?" she cut him off, not slacking her pace.

The steward raised his hands in reassurance. "Still alive, by the grace of the Infinite. Her physician tends her even now. I can say no more. Your uncle, the Most Wise Regent, has been apprised of your return and has bidden me to—"

His voice faltered as she glared at him. A high flush swept her cheeks and her skin glowed with the exertion of her hard ride and her present emotional state.

"—to bring you to him," the steward finished uncertainly. "If it is your pleasure."

"It is my pleasure," she repeated the phrase, but without any malice, for the steward could not be blamed for the situation or her own temper, "to see my grandmother while I still can."

The steward's reply was cut short by the arrival of a second young woman, this one nobly dressed in a sleeveless vest, encrusted with pearls and rubies, and loose trousers of crimson silk gathered around her delicate ankles. Strings of tiny silver bells chimed from her wrists and earlobes. Veils fluttered from the elaborate curls on top of her head. She did not so much walk as glide along the carpeted hall; half a dozen ladies, dressed in more subdued colors, followed a pace behind.

"Maridah!" the young woman exclaimed. "You've returned! So suddenly! And without sending word so that a proper reception might be prepared for you!"

Maridah forced herself to stand still long enough to greet her cousin with reasonable courtesy. They bowed and kissed each another's palms, according to custom.

"Hadidjah, I am pleased to see you," Maridah said, "but I cannot linger. Grandmother—"

Hadidjah's eyes, a beautiful hazel that contrasted with her golden skin, betrayed no alarm. "She is not well, that much is true, but her health has never been good since you left us for Samarkhand. You need not have interrupted your studies to rush home."

She touched Maridah's cheek with one hand. Her fingertips were soft, uncallused, scented with rosewater and cloves. "I cannot say I am sorry. How I have missed you! Come now, you must bathe and put on something decent. Then I will take you to my father so that he may set your mind at rest. Tomorrow, we will feast in your honor."

Maridah wavered on her feet. Her muscles ached and her stomach had long since hardened into a knot of hunger. She saw herself reflected in her cousin's eyes, unkempt and filthy. Doubtless, she smelled of horse and sweat. She could not possibly appear in court with her hair in such disarray, wearing the same shapeless robe of the most lowly student.

She shook her head to clear her senses. Had her year of study, in a community where ideas meant more than titles or wealth, come to so little, that she would throw it all away at a word? She would remain as she was, dirty boots and all.

"I am happy you are not unduly concerned about Grandmother's health," she said with perhaps more harshness than she intended, for Grandmother's own physician had written of the sudden decline in her condition, "but I will not rest until I see her for myself." Effortlessly freeing herself from her cousin's grasp, she pivoted to go.

"But—but my father—" Hadidjah stammered. "He expects to see you!"

A sudden glint of mischief caught Maridah. Unfastening the clasp of her riding cloak, she tossed it to her cousin. "My uncle will have to be satisfied with *that.*"

She did not stay to see Hadidjah's expression.

As Maridah hurried toward the long wing of royal family apartments, the pearly radiance of the twilight thickened into shadow. An archway brought her to an interior corridor. The scents of sandalwood and patchouli swept away the last hint of roses. The corridor was covered with carpets in dark, intricate designs, arabesques of intertwined vines and stylized birds with reaching wings. Her escort, who had been her mother's sworn men before they became her own, followed her like sight-hounds, lean and wary. Palace attendants with caps of blue and white bowed as they passed.

Her grandmother's chambers were the oldest in the wing. In entering them, Maridah always had the sense of moving from one world to another, penetrating into the heart of some mystery. The outer room was ordinary enough, with low benches for outdoor shoes. The act of removing her boots, with all the dirt of the trail, and pulling on the slippers of soft leather stitched in silk threads with designs of phoenixes locked in combat with winged serpents, was part of the process of leaving the outer world behind and entering into an enchanted realm.

The inner wall had been painted as a forest, a profusion of branches and greenery. Between leafy clusters, birds nested and animals, some familiar and others strange, like miniature imps, peeked out. The artist had rendered the mural with imagination, so that the tiny blue demons were as lifelike and charged with energy as the hunting falcon or the cowering hare.

Beyond the forest wall, through the door of carved ebony, the noises of the rest of the palace fell away. The sitting room resembled a garden, with rows of flowering jasmine and star-blossoms in brass planters and a central fountain of white and pink marble, carved in the shape of winged fishes and river peris smiling as they plucked their harps. In the day, light streamed through the windows, teardrop-shaped panes of clear glass. Now, the room was filled with the same fading, silvery-pearl luminescence as the outer grounds.

From the garden room, doors led to either side, presenting a choice between the scented darkness of Grandmother's personal chambers or the even more enchanting discoveries of her workroom. Grandmother's favorite attendant hovered, hands clasped, outside the intimate quarters. Her intertwined fingers looked like knobby tree roots. Maridah felt a pang that her grandmother's magic had waned so much that she could no longer heal her trusted friend. The old nurse's face lit as she saw Maridah, then darkened into a scowl at her escort.

"Come, child," she tugged at Maridah's sleeve, pulling her inside. The escort remained as they were.

Entering Grandmother's bedroom was like plunging into a cavern. There were no windows. Once Maridah had asked Grandmother about it and the old woman had laughed and said there was more than enough light in the garden room.

Now Maridah paused as the door swung shut behind her. Candles had been lit, a row of flickering brilliance. The royal physician, an elderly Persian who had always been kind to Maridah, and his daughter-apprentice hovered over the bed.

The daughter straightened up as Maridah stepped into the room. Maridah drew in a breath and caught a riot of odors, the smells of medicines and herbs, the smoky tinge of candle wax, the sandalwood that always clung to her grandmother's clothing. And woven in there somewhere, the metallic scent that she always associated with her grandmother's magic.

Light fell across the physician's face as he came forward and bent to kiss Maridah's palm. The wispy hairs of his beard tickled her skin. He lifted his eyes, bright with age and unspilled grief. "By the grace of the Infinite, you have come in time."

In time. Maridah dared to breathe. "How does she?"

"Leave us," the voice coming from the bed was almost a croak. Maridah hardly recognized it.

"But only for a moment," the physician warned.

Grandmother's face gleamed like old cracked ivory in the light of the candles. The room seemed unnaturally still. Then Maridah realized there was no music. Her grandmother always had at least one musician about her. She loved the soft sounds of the *oud* and flute.

"My friend." A hand, spidery in the flickering light, reached out. The physician grasped it. "There is nothing more you can do…for me."

The old man bent his head, kissed her palm, and departed. His daughter followed, a shadow with watchful eyes. The door swung shut.

Maridah went to the bedside, knelt and took her grandmother's hand. The skin felt cool and brittle, the nails had never seemed so hard. Maridah's breath caught in her throat like a sob.

In the back of her mind, a question curled like a wisp of poisoned smoke. *When she dies, I will become Princess of Kharazand.*

"And you," came the whispering voice. "You, I will miss most of all."

"No, it's too soon. Can't you use your enchantments to save your own life?"

Grandmother turned on her pillow so that the light filled all the deep hollows of her skull. "I have." Pause, breath.

Maridah's stomach turned cold.

No.

"Remember. Everything."

"I will."

The long sunlit afternoons, playing in the workroom, handling the things that even then she knew were not toys, the wonderful carved horses that would, at the turn of a peg near the saddle, rise into the air, carrying their soldier riders, the balls that gave off colored lights as they spun, the bird of silver, the dagger that would cry out if anyone but Grandmother touched its jeweled sheath…

"In the stronghold. A casket. Of brass."

Maridah nodded. She had caught a glimpse of it, as long as a child's forearm and half again as wide, the worn patterns glimmering in the shadows. Something about the box had drawn her, as if there were a hidden message woven in pattern of intertwining arabesques like some secret calligraphy.

"Shall I bring it to you?" she asked.

"Safe. Guard."

Something in the way the room settled into a different still-ness shook Maridah from her helpless grief. She felt a tenseness in the air, an expectancy, as if the quality of light had shifted. Grandmother was asking her to do something more than simply keep the old box in a safe place. There was an almost holy quiet in the room like the temple at dawn the morning her mother, who was to have been the next Princess, had died. Maridah had been up all night, fasting and praying, willing to bargain away anything she owned if only her mother might recover. She'd been at the very extremity of hope, for Grandmother had not returned from a long trip East and all the court physicians had said there was nothing more to be done.

And the air had shifted, even as it shifted now, with a welling pressure, an imminence… Whatever was said or done now carri-ed weight beyond mere deeds.

"It will be kept safe. I swear it." Maridah didn't know exactly what she was promising, but she spoke the words like a vow.

"Ah." Thin fingers brushed across the back of Maridah's hands. A sigh like a whisper. "Then I have taught you well."

Maridah opened her mouth to ask what it was that Grand-mother had taught her but the air shifted once more, a lighten-ing of that immense weight. The candle light wavered.

Voices broke in upon the stillness, men arguing at the outer door. Maridah recognized the old physician and her own escort, their voices in protest.

"Stand aside!" another man shouted.

Then came her uncle's voice, lower, calm. She could not make out the words. Her heart leapt in her throat. Her fingers closed around the hilt of her dagger.

"Mari—" Grandmother roused. Brittle fire flared behind her words. "Leave the box. Take what lies within. It must not fall into any other hands but yours. Do you understand?"

"I—I think I do. You mean, the contents are for the Princess alone."

A mute gesture of denial. "What lies within *makes* the Princess. Yussuf searched—when your mother died. He will search again."

My uncle wants the throne? Maridah could not think straight. How could he aspire to such power? Even if he were not a man, he had no royal lineage; his only claim was his marriage to Maridah's mother's younger sister.

"Not for himself," Grandmother gasped.

Maridah could not breathe. *Hadidjah, who could claim rightful lineage by blood. Hadidjah, who had always done her father's bidding.*

"Go. Go quickly. The door behind the ironwood screen. You know the one?"

The shouting intensified. Maridah could not hear the clash of steel, but she sensed the hot reek of adrenalin. She could not leave a sick old woman—

"What can he do to me?" Grandmother whispered.

Maridah brushed her lips over her grandmother's forehead. The skin was dry, like dusty silk. Then, under the lash of a terror she had never felt before, she raced from the bedchamber.

The workroom was filled with shelves of scrolls, bound books, bottles of alchemical reagents, wax blocks of different colors and bars of sealing lead, bins of powdered dragon's bone and whale horn, jars of pickled zoological specimens, telescopes and proximiscopes in their wooden holders, astrolabes and cathagaronemeters.

The stronghold itself was no more than a cavity in the inner wall, covered over with a plain wooden panel. Maridah felt a faint prickle as she touched the panel and her fingertips found the indentation. She held it fast, as Grandmother had taught her. It took no magic to open the panel, only a steady hand. A thief would draw back at the shock and then burst into flames.

The prickling subsided. Maridah pushed the panel aside and reached inside. Her fingers closed around something long and cylindrical, then another. She took them out and laid them on the floor, two scrolls wrapped in heavy silk. Then came a small carved box, apparently a solid piece of rosy quartz. She could detect neither hinge nor lid. This too she laid aside.

The brass casket was about two hands'-span long and half again as wide, its edges sealed with a ribbon of lead. On one side, the lead widened into a circle on which was impressed a seal. The faint coppery tang of Grandmother's enchantments clung to it.

Within the casket, each in a separate velvet-lined compartment, lay the wonderful things she knew so well—the ball of flashing jewels, the top that never stopped spinning until commanded, the horse on wheels that would shake its tail.

The horse's wooden body had gone velvety with age. The tail had been made from real horse hairs, black and gray, and for some reason the black hairs had broken off near the base so that only a few long gray ones remained. Maridah whispered the rhyme that went with the horse, the one Grandmother had made her learn by heart:

I will carry you
Wherever you truly wish to go,
To master me, you must first master your heart.

Maridah slipped the horse and the ball into a pocket of her scholar's robe, beside the folded paper for taking notes, a wrapped length of charcoal, two handkerchiefs, and a flint. The other pocket, equally capacious, held a few coins, a single dried fig, a little folding knife, and a leather billfold containing a needle and several lengths of silk thread.

Smiling at her scholarly provisions, she turned her attention to the top. It was painted in a harlequin pattern of yellow and blue, each diamond shape outlined in black. It felt warm under her touch, hummed slightly as if urging her to pick it up.

Underneath the top, she found a wand of yellowed ivory about twice the length of her hand. Delicate carvings curled like vines around it, but otherwise it looked quite ordinary.

When she reached for the wand, sparks erupted from both ends. Fire lanced up her fingers, sending the muscles of her arm into spasm. Her hand jerked away of its own accord. Sweating and gulping air, she wrapped it in her second-best handkerchief and slid it and the top in the other pocket.

The voices came again, accompanied by crashing sounds. Cursing the impulse that had caused her to linger, Maridah searched for the ironwood screen. She found it, deep in the shadows, leaning against one wall. She tilted it aside to discover a door, even as Grandmother had said. It was no more than a tracery of fine joins in the stone of the wall. If she had not been looking for it, she might not have recognized it.

How was she to get through? There was neither hinge nor latch nor any device for opening it.

Something bumped her hip, as if she had put a live hedgehog into one of her pockets. Puzzled, she drew out the ball. The gems on its surface began to sparkle and then to glow with inner fire. Brighter and brighter they flashed, bringing tears to Maridah's eyes. The multi-hued brilliance seemed to take on a density of its own. Maridah could barely hold the ball aloft, it had grown so heavy.

The door creaked open, as if the light from the ball had pushed it ajar. As Maridah slipped through, the ball's radiance diminished but did not go out. The door glided closed behind her.

Holding the ball aloft, Maridah proceeded down the stairs. The light was sufficient, but just barely. A delicious sense of adventure filled her. As a child, she'd slipped away from her tutors and gone exploring. Her grandmother had secretly encourageed it. Maridah loved exploring the network of corridors, cellars, and even danker holes that sent shivers down the back of her neck. Some of these, it was said, were donjeons for the keeping of noble prisoners.

The passage twisted, ever descending. At last, she caught sight of a door of plain wood, somehow preserved from the damp. In the chamber beyond, she found a tiny garden, arched over with a dome like frosted glass and filled with pale, diffuse light. She replaced the ball in her pocket.

Heat lay thick and expectant over the dustless benches. Not a fly buzzed, not a leaf of the trellised roses quivered, not a single fallen twig marred the whiteness of the paving stones.

In the center stood a statue of a young man of transcendent beauty, nude to the hips. He looked to the side and down, revealing the perfect grace of his neck, the triangle of muscle and collar bone. His hands hung at his sides, wrought in stone that had the satiny sheen of marble and the warm hue of flesh. The flowing muscles of his torso ended in a block of uncut stone in place of legs.

Maridah, caught by the masterful rendering of the sculpture, came closer. The air shimmered in front of her eyes, like a mirage, so that the statue seemed to quiver and draw a breath.

She sat down on the nearest bench and rubbed her eyes. Heat seeped along her bones, carrying a sweet lethargy, like opium smoke.

She was weary, so weary. She rested her face in her hands and closed her eyes. Her shoulder and neck muscles ached.

Gradually, Maridah became aware of a noise like creaking leather, faint but distinct. She dropped her hands. The statue— surely its arms had been at its sides, fingers loose, wrists curved slightly inward, as if cradling something delicate. Now one of its arms was raised, the bend of the elbow framing its head.

Then, as Maridah stared in astonishment, the statue took a deep, shuddering breath. The rose vines quivered, releasing a burst of scent.

Maridah scrambled to her feet. One hand went automatically to the hilt of her dagger. The metal felt hot, as it often did when

Grandmother was working her enchantments.

The statue took another unmistakable breath…and groaned. Maridah's alarm vanished at the piteous sound. Moving closer, she saw a tear slip down the statue's cheek.

The statue looked at Maridah. The eyes were creamy, unmarked by any color, not even a pupil. Their blankness gave the statue a quizzical expression, as if it were astonished to find someone else in its private garden.

Maridah opened her mouth, but before she could draw breath to address the creature, the statue lowered its arm and spoke.

"Know, O Princess of a noble race, that I was once as you are. As you will soon become." The statue blinked and two more tears dripped down its face.

This was such an extraordinary way of beginning a conversation, even in the flowery language used at court, even in a place as full of magic as this garden, that Maridah could only stand and gape. Her mind bubbled with the tales she'd loved as a child, of spells woven and broken, dragons slain, evil *djinni* defeated, sorcerers challenged.

"Are you under an enchantment?" she ventured. "Can I—is there some way you can be freed?"

"Not until the seas run dry and the last dragon falls from the heavens." The statue raised its hands and let them fall, as if hope were too great a burden. "She who is my torment and my delight is as ageless as the sky."

The frosted-glass ceiling darkened, as if a shadow had suddenly swept in front of the invisible light source. The garden turned chill.

The statue glanced upward, its beautiful face distorted with anguish. It flung one arm over its face and cried like a stricken deer.

"What is it?"

"The hour of my punishment— Ah! Not yet!" The light steadied as the shadow passed.

"For a hundred years, a great sorceress of old, she who

240

carried me off on my wedding night and imprisoned me in this manner, has visited me daily," the statue said, regaining its composure. "She laughs as her scorpions dig out my heart and feed it to her dogs!"

"Oh, how terrible!" Maridah exclaimed in sympathy. "This sorceress must be wicked indeed! Why would she do such a thing? What does she desire of it, beyond to see you in agony?"

The statue threw his head back. Shudders rippled through his graceful, muscled torso. "Ah! Will I never be free of her?"

Maridah let the question go unanswered, for she began to suspect that if this statue was indeed all that was left of a young bridegroom, he was no longer entirely sane. Tales rose to her memory, poems extolling forbidden liaisons and jealous lovers.

"Perhaps," she said in a calmer tone, "there is something this sorceress wants. She didn't by any chance object to your choice of bride?"

"I've done nothing, I tell you—nothing!" He broke off as the garden shivered as if seized by a sudden gale. "Quickly, depart or be trapped here with me! Remember me when you think upon your own fate!"

My own— Was she, too, in danger of some evil enchantment?

The light in the garden dimmed again. Maridah reached out toward the statue that seemed suddenly far away. "Is there no escape for you? No hope? Let me liberate you by defeating this sorcerer!"

"Save yourself!"

A blast of cold air buffeted Maridah, almost knocking her off her feet. She stumbled backward under its impact. Her eyes watered, tears blurred her vision, and her long hair, freed from its scholar's knot, blew across her face.

The next moment, the wind was gone as if it had never existed. The dome overhead brightened slowly and steadily. Around her, the garden lay as eerily still as before. The statue, too, was motionless, frozen in the same attitude in which she had first seen it. Beautiful as it was, it now seemed cold and sterile, all emotion fled along with its semblance of life.

Beyond the statue, in the far wall of the garden, a door opened. Light, shifting in currents of blue and silver, silhouetted the figure that stood there.

Fingers curled around the hilt of her dagger, Maridah faced the figure squarely. It was unmistakably female, dressed in a loose, gauzy robe that did not disguise the slender waist, strong legs, and full breasts. In one hand, the woman carried a long staff set with crystals.

The woman moved into the garden, bringing with her the scent of sandalwood and copper. The door swung shut behind her. As she approached, the overhead light fell upon her features. Maridah gasped, for this sorceress, who must surely be older than Grandmother, appeared no more than her own age. Clear dark eyes regarded her from a face as unwrinkled and golden as her own. Rose-petal lips curved into a smile.

"Zunayna's grand-daughter! What a pleasure to see you!" The voice was sweet and light, untroubled.

The sorceress, smiling more broadly at Maridah's expression of shock, turned briefly to the statue and gestured with her staff. The statue began writhing, as if in unspeakable agony, but no sounds issued from its mouth.

"Come, sit by me," the sorceress said, leading the way to the bench farthest from the statue, "and tell me how you came into my garden."

Maridah followed a pace behind, but would not sit. "Tell me first why I should not strike off your head for you evil ways!"

"'Evil ways'?" One slender eyebrow arched upward. The sorceress appeared to be trying not to laugh.

Glaring, Maridah tightened her grip on her dagger. "You compound your own wickedness by mocking the suffering of your victim."

"Oh, my dear. Which story did he tell you, I wonder? The curse of the three brothers? Or the punishment for disturbing the tomb of the ancient king of the river?"

Suddenly feeling very foolish, Maridah admitted, "He said you carried him off on his wedding night."

The sorceress nodded, looking pleased. "He's making good progress then." She gestured to the statue. "As you see."

The statue was still moving, eyes closed, body twisting and undulating, arms moving as if to music. For a moment, Maridah imagined a smile playing across the stone lips, but she could not be sure.

"What you see," the sorceress said after a moment, "has all the appearance of a man being turned into stone, but is in fact quite the opposite, as are so many things in the world. This virtuous stone is learning how to be a man. To experience a man's longing and passions, to live a man's history. He undertakes this of his own desire."

Maridah wondered what virtue a stone could have, or why it would want to undergo the painful transformation into mortality. "So the tale he told me—is not true?"

The sorceress pursed her lips, as if considering the nature of truth. "It is a thing that may come to pass, or not. I cannot tell."

Maridah lowered herself to the bench beside the sorceress. "I do not know what to think. I suspected his tale, but I thought you might be a spurned lover bent on revenge."

Merriment rang out like the sparkling of the tiny crystals in the sorceress's staff. "I should not laugh at you, my dear. It is not your fault your head has been filled with such romantic stuff, so that you cannot tell one illusion from another."

Maridah felt unreasonably irritated. She ought not to be wasting time in conversation, when her uncle and his men might be hard on her heels.

"You are as safe here as you might be anywhere," the sorceress reassured her. "Zunayna—who was my student, in case you ask—would not have sent you to me otherwise."

"My uncle, the Regent, wants to seize the throne. Or rule through my cousin, which amounts to the same thing."

Again, that arch of eyebrow and fleeting smile. "I suppose it does."

"You say that as if it does not matter!" Maridah made no attempt to rein in her temper. "Why would Grandmother have me safeguard the contents of the brass casket if she did not fear what my uncle would do with them?"

All trace of amusement vanished from the features of the sorceress. "The brass casket? You have taken what lies within?"

Maridah scrambled to her feet, heart pounding. Had she escaped the schemes of her uncle, only to fall into the hands of someone far more ambitious and dangerous? She knew she could not best this slight, young-looking woman, even if she had a dozen spears and scimitars instead of one small dagger. Nor would escape be easy.

But perhaps one of the other enchanted toys... The horse, to carry her far away...back to Samarkhand. To lose herself once again in books and stories...

"Listen to yourself, with your head stuffed with philosophy! Beware, my child, for the world is far stranger than anything your professors have dreamed of!" With deliberate care, the sorceress laid her staff on the pavement. "I do not expect you to believe me, but I have no desire for what you carry in the pockets of your scholar's robes. I have more than enough magical troubles without seeking out more. For the sake of your grandmother, and the love I will always bear for her, I will help you."

Caught between anger and confusion, Maridah forced herself to consider her situation. She did not think she would escape from the garden on her own...and the sorceress had known her grandmother's name...and the statue had ceased its more vigorous movements and was now swaying gently, head tilted back and to one side, a hint of color across his torso and cheeks. He certainly did not look as he were in pain, quite the opposite.

"I will show them to you, but if you attempt to seize or even touch them, I will use this." Maridah pulled out the dagger.

The sorceress managed not to smile.

The ball had gone dark, all its former brilliance extinguished, but the top hummed slightly as Maridah placed it on the bench beside the ball. She set the horse on its wooden wheels. The wand was still wrapped in her second-best handkerchief.

"Ah," the sorceress said, bending over the toys but making

no attempt to touch them. "The ball was once bespelled to shed its light upon that which is hidden, but I do not think you will be able to use it in that way a second time. This top, when sent spinning, will turn you around to the place to which you least desire to return."

Maridah's suspicions began to lessen as soon as the sorceress began speaking. Something in the woman's tone, her confidence, her turns of phrase, reminded Maridah so strongly of her grandmother that she no longer doubted the two had known one another.

"This fine little steed, on the other hand, will take you far away, but only if it is your heart's true desire." Dark eyes regarded Maridah levelly, as if cautioning her to use great care in exercising that desire.

"And what is this?" the sorceress pointed to the wrapped bundle.

Being careful not to touch it with her bare fingers, Maridah unwrapped the wand. It glistened as if wet in the diffuse overhead light.

"I think this is what my uncle is searching for," she said, "what my grandmother wanted me to keep safe from him."

"It is the key to the city, yes, and will grant to her who holds it rightly the power to keep the city safe and prosperous. Certainly. your uncle cannot use it. And it seems you do not wish to."

"Why—" Maridah opened her mouth to ask, *Why do you say that?* If she had truly wanted to rule, as her grandmother had, as her mother might have, would the wand have stung her with sparks? Or would the pain have paled as a small price for her heart's desire?

"It seems I must take it up," Maridah said wearily.

"Yes, that seems as good a use for your handkerchief as any," the sorceress replied obliquely. "But the question is, will you then choose the top to spin you back to the palace, or the horse to carry you to Samarkhand?"

Maridah rewrapped the wand and settled it in her pocket.

The ball followed. She picked up the top and the horse, one in each hand, weighing them.

"I will carry you," the horse sang in her mind,

"Wherever you truly wish to go,

To master me, you must first master your heart."

When she looked up, the sorceress was gone. An empty dais stood where the statue had once been. All about her, rose petals drifted to the ground. Little currents of air carried their sweet, quickly fading scent.

She put one of the objects in her pocket, folded her hands around the other, closed her eyes, and wished...

...and found herself in the grand audience chamber of the palace, surrounded by courtiers and facing the empty throne. She stood on the intricate mosaic pattern, interwoven symbols representing the city, the royal lineage, and the power of the heavens. To her surprise, she noticed a little horse, a ball and a top nestled among the heroic figures. She had little time to contemplate them, for almost immediately, cries of surprise and alarm filled the chamber. Someone—a man with a trained, stentorian voice—shouted for order.

"It is Lady Maridah, come back to us!"

For an instant, Maridah saw herself reflected in their astonishment, her hair wild and loose about her shoulders, wearing a scholar's gown, hardly suitable attire for such a place. The courtiers shimmered in their silks and jewels. Some she remembered from her time at court before Samarkhand, but many others were strangers. Something was subtly wrong, though. She saw no trace of mourning, which meant Grandmother must still be alive—and yet, surely the steward who had greeted her upon her return had not been so white of beard, nor so frail.

"My uncle!" she called. "Where is Yussuf the Regent?"

The courtiers and nobles drew back. A man rose from where

he had been seated in the chair to the left side of the throne. At first, Maridah did not recognize him, he seemed so thin and somber, so care-worn. Beneath the robe of gray-figured silk and the heavy gold-link collar, his body seemed to have shrunk. The bones of his skull stood out, and his skin had turned sallow, his eyes red-rimmed.

From the other side of the throne, a woman emerged to stand at his side. She, too, was grave, dressed in silks of muted hue. She wore no jewelry except a coronet bearing a single blue topaz. When her gaze lit upon Maridah, her countenance brightened. She moved forward, smiling.

"Maridah! Returned to us after all these years!" Hadidjah seized Maridah's hands, and kissed them formally. "I never believed you were dead. You look so young—not a hair different from the day you disappeared! I knew some magic must have hidden you away. Have you freed yourself from an evil enchantment? Is that how you have come back to us?"

"I—I don't understand." Maridah's thoughts whirled. "I have been gone no more than an hour or two. Is Grandmother still among us? Is that why no one is in mourning?"

Yussuf now stirred into action, gesturing to a man wearing the sash of a chief vizier. "Clear the chamber! And let no one speak of what has just happened."

Immediately, the guards who usually stood at the entrance began escorting courtiers from the room.

"Come, my niece," Yussuf said, holding out one hand to her. "Let us speak of these things in private."

"Let us speak of them right now!" Maridah shot back. She had not returned to put herself in his power. "Right here!"

Yussuf and his daughter exchanged glances. When they were alone, he began. "Very well. It has been five years since Zunayna of the Blessed Memory departed our midst, and five years since you yourself vanished."

Five years! How was that possible? With magic, was anything impossible?

Oh, Grandmother...

Maridah shoved aside the pulse of grief. "And you, I suppose, have been ruling in the interim?"

Under the vitriol of her words, Yussuf paled but did not flinch. "I have been serving as Regent—"

"But he has not been ruling," Hadidjah said, her voice edged with steel.

"You? You dared to take my place?"

"Yes, I dared!" Hadidjah admitted. "What else could I have done? When you disappeared, there was no one else. No one to rally our people when raiders came swarming upriver. No one to negotiate trade agreements, to settle disputes and inheritances. No one to—"

"Do you challenge my right to rule?" Maridah faced her uncle.

"No, *I* do!" Hadidjah exclaimed. "My father would be happy to lay down the Regency, if only there were a rightful heir. He's old and sick, even a simpleton can see that! For the past five years, for good or ill, *I* have made those decisions. *I* have exercised that authority. I have made mistakes, and I have learned from them. I have done everything needful, no matter the price."

She paused, her breast heaving, and went on in a softer tone. "I have always loved you, my cousin, and I rejoice to see you whole, but I have no intention of stepping aside—throwing away everything my father and I have sacrificed—for an inexperienced, irresponsible fledgling who has already abandoned this city and its people not once but twice!"

Maridah glared at her uncle. "This is all your doing! Grandmother warned me of your ambition. If you cannot rule in your own right, you seek to do so through your daughter. I hear your words from her mouth!"

"You hear my own!" Hadidjah cried. "Oh, it is no use reasoning with her, Father. She has made you into a villain and me into your puppet, even as Grandmother did in her final illness." She faced Maridah, her emotions once more under control.

"Yours may be the stronger right by lineage, but I have the

advantage of experience and merit. I will not yield to a lesser claim. And when the wand of office is found, I will release my father from his burden."

"Then take it, if you dare!" Maridah reached into her pocket and drew out the wrapped wand. She pulled away the coverings. The wand lay, gleaming as if moist, on the unfolded handkerchiefs on the palm of her outstretched hand.

When Hadidjah reached out her hand, her father grabbed her wrist. "Wait, there must be a trick. Why else would Maridah take such care to prevent even a casual touch? See, even now she shields her own skin."

Hadidjah met Maridah's gaze with a troubled expression. "Would you poison me? Slay me by treachery? Has your own ambition grown so vast? Have you no memory of the love we once shared? Does the throne mean more to you than blood, than friendship?"

Maridah opened her mouth to protest that they had never been so very dear to one another. Memories swept away her words, of playing together in the palace gardens, braiding each other's hair, giggling over the newest gossip and handsome visitors to court. She had thought Hadidjah lacking in seriousness, too vulnerable to her father's guidance, but never vicious.

More than that, did she want to rule? To forsake the world of stories and dreams? Stories that were her very life…

"I touched it once," Maridah admitted, "and it pained me, but caused no lasting harm. Its power answers only to one who truly desires to keep the city safe and prosperous."

Hadidjah's rose-gold complexion paled. She reached trembling fingers toward the wand.

"My dear, think what you are risking," Yussuf said. "Do not do this for me. I can manage for a while longer. And here is Maridah, come to take up her heritage."

Maridah saw tears glimmering in Hadidjah's eyes as her cousin shook her head. Before Hadidjah could touch the wand, Maridah grabbed it in her free hand.

Fire jolted up her arm. Every nerve flared into white agony.

Her throat clenched around her breath. Her back arched in spasm. Waves of pain shook her. All she had to do was to let go…

The wand clattered to the tiled floor.

Maridah bent over, gasping. Her vision blurred crimson, as if her eyes had been washed in blood. A gentle touch steadied her. She inhaled her cousin's perfume, the scent of rosewater and cloves.

Maridah was still unable to speak, but could stand on her own, when Hadidjah released her. Slowly, with resolve taut in every line of her body, Hadidjah bent to pick up the wand.

Slim fingers closed around the ivory rod. For a moment, the delicate engravings glimmered as if they wept. Then the light passed from it. Hadidjah straightened up. Her cheeks were still very pale. Trembling shook her body. She looked up, an unnatural brightness in her eyes. She opened her mouth as if to speak, but no words came.

Maridah found herself unexpectedly moved by the sight of Hadidjah, ashen and resolute. She could not imagine what her cousin must be suffering. Moving stiffly, for her muscles had not yet fully recovered, she fumbled for her handkerchief.

Hadidjah waved it away and clasped the wand against her body. The chamber, empty except for a guard at the doors, had fallen very still. Maridah could hear nothing above the rasp of her cousin's breathing and the thrumming of her own heart.

Color seeped out of Hadidjah's skin, her hair, her beautiful hazel eyes. For an instant, it seemed that she had become part of the wand. Ivory, once living but now with only the memory of that life. Enduring, enslaved. Glistening with magic as if with tears.

Yussuf had covered his face with his hands, his shoulders shaking, making no sound.

Although the gesture brought her a sadness she could not explain, Maridah bowed to her new sovereign. "You are now the Princess of Khazarand, and so I will say to the whole world!"

Later, much later, the two cousins stood on a balcony overlooking the twin rivers. Dusk perfumed the shadows as Khazarand's thousand gardens released the heat of the day. The moon, just past full, cast a softly golden light.

Maridah, still in her favored robe of soft cotton over riding boots, her hair simply dressed, breathed in the lingering sweetness.

"You have not yet made your plans to return to Samarkhand," Hadidjah said.

"No…not yet." Maridah paused. She dreamed of Samarkhand and, sometimes, a statue who had perhaps become a man who still spun tales of wonder more real than the stones beneath her feet. A wooden horse waited, ready to carry her to her heart's desire, if only she knew what that was.

"There is something I would ask you," Maridah said, "although you may think it presumptuous."

Hadidjah's smile was a ghost in the gathering dark. "Dearest cousin, we know each other too well for artificial courtesies."

"Well, then. When you took up the wand—you saw what it did to me, and I had come here determined to take the throne. I never realized how much greater was your own desire. I had never seen you as ambitious, not in that way. I thought you content with pretty clothes and ardent suitors."

"Of which I have many, all of them interested in obtaining power," Hadidjah interjected. "I must marry and provide our city an heir, but I will choose carefully. I didn't pick up the wand in order to give away everything I'd worked so hard to achieve."

"Why, then? Why did you do it?"

"Did I have a choice? How else could I put forth a lawful claim to the throne? I never sought to rule. I took it up because there was no one else, and to spare my father."

Maridah nodded. Uncle Yussuf would not have lain down the Regency until Khazarand had a rightful Princess. Now that she had abdicated in Hadidjah's favor, the throne was secure.

"I saw what the wand did to you," Hadidjah went on. "I had not the slightest doubt it would bring me even greater pain." She paused, blinking hard.

From the way her cousin spoke, and the coiling silence that followed, Maridah had no doubt the pain had not abated, but it was of the heart and spirit, not of the body. She said, "I cannot envy you."

"You need not." Hadidjah paused. "Did Grandmother ever tell you—do you know what the wand does? How it grants power?"

Maridah supposed the wand bestowed some supernatural ability—prosperity, extraordinary health, good luck, or invincibility in battle.

"It reveals the truth," Hadidjah said quietly.

"Surely that's a good thing. To know when your adversaries or even your own advisors are lying."

"You may say so, you who have lived for your philosophy, who breathed in Grandmother's tales of enchantment as a fish breathes water. It is easy to believe when such stories are beautiful and bewitching. To forget that not every true thought or every true word spoken in haste or anger, is kind."

A sound escaped Hadidjah's throat, a groan of unendurable anguish, of crushing weight, or perhaps Maridah felt rather than heard it.

In Maridah's sight, moonlight turned Hadidjah into a woman of silver-washed ivory. Maridah remembered the wetness of the wand, how it had appeared to weep. She thought of the statue, animated by passion. Even as the stone had come to life, life now seeped from Hadidjah's human flesh as ivory, beautiful and hard, took its place.

Maridah's heart shivered. Were they not two sides of the same hand, the dark moon and the light? Truth bound one with barbed chains, scouring away trust and love; the other was seduced by a world of easy dreams, of riddles that tantalized and intoxicated.

By the grace of the Infinite, what were stories *for*?

All her life, she had wandered through a world of dreams. Of stories. And what use had they been, except to make her entirely mistaken about her uncle, the sorceress, the statue? Even Hadidjah.

Even herself.

Yet…if stories had the power to give life to stone, to comfort a dying old woman, to ease the loneliness of a royal child, might they not also give life…and hope…to this woman she loved, who was even now turning into ivory?

Smiling, Maridah laid her hand upon her cousin's arm. "I think we have, between us, more than enough truth and more than enough dreams, for any one lifetime."

Together they went into the old work room, where the brass casket whispered poisoned secrets in the wavering candle light. Together, they opened it. The ball and the top were in their proper places, no longer inert but charged, waiting.

Together, they put away the ivory wand and the little wooden horse, closed the casket, and sealed it with molten lead.

Together, they placed it back in the stronghold.

The next morning, Hadidjah would sit upon the throne, judging with her own mind. And Maridah would enter Grandmother's painted garden and throw open the doors to the clear light of day. She would study, as was her talent; she would tell all the stories she knew, not to insulate and cripple, but to bring life to all the ivory statues of men's hearts.

I will carry you

Wherever you truly wish to go.

Hadidjah would dispense justice, and Maridah would spin out dreams, and together they would create such an age that there would be no end to the tales of wonder.

The Hero of Abarxia

When word arrived that the war was over, the kingdom went mad with joy. The enemy had been soundly defeated at the Vale of Abarxia and their Prince-general, Jarez, had been slain. Each report was more extravagant in its praise of Prince Givors than the one before. Surely, everyone said, he was the bravest of men and the most shrewd and resourceful of military leaders.

The triumphal procession made its way into the capital city and down the broad, straight avenue festooned with pennons of crimson and silver-edged blue. Unmistakable by his golden hair and the noble carriage, Givors rode at the head of his company where all the city could see him and feel themselves part of his glory.

King Mornand watched from the balcony of the Hall of Justice. His chest had been paining him more than usual, his breath failed him with even the smallest exertion, and so he had taken advantage of an old man's privilege and waited for his son to come to him. If his hopes had been fulfilled then he would soon be able to rest, knowing the kingdom was at last in good hands.

The cortege advanced a little further and now, even with his aged eyes, Mornand saw that Givors no longer rode the heavy-crested black stallion that was the best warhorse within living memory. No, this steed was tall and slender, and its hide caught the light like a shimmering pearl, cream and blue and polished silver. Mornand murmured under his breath, praising all the gods that had ever graced his realm, for this must be one of the legendary *aswa* horses of the Sahael Desert, famed not only for their speed and beauty but for their fierce loyalty to their masters. He had never heard of one allowing any other than its beloved to ride it, but clearly his son had inspired this one to accept him. It was said that battle tempered men like steel, and what greater proof could there be that Givors had at last risen to the greatness of his heritage?

How Mornand wished he could have been there to witness the final moments of the battle—to see the fall of the enemy and the red flags of victory. To watch Givors raise the victory cup and drain it, the wine overflowing and running in rivulets down his chest—such a sight as had never been seen in all his days. In his younger days, Mornand himself had led his armies and ridden at the head of his horsemen but in all that time, the cup had remained tied to his belt, empty despite his best efforts. All he'd achieved had been an uneasy stalemate that drained vitality from land and men alike. A few deaths here, a few fields overridden there, were followed by funeral pyres and skirmishing back and forth across the trampled land until no crops grew there. And now the son had done accomplished what father and grandfather could not.

Mornand's joy mounted as the parade approached, so much so that he barely noticed how Givors displayed the horse's paces. He saw only the radiance of his son's face and the light that seemed to emanate from his entire body, as if the gods had truly blessed this moment. The prince dismounted, threw the reins to a waiting aide, and bounded up the stairs. A few moments later, he reached the balcony. Tears blurring his sight, Mornand wrapped his son in his arms. The resulting sounds of rejoicing must surely have deafened the heavens.

Then came the necessary pageantry of victory, during which Mornand had scarcely two consecutive private moments in his son's company. On the rare occasions when Givors presented himself to Mornand's chambers, he seemed unable to sit still. He moved about restlessly, gazing out the window or twisting a stray lock in his fingers and then dropping the tangle of hairs on the carpet. Afterward, Mornand gathered up the hairs, fine and gleaming as golden wire, coiled them tenderly, and placed them in a keepsake box.

I entrusted this command to him, Mornand thought, *that he might prove himself. Now that he has returned victorious, now that my kingdom will be safe and well-governed, what more can I desire?*

This eclipse of a father by his heir was a good thing, a triumphal thing, and if Mornand the man felt a little wistful at times, he was too sage a monarch to complain.

At last came the night of the victory feast. The royal stewards and chefs, the entertainers and musicians, and the wine-sellers and pastry-makers outdid themselves for the feast. Garlands of the finest hothouse roses and ribbons stitched with silver thread adorned the hall, and the tables had been so arranged that the entire assembly had a clear view of the prince. Mornand took his seat and bade the revelers rise from where they knelt. Then a fanfare composed especially for the occasion shivered through the air, phrase upon rising phrase of wordless acclaim. When Givors entered through the royal door, the people did not bow as they had to Mornand. They leapt to their feet, cheering and waving, practically dancing in the extremity of their rejoicing. Even as a boy, Givors had always had an instinct for the theatrical gesture, the heroic pose, and now his talents were put to their proper use in generating inspiration and hope.

The feast proceeded with one delicacy following the next, with music and laugher and free-flowing wine. Afterward, there was dancing. Mornand did not lead out the first promenade, leaving that honor to Givors, who selected the loveliest noble-born lady as his partner. Rumors would doubtless spread like wildfire, but the prince went from one lady to the next, always choosing those beauties whose families were rich and powerful. He must wed and he clearly intended to do so advantageously. Mornand had not married for love, for what king had that luxury? Givors had every right to indulge himself with beauty and charm while he could. At one point, Mornand noticed his son's old nurse, who had been granted the favor of a place in the corner, watching the dancing. It was just as well the prince did not notice her, lest even a moment of regret mar the evening.

Mornand retired early, as had become his wont in recent months, with the command that the revelers should continue enjoying themselves, for how many such occasions would any of them see in their lives? He dismissed his usual retinue, save only his oldest and most faithful body-servant and two ceremonial guards. They passed through the royal entrance and into the private corridor that would take them to the king's suite. As the door closed behind them, the sounds of the merry-making dimmed. The light from the fine beeswax candles seemed subdued and they gave off no scent. A man waited beside one of the side doors, shifting from one foot to the other. Mornand knew him, one of the under-stewards.

"Yes, yes, what is it?" Mornand heard the snappishness in his own voice. His joints ached and his heart labored in his chest.

"Your Majesty, I am sorry to—"

"Just say what it is." *And get it over with.*

"The groom, sire. The one who looks after the prince's horses. He says—it's about the *aswa* stallion. There's something wrong with the horse, he says. It's languishing."

Of course the horse would languish, if it were as steadfast in devotion as the tales said. For a moment, Mornand felt annoyed at being plagued with such a triviality. And yet, he reflected more soberly, it would not do for the beast to pine away, simply because its new master had other responsibilities. "My own head groom will attend to it," he said, and went on his way.

The next morning, at an appropriate hour and at the appropriate place, the royal groom presented himself, and Mornand knew at first glance that all was not well. The groom's report carried a hint of alarm. The horse was indeed *languishing*, but not from any physical cause. It might be grief or it might be due to some malign supernatural influence. Would His Majesty care to observe the horse for himself?

258

His Majesty would not, nor did it please him to diminish the prince's enjoyment of his triumph. Besides, what was the welfare of an animal, even one as rare and noble as this one, compared to the happiness of the heir to the realm and the conqueror of the enemy? The court sorcerer, sojourning these twenty years from his own far-off mountainous land, long noted for arcane arts, would surely know what to do.

Two days later, days in which Mornand had forgotten about the matter, the court sorcerer begged a private audience. For the man, normally so stern and distant, to beg anything was extraordinary. With trepidation, Mornand received the sorcerer in the smallest of his chambers.

It was customary to remain standing in the presence of the king. The sorcerer sat. "As best I can determine, the malady is of the soul, not of the body."

"Horses have souls?"

Dusky brows furrowed. "All that lives partakes of spirit, to a greater or lesser degree. Thus are we joined to all other beings."

Mornand had never felt joined to anyone or anything. Normally he had no taste for philosophy. Yet the idea intrigued him enough to ignore the sorcerer's lack of respectful address. "Go on."

"Something happened to this horse, most likely during or directly following the climactic battle. Perhaps it witnessed the death of its former master. Without further investigation, I cannot say."

"What form might this investigation take?"

"It is possible—although not entirely without risk—to witness what the horse experienced."

The battle…the moment of victory…Givors dealing the fatal blow to the enemy, Prince Jarez…Givors lifting the victor's cup and draining it… All the things Mornand wished he could have seen for himself.

"You can do this?" Mornand asked, his voice roughened with the intensity of his yearning.

"No, not I. I cannot be both witness and conduit. Some other must undertake the role. Perhaps the head groom?"

Caught by the implications, Mornand ignored the suggestion. "To be party to the memories of another? Why have you not informed me of such a capability? What an asset that would be, to be able to read the mind of another man—to ascertain his loyalty, his motives! Who could conspire or engage in treachery were such a method to be used?"

"Who indeed?" the sorcerer replied, frowning. "Upon a little reflection, it will become clear why knowing another man's thoughts is to be shunned, not sought. In any event, it is not possible. My order has essayed such an exchange for more than two hundred years, with naught beyond the most humiliating of deaths as a result. The exchange can occur only between beast and man."

"Exchange, you said?"

The sorcerer looked as if he were restraining a sigh of impatience, or perhaps remembering the many times he had attempted to interest Mornand in metaphysical study, and failed. "Two beings cannot share the same memories, the same thoughts, the same consciousness."

"So whoever participated in this enterprise would go into the horse's body, and the horse's mind into his?"

"That is the general idea." The sorcerer seemed to take heart from Mornand's expression of interest. "Precautions would be necessary to ensure that neither physical body is injured. It would be best to sedate the man and place him under restraint, although the horse might merely be confined to a comfortable box stall. There is no need for close physical proximity, once the proper preparation is made."

To see Givors in his finest hour...

"I will undertake this foray into the mind of the *aswa* horse myself."

For the first time, the sorcerer's calm demeanor wavered. "Your Majesty, you cannot—the risk—that is, it would not be seemly." Visibly, he remembered his position as a foreign courtier, dependent on the king's favor. "For a man of your royal position."

"People have been telling me that since my older brother, who would have been king, died a-hunting when I was five," Mornand snapped. "I *must not* do *this* and it is *not seemly* to do *that*. I am old enough to know my own wishes, and when last I looked, I still wore the crown. You say that it is possible to witness my son's victory, though it happened a month ago and two hundred leagues away. I say that no man shall have that privilege but myself."

There was no need at all for him to see the horse, but he could not imagine such an intimate encounter without first acquainting himself with this particular animal. Perhaps, in his heart he knew he ought to ask permission. That, or forgiveness.

The *aswa* stallion had been housed in the most luxurious portion of the stables. The posts and railings of the box stall were carved with the royal crest. Mornand lifted the latch and the door swung open, silent on its well-oiled hinges. Inside, the bedding was scrupulously clean. The smell of sweet fresh hay overlay something unsettling, not the sour reek of disease but something more insidious.

The stallion stood near the far wall, head lowered, muzzle almost resting on the straw. He did not move when Mornand stepped inside, not even a flicker of those perfectly shaped ears. The brightness of his coat seemed quenched in the diffuse light.

Mornand was not an expert horseman; he could ride well enough, although he had never had to look after his own horses. As a boy he'd loved them, their power and grace and the joy of their speed, the exhilaration of seeing the world from their backs. He knew enough to realize that he now looked upon a horse so sunk in despair as to welcome death. That would be a shame, to be seen as taking such poor care of a rare and priceless steed, not to mention a pity, now that he saw the horse. As he drew closer and laid his hand on the horse's neck, he became aware of the intelligence in the eyes. The gold was dulled, to be sure, but the misery reflected there struck him as unusual, as if the animal were considering his plight in some deep and complex fashion.

He had issued his orders out of purely selfish motives, his own desire to see the battle he himself had never won. The welfare of the horse had been of lesser concern, although as a symbol of his son's greatness, the beast must be seen to flourish. Now it occurred to him that surely this horse, however dim the awareness or misguided the former devotion might have been, was in himself worthy of compassion. Having transferred his loyalty to Givors, the horse might well be suffering the prince's absence. That, too, could not be helped. The demands of royalty and the welfare of the kingdom, as Mornand knew all too well, took precedence over personal concerns.

He ran his hands over the horse's mane and came away with three long coarse hairs, the exact number required for the transfer spell. The hairs shimmered a little, as if some costly metal—white gold or platinum—had been spun into them. These would be knotted with his own in a particular pattern and accompanied by esoteric incantations.

A short time later, when Mornand arranged himself on his bed, his thoughts were already leaping ahead, so eager was he to witness the pivotal and glorious event. The sorcerer wove the hairs, human and horse, together with multicolored strands of vegetable fibers and a few other stringy things Mornand didn't inquire about, and then placed them in a silver box.

"Rest assured, I will guard these with utmost care," the sorcerer said, "for they open the gateway in both directions."

"You mean the horse will enter my mind as well as I enter his?" Mornand asked.

"That. But also for each of you to return."

Instead of the foul-tasting brew Mornand expected, the sorcerer offered a warm drink, pleasantly sweetened with honey and smelling of ripe apples. Surely, nothing but good could come of such an appealing rite.

The potion took hold and he found himself drifting.

His first impression was that the world had changed in hue, as if he had suddenly gone color-blind, and turned very bright. He could see nearly completely around his body without moving his head, and everything smelled and sounded more vivid than he remembered. The effect was so disorienting that he responded without thinking. His muscles tightened for flight. Walls loomed on every side, penning him in. A strange cry shuddered from his mouth. The next moment, several men rushed into the stall and grabbed the straps around his head. They reeked of dead flesh. He tried to pull away, but his rump slammed into the wooden wall and there wasn't enough space to kick. Dimly he realized that the hands and voices were meant to soothe, but he was in too great a panic to control himself. Then, as if the world had given itself a little shake, everything settled into a neat order. He heard a reassuring nicker from the other side of the wall, but it was from one horse to another, and he was not a horse. Or, not entirely.

With that, he stopped fighting the grooms and allowed himself to be walked up and down the neatly-swept dirt aisle until he'd stopped sweating. He relaxed enough to let the horse's own training and instincts take over, so much so that when he was once more returned to the box stall, he thrust his muzzle into the bucket of clean water, drank noisily, and then urinated in the opposite corner. The stall smelled of fresh straw, sweet hay, and the horse's own waste. By this time, he had become accustomed to the animal's thoughts, such as they were.

Remember... he nudged the horse's mind.

The horse's initial response was a wordless version of *Now is all there is*. With a little experimentation, Mornand discovered that what he sought lay not in the horse's present consciousness. He suggested sleep, and the horse folded his legs and lowered himself to the thick padding of straw. Drowsiness came in waves, and through them Mornand inserted his own thoughts, swift and sure like a hawk on the hunt.

As if from afar, he heard the muted sounds of fighting. They came nearer, and with them came vision—vignettes of motion rather than form—and smells. His nostrils filled with the familiar scents of silk and leather, the whiff of sandalwood and clove that perfumed his rider's skin. Try as he might, Mornand could not follow the progress of the battle, although he discerned the shape of his rider's curved sword as it slashed downward and the knots of rapid movement to either side. For long stretches of time, it seemed the horse was either too excited or rushing about too fast to comprehend what was happening. On occasion, he stood with other horses and their riders while his master issued orders and stroked his neck to calm him. During these moments, Mornand felt a pulse of such fierce tenderness, such a sympathy of spirit, that he thought he would be willing to risk any peril, to gallop through walls of fire or swim through lakes of blood, were his master to ask.

I must observe carefully, Mornand remarked to himself, *or the horse's animal nature will distort what comes next.* His son deserved such a steed, as Prince Jarez surely had not.

The battle settled into a rhythm like the waves on a shore, noise and smells rushing toward the-horse-that-was and then receding, times of movement and of stillness. Always Mornand felt the steadying presence of his rider, the bonds of trust, the response to the occasional stroke of his sweating neck, the gentle pressure of knee or rein. Prince Jarez did not use spurs, nor did he need any. Now and again, Mornand sensed the prince's dismay at the death of his comrades, the flash of hope as the forces of Givors receded, the drenching wash of adrenaline. He heard the screams of men and horses, smelled blood and dust and terror.

The horse advanced, surrounded by the mounted royal guard, prancing with excitement while his rider shouted out orders. Moment by moment, a few strides at a time, they made their way across a field of bodies. Horses stumbled about aimlessly or thrashed where they lay. Here and there, a man sobbed in agony, but many more of them lay motionless. The horse's instinctive revulsion urged him to flee, but the steadfast resoluteness of Prince Jarez calmed his fears.

The racket of fighting diminished as the clash of steel and the shouting of battle cries became distant and scattered. A party of strange horses approached under a ripple of banners. Prince Jarez nudged the horse forward, for a time in the middle of a circle of companions, then alone. From the other party a single rider advanced, mounted on a black stallion. An ordinary horse, sweating with excitement, the black jigged sideways and fought the bit. Ropes of blood-flecked saliva dripped from his jaws.

The two riders went apart from the others, and the *aswa* horse felt a pulse of brightness from his rider, a flare of anticipation like the first scent of spring green. With a shift of weight, Jarez slipped lightly to the ground. He advanced toward the opposing rider, who dismounted likewise, and although he did not take hold of the reins, the *aswa* horse came with him. All was as it should be, horse and man bound by a living river of light.

The horse did not understand human speech, but his memory was keen, rendering every moment so vivid that Mornand could follow snatches of the exchange. Out of hearing of the other riders, the two princes were discussing a truce, and now Mornand saw that the flags were white as well as the silver-edged blue Givors used as his personal emblem. A tendril of puzzlement crept through Mornand's thoughts. Until this moment, he had not known of a truce. Givors had reported nothing of it, only of the battle and the vanquishing of his enemy. Perhaps Jarez would now reject the offered terms and storm away. Perhaps—and Mornand in the horse's mind quailed at the thought—perhaps Jarez had violated the traditions of the parley. But the horse felt no trace of alarm, and he would have sensed the flare of anger in his master.

Now the words were harder to understand as the tone of the men's voices became strident. The horse bent his head and touched his muzzle to Jarez's shoulder. Mornand felt the reassurance offered and sought, the memory of the thousand times the gesture had previously united the two. He felt the answering warmth and saw the smile as Jarez turned to stroke the horse's neck.

And watched, through the wide-sweeping vision of the horse, as Givors drew the dagger at his belt and plunged it into Jarez's heart.

The world fractured into chaotic shards, a jagged whirl of color and sound, the strange man—*Givors!*—shouting, "Treachery! Treachery!" and swinging up on the black horse, wheeling him, digging spurs into his sides...

"To me! To me! Strike them down!"

...the black stallion whirling, trampling Jarez's fallen body...

...the *aswa* horse himself in a convulsion of rage and madness, hooves flailing, striking flesh and smashing through bone...

...the reek of blood—horse and human—drenching the air, the black horse falling, the rider leaping free...

...a rope, no three, no ten, pinning him to the earth...the strange rider on his back, raking his sides with spurs, his mouth torn by a savage bit...

...loss wailing through the chambers of his mind as if through a desert...

...the slow sinking into darkness...trudging through an eternity of unchanging misery...

...endless...

The land changed and the dust beneath his hooves changed and the harsh, sterile voices of the men changed, and the grief that numbed his spirit die not change...

...endless...

And then it came to an end, and Mornand sat up.

His mouth was dry and his heart felt as if he had wept for a month. He stared at his surroundings, for a moment alarmed that he recognized nothing. With painful slowness, memory returned. He knew where he was—in his own bed, in his own body. Part of him knew who he was—sovereign, father, an old man not far from his own death. He nonetheless grieved for the master he had lost, and also for the son he had never had. Sending Givors to war had not changed him.

His joints protested when he attempted to free himself from the bedcovers and swing his legs over the side. He could have sworn he'd been gone for longer than a single night. By the light slanting through the eastern windows, it was still early in the day. A moment later, a single body servant instead of the usual bevy presented himself, inquired whether the king required his services, and departed with a bow when Mornand declared he wanted to be left alone. The impression of change and the passage of time increased when Mornand, having washed and dressed himself, ventured into his sitting chamber to find a table laid with a simple meal of brown bread, sliced apples, and cold mint-tea. He went to the door, spied a guard not directly outside but a short ways down the hallway, and demanded to see the sorcerer without delay.

Once they were alone behind two sets of closed doors, Mornand confronted the sorcerer. "How long have I been—" despite the impossibility of being overheard, he lowered his voice, "—a horse?"

"A month."

"A month?"

The sorcerer folded his arms over his chest, his brows knotted in a scowl. "I informed you of the risks."

"You did not tell me I'd be lost in that horse's slough of grief for a *month*!"

"Hmmm."

Mornand heaved himself to his feet and began to pace in order to compose his thoughts. The sorcerer watched, apparently assessing Mornand's mobility and perhaps his soundness of mind as well. With a sigh of resignation, Mornand eased himself into one of the many chairs and schooled his features into civility.

"I have no reason to be angry with you. You did indeed warn me. As was pointed out, the horse had been *languishing*. I suppose I should be grateful I myself did not *languish* any longer."

"Indeed," the sorcerer replied with a grunt that indicated he had accepted the apology. "It could have been indefinitely."

Mornand closed his eyes, offering a silent prayer to whatever god had been watching over him. "So tell me what has been happening."

"You may suspect from your physical condition that you did not simply lie abed." Now the sorcerer's expression lightened. "You've been busy."

Mornand thought acerbically that he had indeed, but not in the way the sorcerer meant. He'd been discovering things he would rather not have known. He gestured for the sorcerer to continue.

"You've arranged a peace treaty with Prince Jarez's heir, offering surprisingly compassionate terms. You've given food and medicine to the returning soldiers and made exceptional provision for the families of those who did not return."

Foals must be protected. Once an enemy stallion has submitted, the battle ends. There is enough grass for all.

"You've flatly refused to authorize any new taxes to pay for the rather extravagant festivities in the honor of Prince Givors. In fact, you cut his allowance and reassigned most of his personal retinue to help with the charitable distributions."

"I have? I wonder what Givors said to that."

"The shouting could be heard throughout this wing of the palace. It recurred at even higher volume when you pardoned all thirty men the prince had sentenced to death for sedition, and then removed the prince from his seat on the courts. Shall I go on? I'm sure your own secretary can supply the details of your other decisions."

"I have a secretary?"

Something glinted in the sorcerer's eyes. "I believe Your Majesty set a great many things in order."

Mornand sat in silent amazement. He had done nothing, as the sorcerer well knew. What could a horse know of mercy or justice or the orderly running of a kingdom? Even one of the *aswa* breed, renowned for loyalty and selfless devotion?

How could a horse in a man's body even talk? The magic must be powerful indeed, or perhaps Mornand's human mind had remembered, even as the *aswa* horse's mind had done.

Now that he was back in his right body, he must strive to continue what had been so well begun. Yet even as he vowed to himself to be steadfast, he knew that he would fail. He had never been able to deny his son's wishes, not since Givors had been a small boy. It was his failure as both father and king. Had he been able to enforce a healthy discipline, to teach the principles of service, then Givors might have turned out a different man.

How had it all gone wrong? Givors wasn't inherently bad, was he? Mornand remembered the toddler in his lace-trimmed cloak, his hair like flax, flailing about with his tiny bejeweled sword…his face red with fury after he'd slid off the rounded back of his pony, clambering back on, digging in with his spurs and jerking the reins until blood stained the froth from the pony's mouth…

…Givors older now, with a sly tautness around his eyes that smoothed into innocence when he lifted his gaze to his father's…the way the other noble boys would grow silent and hunch their shoulders at his approach…the fuss about the little maid who threw herself from the tower…

Blood rushed to Mornand's head. He felt faint with it, breathless. Chilled. It came to him that the *aswa* shared some human feelings—loyalty, certainly, and grief—but not this paralyzing fear. The beast had been numb with grief when Mornand had first entered his mind, but the horse had not remained there. Through Mornand's own body, he had dispensed mercy and kindness.

Protect the foals. Respect the older mares. Defend the weaker members of the herd…

269

Fear shook Mornand, not only at his own failings but at how little time he had to set things right. He could ask the sorcerer to send him back, to give the *aswa* a small measure of additional time, but it would not last long. He was an old man who had a few years at most to live, perhaps only months.

No, he thought as he felt an ominous sense of pressure behind his breastbone. *Not even that long.*

And then Givors would take the throne, without even the ineffectual restraining influence of his father.

Mornand's gaze, which had drifted unseeing about the room, now fixed on the table bearing his private keepsake box. He remembered his own sense of grief that although he and his son might be in each other's physical presence, all pretense of intimacy had long been forsaken. As if the spirit of the *aswa* horse animated his limbs once more, he went to the box, opened it, and removed the coil of gleaming golden hairs.

His hand did not tremble as he turned to the sorcerer. "Could you make a second charm...with this?"

The sorcerer's black eyes narrowed. "Without the consent of the other party?"

"At the command of his king." *Who has too long neglected his duties to his people and his heir.*

When it was done, the potion delivered to Prince Givors and all else accomplished, Mornand bade the sorcerer to leave behind the bundle of hairs and dried plants. For long moments, he studied the intricate knots, so like the way the lives of people...and of steeds...might be woven together. As if in the most solemn ritual of office, he carried the bundle to the fire and let it fall into the flames. With that, the power that had sustained him failed and he sank into the nearest chair.

He was dozing when a servant—he could no longer concentrate enough to remember which one—brought a message that Prince Givors requested an audience.

Givors?

The prince entered, not with his usual swagger but lightly, as if he danced over the earth. Just inside the door, he halted and bowed deeply, waiting to be recognized.

"Come closer, my son. My sight is failing."

Before Mornand could draw another breath, Givors knelt before him. Or was it Givors? Mornand could not think clearly. There was some reason why it might not be. But no, the hair like a crown of spun gold was the same, the eyes like the sky on a clear summer's day.

But what was this? Tears? From Givors, who never cried?

Or Givors as he should have been?

"I leave my..." he could not say *kingdom*, for what meaning did that have for this Givors? "...my herd in your care."

Protect the foals. Respect the older mares. Fight only when you must.

The chin lifted and a ray of light lit the eyes that were so familiar, and for a moment Mornand could not tell to whom he had been speaking. Then it came to him, as the hero of Abarxia bent to kiss his hands, oh so tenderly, oh so surely, that it did not matter.

About the Author

Deborah J. Ross is an award-nominated writer and editor of fantasy and science fiction, with over a dozen traditionally published novels and five dozen short stories in print. Recent releases include *Thunderlord* and *The Children of Kings* (with Marion Zimmer Bradley); *Collaborators* (Lambda Literary Finalist, as Deborah Wheeler), and *The Seven-Petaled Shield* trilogy. Her short fiction has appeared in *F & SF*, *Asimov's*, *Star Wars: Tales from Jabba's Palace*, and the Book View Café anthology, *Nevertheless She Persisted*, and has earned honorable mention in *Year's Best SF*. She has served as Secretary to the Science Fiction Fantasy Writers of America (SFWA), is a member of Book View Café, and chaired the jury for the Philip K. Dick Award. When she's not writing, she knits for charity, plays classical piano, and studies yoga.

Also by Deborah J. Ross

Darkover novels (with Marion Zimmer Bradley)
The Laran Gambit (forthcoming)
Thunderlord
The Children of Kings
Hastur Lord
The Alton Gift
A Flame in Hali
Zandru's Forge
The Fall of Neskaya

The Seven-Petaled Shield trilogy
The Heir of Khored
Shannivar
The Seven-Petaled Shield

*Collaborators** (forthcoming)
*Northlight**
*Jaydium**

Collections
*Transfusion and Other Tales of Hope**
*Azkhantian Tales**
*Other Doorways: Early Novels**

Nonfiction
*Ink Dance, Essays on the Writing Life**

*available in BVC editions

About Book View Café

Book View Café Publishing Cooperative is an author-owned cooperative of over fifty professional writers, publishing in a variety of genres such as fantasy, romance, mystery, and science fiction.

BVC authors include *New York Times* and *USA Today* bestsellers; Nebula, Hugo, and Philip K. Dick Award winners; World Fantasy Award, Campbell Award, and RITA Award nominees; and winners and nominees of many other publishing awards.

Since its debut in 2008, BVC has gained a reputation for producing high-quality e-books, and is now bringing that same quality to its print editions.

www.ingramcontent.com/pod-product-compliance
Lightning Source LLC
Chambersburg PA
CBHW020912130726
47904CB00006BA/1843